The Hounded Hoopster

Doro Banyon Cozy Historical Mysteries-Book 7

D.S. Lang

Paperback ISBN: ISBN: 978-1-962039-22-2

Cover designer-Karen Phillips

Editor-Alyssa Colton

Chapter One

A sigh left Dorothea Banyon as she gazed out the mullioned windows of Michaw College Library. Late November was usually a time when students and faculty would be crisscrossing the campus on their way to classes or activities. Not so this year. The paths of College Commons were empty, and so were the benches scattered along the way. As she looked onto College Hall, Doro saw a fellow professor toting a box. The man turned toward the parking area, put the crate in the trunk of a vehicle, and drove away. He was not the first faculty member to leave the school in recent months, and he would not be the last. Not unless conditions changed dramatically.

"You look glum, Doro," her boss, Floyd Quartine, said. "Anything in particular getting you down? You're usually chipper on a Monday morning."

Doro turned to face the library director. "It's so quiet in here and out there." She gestured toward the expanse beyond the windows. "I just saw Professor Maynard put some belongings in his car and leave."

He frowned. "Not the typical way of things, but the Board of Trustees made a sound decision in closing down for a few weeks. Not needing to keep the buildings warm during the coldest part of the year will save money. Just enough heat so that the pipes don't break is the ticket." The library director smiled. "By mid-January when classes resume, the economy may be better. In any case, Maynard will be back then. He's spending the break with his family."

"I hope things are better." Although she nodded, Doro wondered if conditions might not be worse next year. Since the stock market crash in October 1929 just over a year earlier, the financial crisis had deepened, leaving many without work. Many private colleges, like Michaw, now dealt with lower enrollments. About ten percent of the student body had not attended this fall. What if some of the current students did not return after the first of the year? That could spell disaster for the school.

Floyd cleared his throat. "I wanted to talk with you."

With her heart hammering at her ribs, Doro struggled for breath. Was her job being cut? If so, what would she and her fiancé do? Could they still marry in January? Both of them worried about his position as campus security officer being eliminated, especially since the town had gotten rid of his part-time deputy constable job. How would they manage with no income at all? Her boss's voice broke into her thoughts.

"Let's go into my office."

"All right." Doro's legs wobbled as she followed him into the small room behind the circulation desk.

"Take a seat," Floyd said, gesturing to the only empty chair. Although two others faced his desk, both were piled with books.

As Doro glanced around, she noted that the shelves were nearly bare and boxes were stacked in the far corner. The office was usually neat as a pin with nothing out of place. During the workday, he typically only had a book or two out and perhaps a few papers. At the moment, stacks of books from his personal collection covered it. Why weren't they in his bookcase? Dismay rippled through her as she noted its empty shelves. "Is the library reopening after the two-month break?" What if it didn't? What would she do? Being without a job was a fate faced by many Americans now. Was she about to become one of them?

As he sat down, the older man's expression softened. "Of course, it is. I should've made that clear. Take a seat."

Despite her boss's reassurance, Doro did not relax as she sat down. "Why are you packing?"

He leaned back and laid his arms across his chest. "I'm retiring, effective at the end of the year. If things were different, I would've waited until May. As they stand now, more jobs will be eliminated, and I'd rather make way for someone younger to take over immediately." His grin took years off his narrow, lined face. "I hope you're still interested because President Adams is putting your name forward at the Board of Trustees meeting a week from Wednesday. I'm sure they'll approve you as the next director, so you need only make plans to celebrate. If you still want the job."

Caught between surprise and excitement, Doro could only stare at the library director. Moments passed before she found her voice. "You know it's been my dream since I was a little girl."

"I'm aware of that," Quartine replied. His hazel gaze shone with pleasure. "I remember when your dad first brought you to the library. You were beyond excited to see so many books. We couldn't hold you back."

Memories sprang into Doro's head. "I was four. My mother took me to the town library often, but this place was much larger. I was enthralled from the first moment." She studied his face. "You were so kind to me in answering all my silly questions, not just that day but every time I came." Although more than twenty years had passed, Doro remembered the library director's warmth and kindness. While his light brown hair had turned to gray and his familiar face was now lined, she pictured a much younger man, one who had been patient with a little girl in love with books.

"You were a sponge for knowledge, and you still are, which makes you a wonderful librarian." His smile faltered. "There's little doubt you'll get the job, but your current position won't be filled, which means a lot will be on your shoulders. Charlotte plans to retire, too, so there will be a new secretary. Not sure who it will be yet. Unfortunately, you'll only be able to hire one student worker next term. With luck, enrollment will pick up in the fall."

Luck would help. Good luck. For the past thirteen months, too many Americans had suffered only misfortune. "Probably so," she replied before bringing her attention back to the immediate future. "Did you speak with President Adams already this morning?"

"I did, and I'll be moving out of my office this week."

Fresh surprise made Doro blink. "This week? The end of the year is a month away."

"True, but starting in ten days, heat will be cut way back in most campus buildings in a cost-saving effort. That includes the library."

"What about Maple and Wheaton Halls? Will they close? I hadn't heard about that possibility." If so, the male and female faculty members living in the two buildings would have to move out, Doro included. Maybe she would be moving to her grandmother's home in nearby Sylvania before her marriage, which was less than two months away. At least she had a place to go.

He braced his elbows on the desk edge and leaned forward. "I'm afraid so. When I spoke with Adams, he felt sure the board would approve his decision to cut heating as much as possible. I'm certain he's right. Residents of Maple and Wheaton Hall will have until December tenth to find other housing. With several of the boardinghouses in town losing student boarders, there are options. The hotel isn't likely to be busy, so some of our colleagues can stay there. Others may live with relatives for a time." He sighed. "A few may not be back in January. We won't know for sure until after the board meets."

Doro clasped her hands and put them on her chin. "Because enrollment will be down even more?"

"I'm afraid so," her boss replied. "A few dozen students have already reported that they'll finish the semester in January but not enroll for spring. Adams and the deans have been looking at what courses and professors will be affected. The concerned parties will be advised of their status after the board makes the formal decision. Rumors have already circulated in some quarters."

The last comment did not surprise her. "There was gossip at this morning's breakfast. A couple of my Wheaton Hall neighbors fear they'll be let go, since they've only been here for two years. Two professors left over the summer, and we've had several secretaries move in. Will any of them be affected?"

"Not the secretaries, since clerical help was reduced at the end of the last academic year. Any professor with fewer than five years may be involved, and some senior faculty will go back to teaching introductory courses." Quartine sighed. "Adams knows the decisions won't be popular, but cutting back is wise. These economic problems will end eventually. Michaw has weathered other storms, and it will weather this one."

Doro hoped so, because she loved the college. "He's in a tough position. Both Wheaton and Maple Halls are free to single professors. They'll have to pay at a boardinghouse or the hotel. Even a few weeks of rent will be hard for some of them." She intertwined her fingers. "I'm lucky my grandmother lives nearby. She'll be happy to have company," Doro murmured. But what about Ev? Her fiancé's sister lived between Toledo and Cleveland. If he had to move there temporarily, would they see one another prior to their wedding ceremony? And what about afterward? They had planned to buy a house. Would that be possible now?

"That's wonderful, but you won't need to pack up until after Thanksgiving, except here. My office will be empty soon. Feel free to move in after the Board meeting next Wednesday."

"After the meeting," Doro murmured. Maybe her promotion was not a sure thing.

Quartine put up both hands. "Only because it wouldn't look right for you to move in until the announcement is made. You deserve the promotion, Doro. You've earned it with your dedication and diligence."

A possible barrier suddenly arose in her mind. "I don't have tenure yet. I've applied, but it won't be approved until the end of the academic year. What if the board turns me down for promotion based on that?"

He shook his head. "President Adams said several faculty members will be given tenure early, due to the special circumstances. You're one of them, unless some of the trustees disagree, but I don't think they will. It's the least the college can do when times are tough, and it will give people some sense of security."

"I'm grateful." Doro glanced around the office. "Can I help you pack? With the students gone, there's nothing pressing for me to do."

"Violet Jones is coming over, since she's only working half-days until the campus shuts down completely. I couldn't turn down her help, because she'll also help me arrange things in my home office. I'll pay her back with dinner in Sylvania. Maybe a movie, too."

Doro could not repress a smile. The president's secretary and the library director had been seen in each other's company for several months. Most of the campus and town communities saw nothing unusual about it since both had been alone for many years. Doro hoped the connection was more than casual. Her boss had lost his wife more than twenty years ago, and Mrs.

Jones had been a widow for almost that long. "All right. I'll check the shelves and make sure everything's in order."

"You did that a few days ago. Since we haven't had anyone except a handful of faculty members in, I'm sure the books haven't moved. Why don't you take off early? Maybe you and your fiancé can spend some extra time together."

That was a suggestion Doro could not turn down.

As she rushed across the campus, Doro shoved her hands into her coat pockets. An icy wind whipped through the bare trees. Although getting back to her place and snuggling in front of her little fireplace sounded lovely, she headed toward College Hall where Ev might be in his office. Doro hoped he was because she wanted to share her good news.

Her footsteps, echoing in the empty hallway, threatened her high spirits. Usually, students and professors would be crowding the corridor. With determination, Doro reminded herself of what her boss had said. Soon, the economy could be better, and the college and country might return to normal. When she reached her fiancé's door, Doro smiled. *Everett Mallow, Campus Security Officer,* was painted on the frosted glass window. Thank goodness his job had not been cut. Yet. Anxiety sent a twinge through her, but Doro focused on the news about her pending promotion. As she got closer, Doro heard Ev's voice. When no one replied at his pauses, she realized he was on the telephone. Unsure about interrupting, she waited before knocking.

"Thanks, Lowery. I appreciate it, and I'll let you know when I have more information," Ev said.

When he did not continue, she rapped on the door.

"Come in," he called out.

Doro was barely inside when Tee, the little black dog the two of them shared, jumped up from her bed in the corner. Her fluffy long tail wagged as she ran to greet Doro. "Hello, sweetie." Tee danced around and woofed. Doro bent to pet the pup. Now, over two years old, Tee was full-grown but less than twenty pounds.

Ev rose from the desk. "She's always delighted to see you, and so am I." The comment was punctuated by a smile that failed to reach his eyes.

When he did not approach her, as he usually did, Doro shifted from one foot to the other. Maybe she had caught him at a busy time, but a survey of his desk found it bare of papers. "I'm always happy to see you, too." After Tee settled down, Doro perched on one of the chairs while Ev took his seat behind the desk. "I hope I didn't interrupt your conversation," she said.

"No one is here except Tee," Ev replied.

"But you were on the telephone, weren't you? Talking to Lowery Canton?"

His attention moved to the clear desktop. "I was. We chat every now and then."

Apprehension filled Doro. Canton was the senior agent in the Toledo office of the Prohibition Bureau, and Ev's former boss. While the pair was well-acquainted, they were not close friends. "He isn't trying to talk you into another stint with his office, is he?"

A moment passed before Ev responded. "Not at all. He's got a full complement of agents. We're friendly, so I talk with him at times."

"You've never mentioned that," Doro said.

Ev's gaze returned to her. "I should have, because he asks about you."

"How nice. I didn't think he liked me," Doro replied.

Ev scratched his cheek. "He doesn't like civilians getting involved in his cases, but he appreciates your abilities. But enough about him. What brings you out of the library before noon? An early lunch?"

Part of Doro wanted to quiz Ev more, but most of her yearned to share her advancement. "No. Floyd gave me the rest of the day off. With no students on campus, we're not busy, and he thought I'd like to tell you some good news as soon as possible."

"I'd love to hear something positive." His flat tone underscored the statement. "Everyone would."

Doro did not waste words. Instead, she got right to the point. "Floyd is retiring at the end of December, and I'll be his replacement as long as the board formalizes it."

After a second's hesitation, Ev smiled. "Congratulations. I'm so happy for you and very proud of you. I know it's what you've wanted for a long time."

While his words seemed sincere, Ev's tone did not match the excitement echoing inside Doro. She had expected a heartier reaction, along with a hug and a kiss. "Is something wrong?"

He shook his head. "Of course not. I'm just busy and distracted."

Again, she looked at his desk and wondered what he'd been doing. Nothing obvious. Doro sat back in the chair. "You're the first to hear the news. I came here straight from the library."

"I'm glad you let me know first." Ev gripped the chair arms. "Aggie and Wade will be excited for you, and your parents, too. Gramma Rose will be thrilled, as well. You'll have to call your folks."

His assertions sounded right, but his demeanor was off. "I will, but I thought we might go out for dinner to celebrate. If you're not otherwise occupied." Even to her own ears, the statement sounded odd because they spent most evenings together, but Doro could not shake the feeling that something was bothering him. "Maybe Aggie and Wade could join us."

"Sure. That'd be great." Ev met her gaze. "If we eat in Sylvania, we could pick up your grandmother. A celebratory dinner, although I'm guessing she'll want to plan a party for you."

His voice still held an odd note. "Including her tonight would be fun," Doro agreed. "And maybe a party next weekend. The Sunday after Thanksgiving would work well, but we should wait until the Board of Trustees meets next Wednesday and approves my promotion."

"Their decision sounds like a formality, but we can celebrate next weekend. Let's plan on the Sunday after Thanksgiving, if Gramma Rose concurs."

"That sounds good, and an informal dinner tonight. Is that all right?"

Ev nodded. "Why don't you make the calls? With no students on campus, I can leave at any time. There's not much for me to do."

The last assertion was at odds with his earlier statements that he was busy. A flurry of anxiety took flight in Doro's stomach. Since she had already asked if something was amiss, Doro did not inquire again, but she could not dismiss her doubt. His office was next to the president's suite. Had Ev overheard him talking with Floyd? Or spoken with Adams himself? Surely, he would share any new information, especially if it involved his position. "All right. Maybe we can leave for Sylvania around four o'clock."

"Make it a little later. Wade doesn't have the luxury of taking off early. As town constable, he'll stay until the office closes at five."

"He's been working extra hours, so leaving early one day won't hurt, but it's up to him. I'll telephone Gramma Rose, but I want to tell Aggie in person because I want to see the look on her face. She knows how long I've dreamed about being the library director."

"She'll be as happy for you as I am," Ev assured Doro with a more genuine smile.

"She will." Doro hesitated for a moment before voicing one of her concerns. "Floyd heard from President Adams that both Maple and Wheaton Halls will be closed until classes resume in January." She watched carefully to see Ev's reaction.

His mouth flattened. "Adams called me into his office earlier and let me know. He's not even sure Maple Hall will reopen then. He told me I could have the room over his garage for a while, since I used it when I first came to Michaw, but I'll have to be out of Maple Hall by December tenth."

"That's a good plan. I know it isn't ideal, but you won't need an apartment for long, since we're planning to marry in January. If I talk to Gramma Rose tonight, I can tell her the date. Because we talked about having the ceremony at her house, I'd like to let her know as soon as possible."

A frown furrowed his forehead. "We haven't set a date."

"But we can now. We never intended to have a big wedding, so right after Christmas instead of mid-January would be fine. With the holiday break beginning so much earlier than original-ly planned, there won't be two weeks between semesters. Right now, the calendar only has four days between the terms. With that in mind, what do you think about an earlier date for our ceremony?"

Ev leaned back and folded his arms over his chest. For a long moment, he avoided Doro's gaze. When he finally looked back at her, Ev's jaw was tight. "Everything considered, we should probably wait until the end of the school year."

Doro's jaw dropped. "What? Why?"

After steepling his fingers, Ev focused on them. "I just think we should wait until we know what else will happen at the college."

Her heart hammered against her ribs. Was this why he was acting so strangely? "What else did President Adams tell you? Does he think the college won't re-open for next term? Surely, I wouldn't get a promotion, if that was likely." Floyd had told her the exact opposite.

Ev pressed his fingertips together. "He's sure it will re-open."

"Then, why delay our marriage?" She searched his face but found no clues in his schooled features. As Doro studied him, she realized faint shadows had formed beneath his eyes. The previous day, she had noted circles there. But now they seemed darker, and his eyes looked dull. Something more than moving out of his Maple Hall room was bothering him. Something that was disturbing his sleep. Something he did not want to reveal. But why?

As his head fell forward, Ev massaged his neck. "Everything is in turmoil. Most college employees will leave town until classes resume. That means some of your friends couldn't be at the wedding if it's right after Christmas. A small wedding is great, but only a handful wouldn't be much of a celebration. Besides, a spring ceremony would be better in a few ways. It'll be easier for your parents to come when there's no chance of snowstorms, and we'd have more time for a honeymoon. Since I'm not working as a deputy constable anymore, I'll have two months off during the summer. Plus, we could get married in your grandmother's backyard. The ravine with the fish pond and brick paths is lovely, so we could have an outdoor ceremony. Or just use the yard for the reception. She's proud of her garden, so she'd love that. Wouldn't you?"

As Doro considered the points, she could not deny their validity, but his reasons rang like excuses. Delaying bothered her. Or, more specifically, Ev suggesting a postponement was troubling. "Do you really want to push back our wedding?"

A puzzled expression crossed Ev's face. "I just said we should for several reasons."

"But is it what you really want? Are you fine with delaying six months?"

His stoic expression did not lighten. "I'd marry you today if things were different, but we have to deal with reality, not wishes. When we ate Sunday dinner with Gramma Rose yesterday, she mentioned worrying about your parents traveling during the winter."

"I remember." Doro folded her hands in her lap and pressed them together. "I've been a little concerned myself."

His gaze went to the diamond solitaire on her left hand. "I want to put a gold band next to your engagement ring someday."

Someday was vague enough to make her nervous, but Doro asked another question from the back of her mind. "We haven't discussed it, but would you wear a ring?"

"Sure," Ev replied without hesitation.

"Not all men do. In fact, most don't," she pointed out. Doro had always wondered why, just like she wondered why women changed their names. As a girl, she had found it odd. As a woman, she still did—but it was the custom, and one she would not oppose.

"Wade does, and I envy him."

The candor in his voice and expression eased Doro's mind. "You won't have to envy him a lot longer." Ev would be wearing a ring if they married in January, as originally planned. She was about to press her point when a rap at the door interrupted.

Ev stood up before calling out. "Come in."

Mrs. Jones, a slender woman in her fifties, peeked in. "I don't want to interrupt." Her glance went from Doro to Ev and back.

"You're not," Doro assured her. Violet Jones was one of her mother Julia's best friends, and Doro had known her since childhood. Since Julia McLaren Banyon now lived in Colorado, she no longer got together with Mrs. Jones on a weekly basis, but correspondence kept them in touch. And Doro often saw the secretary.

"Of course not," Ev added before gesturing to a vacant chair. "Please sit down."

The older woman waved off the suggestion. "Thank you, but I'm helping Floyd pack his office up." A smile played across her lips. "Doro has shared her good news, I'm sure."

"She has," Ev replied, "so we're celebrating with dinner out tonight. Why don't you and Floyd join us?"

"Please do," Doro put in.

"That sounds lovely, and I'm sure Floyd would agree," Mrs. Jones said.

"As soon as we decide what time and where, I'll let you know," Doro replied. "It will probably be in Sylvania, since we can include my Gramma Rose if we go there."

"Wonderful, but the reason I stopped is that I wanted to make sure you two are coming to the big pre-holiday dinner on Sunday. I planned to ask Ev, but I'm glad you're here, Doro. With so many college employees leaving campus well ahead of Christmas, the meal will celebrate the entire season." Mrs. Jones clasped her hands together. "I'm sad that everyone must move for now. Of course, it's worse that a few more are losing their jobs. At least, it seems that way. Even though I work in the president's office, I don't know what the final decisions from the Board of Trustees will be. I'm only sure more positions will be eliminated—temporarily at least."

The dismay on the older woman's face echoed inside Doro. "It is," she agreed. "But it's kind of you to put the special dinner together on short notice." Usually, two dinners took place: one for Thanksgiving and another for Christmas.

"Come a little early, and we'll put you both to work," the secretary said.

"Sure thing," Ev said.

"We're happy to help," Doro said. "A festive occasion is something we all need. We should celebrate every chance we get." She glanced at Ev. As soon as possible, Doro planned to pin him down on when they would celebrate their marriage vows.

Chapter Two

After the older woman left, Doro turned to Ev. "This dinner is our last big campus event. For a while anyhow." A wistful note entered her voice as she considered how to get the conversation back to a wedding date without sounding desperate. Subtlety was best since he was acting strangely.

"It's hard, I know. I haven't lived in Maple Hall as long as you've been in Wheaton, but I'll miss the camaraderie. For the most part, the guys get along well."

Doro forced back the rising tide of nostalgia. "Even if you insist on delaying our wedding, you and I will be moving out in the spring anyhow. But maybe we can still wed in January." Moving in together as husband and wife had warmth spreading through her.

His jaw tightened and relaxed. "I'll look forward to when that happens."

"Far forward as in toward spring? Or sooner?" Doro injected a light note into her queries, but anxiety compressed her insides as she waited for his answer.

Ev frowned. "It's best if we wait and see what happens. So much is uncertain now."

Despite Ev's reasonable excuses, Doro felt like he was drawing away from her. Why? She was about to quiz him more when loud voices in the outside hallway interrupted.

Ev jumped out of his chair and rushed through the door. Doro followed. Two younger faculty members, Emory Baylor and Carson Longley, faced the basketball coach, Roscoe Munroe. All three were scowling and looking as if blows might soon be exchanged. Doro gasped when Ev stepped into the group. They all looked angry enough to strike out. "Gentlemen, what seems to be the problem?"

Munroe, tall and blonde, glanced at Ev. "Baylor and Longley are mad because my job is safe, and theirs may not be. This isn't the first time they've gotten after me about it. They don't seem to understand that I'm not the one calling the shots."

"Aren't you? We've heard differently," Longley, his face beet red, said.

"Indeed, we have," Baylor put in. "My department chair was told a faculty member had to be fired so your team had funds for travel."

"Ridiculous," Munroe said. "We get plenty of support. More than you two."

"You're the basketball coach. I teach math, and Longley is an English professor." Baylor fingered his cowlick as he glared at Doro. "He should be kept on instead of your friend Aggie, who'll have a comfortable situation, no matter what."

Doro started in surprise after having the fire turned on her. "Aggie just got tenure." She jerked a thumb at one of the fellows. "Professor Longley is four years away from being able to apply. As for Coach Munroe, he also teaches physical education."

When Longley released a snort, his thin mustache bounced. "Hardly a serious academic pursuit. Mathematics and English are far more important, Professor Banyon, as you should know." His dark gaze flashed with anger.

"That's enough, Professor Longley," Ev said, his tone sharp and cutting.

Baylor glowered at Ev. "Of course, you'd stick up for her. If you lose your job, you'll still be as comfortable as Aggie Lammers."

Color swept into Ev's lean cheeks while his jaw worked. Torn between wanting to support Ev but not wanting to make him look weak, Doro hesitated. Relief filled her when he provided the perfect answer.

Ev straightened until his spine went rigid. "What happens between my fiancé and me is none of your concern, sir. However, your behavior is my business."

A chortle rumbled out of Munroe. "You tell 'em, Officer Mallow."

Ev's gray gaze glittered with banked fire. "There's no reason for any of you to be yelling in the hallway. The students act better."

Munroe scowled. "Nobody's around to hear us." He jerked his thumb at the two young professors. "Besides, these guys started it, like they do almost every day. I have no peace at meals, because they're always hounding me. You've seen it for yourself in the Maple Hall cafeteria, Mallow."

When Baylor moved toward Munroe, Ev stepped between them. "That's enough. It doesn't matter who started the argument. It's going to end here and now."

All three men scowled at Ev. For a moment, Doro thought at least one would punch him. Finally, they all shrugged as if nothing amiss had occurred.

"Come on, Bay," Longley said. "Let's get out of here."

After the two professors were out of earshot, Munroe focused on Ev. "This isn't the first time they've harassed me. They even give some of my players a hard way to go in class, just because my guys are athletes and those two couldn't lift a twenty-pound weight together. Milquetoasts." He spit out the last word like it tasted nasty.

Since neither Baylor nor Longley was in top-notch condition, Doro could not disagree. However, name-calling was obnoxious. "If students are being treated unfairly, they have every right to complain to a dean."

His green gaze shifted to Doro. "We handle things within the athletic department. If there's a major issue, I go straight to Adams."

Doro was about to ask how things were handled when one of the custodians came along with a big box. Stan Jackson, a young man of medium height and build, had only been at the college for a few months, so Doro did not know him well.

"Excuse me, Officer Mallow, but this was left in the mailroom for you," the young fellow said.

Munroe spun toward him. "You're interrupting, Jackson."

Color suffused the younger man's face. "I'm doing my job," he shot back, "and you're gonna have to do yours when you don't have an assistant to do it for you."

"Why you little twerp," Munroe muttered. "You don't know anything about basketball, and my lackluster assistant is more interested in your sister than his job."

"Leave my sister out of it," Jackson, his lean face going pink, muttered.

"But she's in it," Munroe said with a sneer. "They think they're smart with the way they got the athletic director on their side. His kids are in her class, and they think she's wonderful. I don't appreciate being sandbagged."

The custodian's jaw dropped. "I don't know what you're talking about."

The coach's green eyes glittered. "Tell your sister and my assistant that they aren't fooling me."

Doro watched in disgust and confusion. Coach Munroe had a quick temper, which was often on display during basketball games. His penchant for loudly nitpicking referees' calls was well-known across campus, and something Doro had witnessed on more than a few occasions.

When Jackson stepped forward, Ev laid a hand on his forearm. "Coach, why don't you go on your way?" Ev suggested.

For a moment, Munroe stared at the young custodian before nodding to Ev. "Good idea," he said before stomping off.

Relief rippled through Doro. Coach Munroe was a muscular man who stood a couple of inches taller than the lean, shorter custodian.

"Sorry," Stan murmured.

After clapping the other man on the shoulder, Ev smiled. "Munroe was already upset before you came along. It's not your fault."

"He doesn't like me," Stan said.

"Does he like anyone?" Doro asked. Despite her love of basketball, she was not a fan of the coach.

A half-shrug lifted one of Stan's shoulders. "He's not fond of Clint Spalling, from what I can tell."

The comment puzzled Doro. "Clint seems to be a good assistant, and they acted like they hit it off last year." Spalling had been hired prior to the 1929 school year, and Munroe had seemed happy with his choice.

"Clint's a real nice guy," Stan said. "If I'm working in the fieldhouse, which isn't often, he always talks with me. We've even shot baskets a few times."

Memories returned to Doro. "He started stepping out with your sister in September, right?"

Stan looked away from her. "Yep, he did."

"Ev and I saw the three of you in Sylvania at the picture show," Doro said.

"I remember." A slight smile played across Stan's lips. "My sister and Clint are nice to take me along as a chaperone."

In the current day and age, Doro found the idea of an unmarried couple needing oversight archaic, but she bit her tongue. She and Ev stepped out without someone watching their every move, not that there were moves to watch. Heat scorched her cheeks as she forced her mind back to Stan.

"Very good of you to go along," Ev put in.

"My sister was only sixteen when our folks died from influenza. I was twenty, but I quit college and went to work, so I could look out for her like I promised them," Stan said.

"And you still are." Doro considered what she knew about the siblings, which was not a lot. "You and your sister came from Toledo, didn't you?"

"We did," the custodian agreed.

"So did Clint Spalling. Did you know him there?" she asked.

For a moment, Stan looked startled. Then, he shook his head. "It's a big town."

"It is. I've always lived in a city myself, so moving to Michaw was a big change. Everyone knows everyone." Ev grinned at Doro. "I'm glad I did."

"As am I," she murmured. His lightheartedness eased some of her earlier concern.

Stan cleared his throat. "My sister and I like Michaw. We were lucky to both get jobs. She taught English there, but I lost my position as a bank teller. With so many folks out of work, I feel real fortunate to get hired here."

"You do a great job," Ev said. "When things improve, I'm sure you'll have a chance at a better position."

A grin lit Stan's face. "That'd be nice. For now, I count my lucky stars that I have work."

As the custodian started to turn away, Ev spoke again. "I talk to Clint pretty regularly, and I know he's down over losing his job. I told him to hang on because he may be hired back, especially if the team wins the big tournament next week."

"I wish that'd happen. As things stand now, Clint may be moving away." Stan looked morose. "Bonnie will be heart-broken if they're apart."

Sympathy filled Doro as she considered how she would feel in a similar situation. "Basketball is big at Michaw College. Most of the trustees will be at the tournament, and so will many donors. Even though the assistant coaching position has been cut, it could be restored."

"I'll tell my sister," Stan said. "Maybe that will ease her mind."

"Useless worry never helps, so I hope it does," Doro murmured. The comment was as much a reminder for herself as advice for Stan. She took a reassuring glance at her engagement ring. She and Ev would marry. It was only a matter of time.

"Not all worry is useless," Ev put in. "Sometimes, it helps plan for the future."

When Doro studied his face, she saw a host of emotions there. Uneasiness crept through her. Although the economy was bad, focusing on better days ahead seemed like the best strategy to her. But Doro had not experienced the struggles Ev had, and she needed to be empathetic to his feelings. "That's true."

Stan shifted from one foot to the other. "We'll manage, no matter what, but my sister deserves to be with her...with her sweetheart. She deserves a happy marriage and a family."

The young man's sincere concern touched Doro. "You're a good brother."

"I promised my parents to take care of her, and I will," Stan vowed. "Now, I gotta get back to work."

After Stan ambled away, Doro turned to Ev. "He's usually quiet. When I've seen Stan in the past, I've barely gotten a phrase out of him."

"It seems like he wanted to explain his reaction to Munroe, who was out of line with his comments about Clint caring more about Miss Jackson than about his job. He's smitten, so of course she's important to him. That doesn't mean he isn't doing his job." Ev shook his head. "It's hard to understand the animosity between Munroe and Clint. Last year, they got along fine. Now, they seem to be at odds often."

Doro stepped back and tried to concentrate on what Stan had told them. "The Jackson siblings moved here in early August, and she started stepping out with Clint around Labor Day."

"Right," Ev agreed.

"Did the friction between Munroe and Clint start then?"

Ev scratched his head. "Shortly after that."

"Maybe Clint really is focusing too much on Miss Jackson. We don't know how he acts at practice, but he could be distracted. The team has only had one exhibition game, and I couldn't be there. You went, didn't you?"

Ev nodded. "I was there."

"Did you notice Clint seeming sidetracked?"

For a long moment, Ev stared into the distance. "He glanced into the stands a few times. Miss Jackson and Stan sat directly across from me, and I noticed her giving little waves every now and then."

"They're already in love," Doro observed.

"I guess so. Some people don't let obstacles stand in their way."

His remarks reminded Doro that Ev had wanted to step out long before she had agreed. "You were patient when I thought being the library director was more important than anything else." She sighed. "I never had a beau and never wanted one because I didn't intend to marry. Not when the college wouldn't employ married women."

"I understand that."

When she studied his set features, Doro wondered if he did. Was her earlier reluctance to step out bothering him now? How could that be? They were engaged. Doro laid one hand over his heart. "Like I've told you before, when I was kidnapped from the train over a year ago, I didn't think about the library, I thought about you and how sorry I was that we'd parted two months earlier on bad terms."

He stood stock-still. "Sometimes, a calamity heightens emotion. Being held hostage by a killer would be in that category."

The comment puzzled her. Was he saying she had made a rash decision in the aftermath of the kidnapping? That made no sense because they had not moved from stepping out to courting for months, and their engagement came even later. "Or make someone come to a realization, which is what happened to me. We're fortunate," Doro murmured. "Clint and his sweetheart may not be. If his job isn't restored, he may have to leave Michaw." When Ev did not touch her, she stepped away. Even though few people were on campus, getting caught flaunting propriety was not wise. And College Hall's main corridor was a public place.

He shrugged. "Sometimes circumstances keep sweethearts apart for a time."

The cryptic comment disturbed her, but Doro focused on what they had just heard. Maybe a more general conversation about other people's troubles would lower the barrier between them. Personal reflections should come off-campus and in private. Not here and now. "That's true, but it would be a shame if Clint had to go elsewhere. He seems like a good assistant, and last year, it looked as if Coach Munroe got along well with him."

"I thought the same thing, although Clint has mentioned being at odds with the coach on a few occasions. Stan may not realize the position was cut by the college not Munroe."

"Probably not, but Munroe could fight to keep Clint on."

Ev rubbed his forehead. "Winning the tournament next weekend might help, but I'm not sure President Adams will support hiring an assistant back when professors may be out. The economy being weak is hard on everyone."

"It is. I'm sorry Longley and Baylor are likely to lose their jobs, but Baylor's comment about Aggie infuriated me."

Ev grimaced. "Me, too, but both professors can be belligerent. So can Munroe. The three of them have had words more than once at meals in Maple Hall. You heard Coach complain about being hounded. I'm not sure I'd use that term. Usually, Longley and Baylor rant like just now, and Munroe returns the same fire. All three seem to enjoy bickering."

Doro shifted from one foot to the other. "A couple residents of Wheaton Hall are angry, too. It has to be hard to be let go, especially when finding faculty jobs elsewhere will be difficult. Clerical workers have already been reduced in number. The several who moved into Wheaton last summer complain constantly about having to do extra work."

A grim expression hardened Ev's handsome features. "Getting work any place is becoming harder and harder."

Doro laid a hand on his forearm. "You and I are fortunate."

Several moments of silence preceded his reply. "We are." His tone did not match his words. "I'm not sure how Sunday's big campus dinner will go if all three of those guys come. They could make a scene."

"President Adams and the deans will be there, so I would think everyone will be on their best behavior."

"We can hope." Ev looked at his wristwatch. "I want to catch up on paperwork before I leave. When you know what time we'll all go to dinner, call me here. All right?"

After studying his face for a fleeting moment, Doro nodded. "Of course. I'll see you later."

"Yep. Now, I need to get back to work." Ev returned to his office and closed the door.

Doro stared after him in stunned surprise. Ever since their engagement in April, they had not parted without a kiss or, if among other people, a casual touch. At least they hadn't until now. What caused the change? Was it related to his conversation with Lowery Canton? Or was Ev having second thoughts about their impending nuptials? Did he only want a delay? Or was something worse afoot? The questions disturbed Doro.

Chapter Three

Over the next few days, Doro saw little of Ev. While he acted normally at dinner with their friends and her grandmother on Monday evening, he was quieter than usual. Whenever they spoke late in the week, attempts to draw him out proved futile. When she asked what was wrong, he claimed to be coming down with something but never seemed sick. In the slightly more than two years since they met, Ev had never acted so oddly. But times were hard, and many folks felt the stress even if they had not been directly affected. Doro figured that was the case with him, since he knew firsthand how it was to struggle financially.

With no classes in session, she worked on organizing her materials for the move to the library director's office while also helping Floyd and Mrs. Jones pack his belongings. Despite her joy over the promotion, bittersweet memories filled Doro. She would miss her boss.

By Friday afternoon, most of his belongings had been boxed up, so Floyd was in the process of moving them to his Ford Model T, which he had parked outside the library's storeroom. While her boss put a large crate in the trunk, Doro slid a smaller one on to the back seat.

"You'll stop in the library, won't you? You aren't leaving town," Doro said.

"Of course not. Michaw has been my home for many years, and I have a lot of reasons to stay," Floyd replied. "But you deserve to take charge without me hanging around this place."

"I'd love to see you here," Doro said with complete sincerity.

Floyd smiled. "I'll stop from time-to-time. But now, let's finish getting my things packed. After the announcement of your promotion, I'll be happy to return and assist you in your move. There might be almost as many boxes, but we won't be moving them as far."

After going back into his office, they worked amiably for about thirty minutes before they were joined by Agatha Darwine Lammers, Doro's best friend. Aggie, a flush on her freckled face, rushed in. "Sorry I didn't get here sooner, but Davey forgot his lunch, and I took it to school for him. I still could've gotten here on time, but the principal asked me to step into his office. With many folks out of work, Mr. Smith is concerned that some of the children won't get even one present, so he wondered if I could organize a group to gather items. Knowing how our children look forward to Christmas, I said I would." Aggie sighed. "Now that I'm here, what can I do?"

"We're hauling boxes to Floyd's car, so grab one from his office," Doro replied.

"It's not mine anymore," her boss put in.

A short, quick breath escaped Doro. "It'll take time for me to get used to that." And she didn't want to count on the new job until it was formalized, not with so much uncertainty shrouding the campus and the country.

After they finished, Floyd said he planned to take off and told Doro to leave early, so she and Aggie headed out. When a frigid breeze blew across the empty campus, Doro thrust her hands into her coat pockets. "It's unnerving to see no one out-and-about. Even in the summer, there are a few people around."

"I know. It's sad." Aggie pulled her knit cloche over her auburn waves. "Not everyone has left for the long break yet. When that happens, it'll be even quieter."

"That seems impossible." Chilled to the core but not wanting to be alone, Doro continued. "Why not stop by my apartment for tea and cookies? You have a little time before the children get home from school, don't you?"

"I have plenty of time. This is the last day before Thanksgiving Break, which is longer than usual. There's a party in every class, and they'll stay after, if I know them. Like the college, the local schools are trying to save money by cutting the heat back for a while—although not as long. The kids will go back after only a week's vacation. Christmas vacation may be longer than normal, too."

"There are only two schools in town, and they're smaller, so that makes sense," Doro replied. One building housed grades nine through twelve while the other contained grades one through eight.

Aggie addressed her friend. "I figured Ev would be help-ing you. He can't be too busy with no students on campus."

A sigh escaped Doro. Since Aggie had married and moved out of Wheaton Hall in July, the two friends did not chat as often as they had in the past, so Doro had not mentioned Ev's withdrawal. Getting Aggie's perspective would surely ease her mind. After Floyd was out of earshot, she went ahead. "I haven't seen much of Ev over the past few days. When we're together, he seems distracted at times. I know there's been unrest among some of the junior faculty in Maple Hall." Doro relayed the contretemps outside Ev's office earlier in the week. "Since then, I've asked if they're still bickering, and he says he's handling it. I don't know what that means."

A frown furrowed Aggie's forehead. "Neither do I." She chewed on her lower lip. "Wade mentioned Ev coming to his office, and they talked a little about the problem."

Doro's jaw dropped. "They did?" Why was Ev seeking out his best friend, who was Aggie's husband, and not her? The question made her heart lurch. Usually, she and Ev discussed all their concerns. Lately, that was not the case.

"Professors Longley and Baylor got into an argument with Coach Munroe uptown. Wade was afraid they'd come to blows, but he separated the three. He wanted to discuss the problem with Ev." A sigh escaped her. "Evidently, the professors have confronted the coach individually and to-gether. Wade mentioned several incidents."

The news did little to allay Doro's qualms. Why hadn't Ev told her? "Uptown and on campus?"

Aggie nodded. "One other incident on Main Street and several in the Maple Hall dining room. The latter was according to Ev. Wade understands how upsetting it must be to lose their jobs, but they're blaming Coach Munroe. It doesn't help that he's...let's say somewhat arrogant."

A chortle left Doro. "Somewhat? That's kind."

"True. The man often throws fuel on the fire with his remarks." Aggie released a harsh breath.

Thinking back to the confrontation outside Ev's office, Doro could only agree. "Coach egged them on when I was watching." She did not mention Baylor's comment about Aggie. "As much as I hate to think about moving out of Wheaton Hall, I'll be relieved when the troublemakers are off campus."

A smile brightened Aggie's expression. "You'd be moving out in January anyhow. Have you and Ev set a date? You could make it earlier than you originally planned since the campus is closing down in a couple of weeks. A wedding right after Christmas would be special."

"Ev doesn't seem interested in an earlier date," Doro murmured, unable to keep her anxiety from her voice.

"Is something wrong?" Aggie asked. Concern blanketed her delicate features.

"Not really. Ev and I ate Sunday dinner with Gramma Rose." But something seemed wrong. She just did not want to admit it, even to her best friend.

"I know," Aggie said. "All three of you mentioned it on Monday evening."

"Of course. Anyhow, she brought up fretting about my parents taking the train when heavy snow and bitter cold are possible. I've worried myself. What if they got stuck like we did a couple summers ago? My mother's health could be jeopardized if the delay was lengthy." Over a decade earlier, Julia McLaren Banyon had contracted consumption. When the disease lingered, doctors recommended going to a sanitorium, so Doro's mother had left for Colorado Springs where her brother, Doro's uncle, then lived. After her health improved, physicians suggested she stay on since the dryer climate was better for her. Eventually, Doro's father took a job at Colorado College to be with his wife. Although her parents had encouraged her to move with them, Doro chose to stay in Michaw, partly due to her grandmother living in nearby Sylvania. And partly because as her grandmother often said, both she and Doro had deep tap roots in their hometowns.

Aggie nodded. "I suppose there could be weather problems, but you want them here for your wedding."

"Definitely, and they'll come at any time of year." Doro chewed on her lower lip. "On Monday, Ev and I discussed it, and we may wait until May when the next semester ends. I suppose it makes sense. A lot of our college colleagues will be gone until mid-January, and we want to celebrate with everyone. We won't have a lot of guests at the wedding, but we discussed a bigger party following it. Plus, spring is so much prettier. We can get lots of fresh flowers right around here. We can even have the ceremony and reception outside at my grandmother's house." When she started sounding like she was selling the idea of postponement, Doro offered a slight smile. "It seems like the best idea, so I wrote my parents last evening and telephoned Gramma Rose, too. She agreed May would be a fine time."

For a long moment, Aggie searched Doro's face. "You're not disappointed?" It was more question than statement.

Hot tears pricked the backs of Doro's eyes, and she bit hard on her trembling lip. "I am, but it is sensible."

Aggie slipped an arm around her friend's shoulders. "Being sensible isn't what it's cracked up to be."

"No, it sure isn't." Doro swiped the moisture from her face. "When Ev and I talked this morning, we agreed to wait and see what happens over the next few months." The conversation had been brief since Doro was headed to work, and Ev had a meeting. She would have liked a longer discussion, but establishing a valid argument to go ahead with the wedding proved difficult. The main reason for marrying in January had been the two-week long break. Because the current term had ended early, the academic calendar had changed, and that motive no longer existed. "Earlier in the week, I tried convincing him to move the ceremony up. We could always have a party later. He refused to budge. Mostly, he used my parents being able to travel more easily in the spring."

"That part is true."

"I know, but he acts almost remote at times. Maybe he's having second thoughts."

"Nonsense," Aggie shot back. "He loves you. Anyone with eyes can see that at a glance."

Doro wanted to believe her friend, but doubt hampered her. "You haven't seen us together much lately."

"I saw you two on Monday night. While I agree, he acted tense at times, Ev is smitten. More than smitten. I'm sure whatever's bothering him has nothing to do with his love for you.

The town dropping the deputy constable job had to hurt, even though it was strictly due to money, not anything personal with Ev, who did a wonderful job."

"He understands it wasn't his work, but I agree. It has to be hard for him." She chewed on her lower lip. "He doesn't say much about his campus position, but we both know it could be eliminated. In most ways, that seems unlikely what with bank robberies and bootlegging on the increase all over. The college doesn't have a bank, but some students go to speakeasies, and I wonder if any are involved with rumrunning as a way to make extra money."

"It's not impossible, but what makes you think that?"

Doro revealed what she had overheard outside Ev's office on Monday. "At the time, I figured Lowery wanted Ev to come back to the Bureau. Now, I suspect he wondered if anyone here is working with bootleggers. Some were a while back." Ev's excuse that he and his old boss had casual conversations did not ring true. Canton had to be busy with little free time for idle talk.

"That makes sense," Aggie said. "All the more reason for Ev to be kept on as the security officer, so let's not fret about that. Instead, we can start planning your wedding," Aggie said with a smile.

"We can talk about plans," Doro agreed. As May grew closer, would Ev make more excuses to postpone the big event? Getting her mind on something else would be wise. "Right now, we should focus on the big dinner this Sunday. Usually, I look forward to the campus holiday dinners. This year, I'm not so sure. Some faculty and staff have been warned that their jobs may be eliminated for the rest of the school year, as you know.

Even though clerical jobs were cut last May, the secretaries living in Wheaton complain about being overworked. They might not act out at the dinner, but Baylor and Longley could."

"Wade plans to invite Coach Munroe to sit at our table," Aggie said. "With you and Ev there, too, he shouldn't be obnoxious, and the others will likely sit together. Probably not close to us."

"Let's hope they don't." Doro did not want to listen to grown men arguing like schoolboys.

"What does Ev think?"

Doro considered her fiancé's reactions to possible problems at the dinner. "He's a bit concerned, but he'll take care of everything, so I shouldn't worry." She studied her best friend's countenance. Aggie had always been pretty, but since marrying the town constable, she glowed. "What does Wade say? Other than about the arguments in town?"

By then, the two friends were at Wheaton Hall, and they exchanged greetings with several other residents before heading upstairs. Once inside Doro's apartment, the two friends fetched refreshments and went to the little fireplace. Doro got the flames going before sitting on the sofa. "We were interrupted before you could reveal Wade's thoughts."

After perching on the edge of a chair, Aggie held her teacup in her lap. "Ev has told Wade not to fret because he'll handle things on campus. So, pretty much what Ev told you."

For a moment, Doro stared at the plate of cookies on the low table between them. Shortbread was Ev's favorite, but he had turned down her offer of some this morning. She thought back over the two-plus years of their acquaintance. "Ev was somewhat withdrawn when he first came to town, but it's been a long while since he didn't want to discuss a situation in detail." She looked back at her friend. "The four of us have worked on several cases together, and Ev is always open and straightforward. Now, he wants to handle challenges on his own. With us getting married, shouldn't he be more frank, not less?"

Sympathy filled Aggie's hazel eyes. "Wade says much the same about Ev's recent behavior, and they're best friends. I haven't spoken privately with Ev lately, but he was distracted at Monday's dinner. Maybe that goes with his reluctance to get everything in the open. Like I said, losing his post as deputy constable has to affect him."

Two months earlier, the town council had eliminated the part-time position, held by Ev ever since he had come to Michaw. He had been putting that salary in a fund for their future house. If necessary, it could become emergency support for them. They had discussed ideas more than a month ago, but Ev had withdrawn since then. "He expected it, and we discussed how it would affect our budget as a married couple. Both of us are willing to economize however we can. Now that I should be promoted, the increase in my salary will almost make up the difference."

"Did you say that to Ev?"

Doro shook her head. "No. After Longley's and Baylor's nasty remarks on Monday, I thought it was best not to point out that I'll be making more money than he will." She continued by revealing some of what the young professors had said.

"Ev would never live off your salary. He'd find some sort of work."

Her friend's assertion rang true, but it also disturbed Doro. If Ev lost his job as campus security officer, what else could he do in Michaw? She thought about their trek across College Commons again. Bare trees, vacant benches, and empty paths dominated the landscape. Little security was needed when no one was around, and that fact disturbed Doro. So did Ev's on-going conversations with Lowery Canton. While the Prohibition Bureau was active in tracking bootleggers, would the Board of Trustees keep a campus officer on the chance that students or employees were involved in rumrunning? And what about other disciplinary problems? With fewer people on campus, they might think the town constable could handle any issues that cropped up. Unsure what to think, Doro made a general observation. "With so many folks losing jobs, it's hard for every-one."

Aggie nodded. "Even though we're all lucky to have work, many people around us aren't so fortunate. It bothers me be-cause my family had trouble making ends meet at times, and it's hard. I hate to see others going through the same strug-gles. Sometimes, I even find myself wool-gathering about the future—and not in a positive way."

The explanation solidified Doro's conclusion. Ev was uneasy due to general problems, not anything in their relationship. But her heart still felt heavy. And her mind remained troubled.

Chapter Four

S unday morning, Doro went to the Wheaton Hall kitchen and put the cranberry relish, made the previous night, in a big basket before gathering shortbread and piling it into small bags. She placed everything on the dining room table and dashed upstairs to dress for the campus dinner. Usually, she eagerly anticipated the event, but this year was different. Since Monday, word had spread far-and-wide about more jobs being eliminated. At a faculty meeting the previous week, President Adams had framed all cuts as temporary, yet doubt permeated the campus community. Not knowing for sure until after the Board of Trustees meeting the following Wednesday added to the apprehension. Although her promotion seemed safe, Doro would not rest easy until it was formally announced. And until she knew Ev's job was safe.

After donning her favorite blue dress, at least it was Ev's favorite, Doro peeked into the mirror by her front door. A pair of sea-blue eyes just like her mother's and her grandmother's looked back. With one hand, she smoothed her light brown hair away from her face and covered the stylish bob with a felt cloche. The hat, in the same deep azure as her dress, boasted a small silk flower. Doro touched the faux bloom. When buds again came out in spring, would she and Ev be married? She hoped so. Buoyed by Aggie's reassurances on Friday, Doro smiled at her reflection. All would be well.

Since Tee was staying with Ev over the weekend, Doro left the apartment without a backward glance. At exactly eleven o'clock, she waited for Ev by the front door of Wheaton Hall. When he arrived, Doro gestured to the dinner supplies. "I'm glad you could help me."

"Sure thing," he replied before scooping them up.

His lack of comment on her outfit sapped some of her already weak enthusiasm. In an effort to draw him out, she scanned his lean form. "You look dapper this morning."

"It's the same navy suit you've seen a few times," he replied.

"I know," she murmured. "But it's nice to see you out of uniform."

His brow wrinkled. "You saw me in pants and a sweater last evening at Wade's house."

The response did nothing to lift the conversation or her spirits. "I didn't see much of you, since Aggie and I were baking." The two friends had made cookies to take as little gifts for today's dinner guests. The usual campus gift exchange would not take place, so this was a small gesture in its place. Doro had baked shortbread while Aggie whipped up chocolate chip. "Now, we should get going."

Ev laid the boxes aside and took her arm. "I'm sorry I'm on edge. It has nothing to do with you."

His apology resonated inside her. She laid her free hand on his chest. "It's a difficult time for everyone." She paused for a moment. "Last evening, Aggie and I caught snatches of you and Wade talking when you weren't playing with the children, so I know Longley and Baylor are still arguing with Munroe. Coach has done nothing to calm them down, which means you've had to intercede." While they baked, her friend had shared additional information about the problems, which made Doro wonder again why Ev had not told her.

A long, low breath rumbled out of him. "There have been more confrontations at meals and one near the fieldhouse. With the boys out of class, they practice twice a day. Anyone who wants to berate him can figure out the schedule, so I've headed over myself when Coach is apt to be coming or going."

That explained part of why she had seen so little of him. "You were able to calm troubled waters?"

"Pretty much, which is why I've also stayed during all the meal hours in Maple Hall," he admitted. His voice softened. "I should've told you."

"I wish you had, but we're all on edge." Doro smiled. "Now, let's go, so we're there before the crowd comes."

"And any of them cause chaos," he murmured.

"You and Wade will handle whatever happens," Doro said.

"We'll try."

As they made their way across campus, Doro and Ev encountered Aggie and Wade. After the group exchanged greetings, Aggie spoke. "It's good you took all the shortbread, Doro. The kids ate a lot of my chocolate chip cookies, so I don't have as many as I planned." She gestured to Wade who carried far fewer bags than Ev.

"Mrs. Jones and some others will bring take-along treats, too, so we'll have plenty," Doro said.

"Faculty members living in college housing have another two weeks to move out," Wade commented. "I suppose they can enjoy the sweets there."

"They will," Doro agreed, "but most who plan to stay with relatives will leave tomorrow or Tuesday, so they can spend Thanksgiving with them."

"I can understand that. When I worked on the railroad, I did my best to get home early for Thanksgiving and Christmas," the constable said.

Aggie slid her hand into the crook of his arm. "I'm glad you aren't away from home now."

"Me, too," he agreed, patting her hand.

When Ev remained silent, Doro made an observation. "I'm not planning to move out of Wheaton Hall until next week. Since Ev and I are spending Thanksgiving with Gramma Rose, we can load his automobile and take part of what I need. I'll haul the rest later."

"A great idea. Gramma Rose will be thrilled to have you with her," Aggie said. "And Tee will enjoy the yard."

"She will," Doro agreed. The little dog loved Gramma Rose, but she would miss Ev when they moved into her grandmother's home. So would Doro. Thinking about the weeks ahead threatened to lower her holiday spirit, which was not high. Before she could say more, the group crossed paths with Carson

Longley and Edith Farrow, who was one of Doro's neighbors in Wheaton Hall. "Good morning."

Longley glanced around the group. "Probably good for all of you. Not necessarily for many of us. I'll be packing up tonight and heading to who knows where in a few days." His gaze narrowed on Aggie. "I'll be without a home and a job after the board meeting on Wednesday."

Color rose in Aggie's cheeks as she gripped Wade's arm tighter. "You can't be sure you'll be let go."

He scowled. "I saw the schedule of classes for next semester. There are five fewer listed in the English department. As the last person hired, I'll undoubtedly be the first to go, even though I'm the sole support of myself." Longley looked down at Edith. "And even though it will mean delaying any understanding between us."

The petite blonde's blue eyes filled with tears. "It's not fair," she murmured.

Although Doro knew the professor and the English department secretary had been stepping out for a couple of months, she did not approve of the woman sharing information that had not been widely distributed. "I wasn't aware your chairman released the slate of classes. When it's official, I get it since my course on the mystery novel is among them. But I haven't received the schedule."

Pink surged into Edith's face. "It hasn't been released to everyone yet, but Carson was in the office when the chairman gave it to me, so...well, he happened to see it."

Longley patted her hand. "It's hardly a secret, Edie."

"Cuts won't be announced until after the board meeting," Doro pointed out. "You can't be sure your position will end."

The English professor snorted derisively. "Easy for you to say, since you won't be out of work. Coach Munroe wouldn't dare touch your job."

"The coach doesn't make academic decisions." Doro frowned at the man. "You've made a serious allegation twice, and it makes no sense,"

A harrumph left him. "It would if you weren't in your protected world. Munroe has the ears of a couple of trustees. They'll make sure he keeps his job, and they won't take on anyone with a long history here. So, you're safe. Meanwhile, the rest of us have to fend for ourselves."

Munroe curried favor with trustees who were former basketball players. The man would not go to bat for her, but Doro could not overlook her family's lengthy involvement on campus. Maybe it had more influence than she cared to believe. "Even if your job is eliminated, the changes are only temporary. As soon as enrollment recovers, people will be hired back."

"When will that be? The economy has only worsened since the crash, and there's no end in sight. Unlike some of you, I don't have family to rely on. Neither does Edie." Longley stared daggers at Aggie. "You'd think the faculty who have support would step down to help those who desperately need a job."

Recalling his previous similar comment, Doro opened her mouth to chastise the man. Wade beat her to it.

"My wife worked hard to get tenure. Why should she quit?" the constable asked in a cool, crisp tone.

Longley's jaw worked from side-to-side. "I didn't say she should."

Wade's steely gaze focused on the English professor. "You hinted at it."

Silence hung heavily in the chilly air for several moments. When Edie shivered, Doro made a suggestion. "Let's all go to the dining hall where we can warm up. Dinner will be served at noon, so Aggie and I need to get there. We've volunteered to help since no students are on campus to fill that role like they usually do."

"Those basketball players are still here," Longley said. "Why not make them do something?"

"They have a tournament this week, so they're practicing later today," Ev said.

"On Sunday?" the young professor echoed.

"President Adams approved it," Doro said.

A snort left the man. "He approves a lot for his favorites. Like giving tenure to someone a year early."

Doro's gaze went wide because she knew he meant her. After a moment, she glanced at Edie. "As the English department secretary, you see a lot of documents."

The young woman blushed and gripped Longley's arm tighter. Another little shiver rippled through her. "I'd like to get inside. It's cold out here."

Longley smiled down at her. "Of course." He put a forefinger to his hat brim. "Excuse us."

For a long moment, Doro stared after the quickly retreating figures. "Edie had to see the report from the President's office."

"Probably so," Aggie agreed. "She shouldn't have told anyone. Especially not someone as mouthy as Longley."

Ev squeezed Doro's hand. "Don't worry about it. You deserve tenure, just like you deserve to be the library director. Family connections have nothing to do with it. You're great at your job, and everyone with sense knows it."

His sincere support lifted Doro's spirits. "Thank you."

"He's right. You not only work in the library, you teach two sections of your mystery course with no extra pay," Aggie added. "But what did Longley mean about the coach and the trustees?"

Doro provided a summary. "I'm afraid it may be true, because a couple of trustees were on the team as students, and they're friendly with the coach. I love the sport, but I don't like it taking precedence over academics."

The group agreed, but Aggie was the one who responded. "It isn't right, but neither is being so nasty. Now, let's forget those two and enjoy dinner."

"First, we need to help set up," Doro reminded her friend.

"We'll enjoy that, too," Aggie said.

Doro nodded, but doubt dogged her.

꙳

The aroma of roasting turkey, sage, cinnamon, nutmeg, and apples filled the dining hall kitchen when the group entered. Mrs. Fisher, the girls' dormitory cook, stood at the far counter while several other ladies took pies and rolls out of boxes and bags. Violet Jones was one of them.

Wade inhaled deeply. "Everything smells delicious."

"It sure does," Ev agreed.

Mrs. Jones smiled. "Dinner will be served right at noon, but you can put the cookies over on the far table." She gestured to the other side of the room.

"We put them in bags, so people could easily grab one," Aggie said.

"I appreciate you girls pitching in." The secretary's expression grew serious. "With the semester ending early, college personnel won't be here for the town Christmas party."

Doro glanced at Aggie. "I'm not on the committee this year, but Aggie is. Do you have news?"

A soft sigh left the other young woman. "We're meeting again tomorrow. As things stand, the gathering will be much smaller because fewer people can afford to donate, and the town is strapped for funds. It may only be caroling in the park, and no dance at all. If folks pitch in, we can have cookies and cocoa at the church afterward. But no money will come from the town."

Ev and Wade returned to the group in time to hear the last phrase. The constable frowned. "Considering that Ev's job was eliminated and Colleen is only working part-time as my clerk, spending money on a big event doesn't make sense."

"I understand the decision," Doro said. "Maybe next year everything will be back to normal."

Mrs. Jones offered a smile that did not quite reach her gaze. "I'm sure it will be. Now, if you two girls will put gourds and pumpkins in the baskets and get them on the sideboards, that will help. Aggie, afterwards, maybe you'll assist with making side dishes, while Doro puts candles on the tables."

Aggie immediately agreed, and Doro followed suit. When they finished the baskets, Ev came over to praise their efforts. "Very festive."

"Doro has a knack for making things look pretty. You should see her apartment. It's warm and cozy and tasteful," Aggie said.

Her friend's praise warmed Doro's heart, but Ev's next comment heated it up.

"I'd love to see her apartment, and I look forward to seeing what she'll do with our first home. My talents don't extend to decorating," Ev said.

His words painted a reassuring and exciting picture. "I look forward to that, too," Doro said.

"I better get into the kitchen," Aggie said before heading away.

Ev studied Doro's expression. "What's the matter?"

She shrugged. "Aggie gets to help prepare food while my next task is to put candles on the tables because I have no domestic talent."

"Making things look pretty and festive is a talent, and an important one. You were responsible for the decorations for the town Christmas party for the past two years and for the Sweetheart Dance ones."

"Those aren't as important as putting meals on the table," she murmured.

"You won't need to worry about that for a while," Ev said.

The comment, while made in a casual tone, increased her doubt about when they would wed. "Let's get the decorating done."

They were finishing that task when Mrs. Jones came out of the kitchen. "Everything looks wonderful, Doro. You have a knack for decorating."

A smile formed on Doro's lips. "Thank you."

Wade walked up and agreed. "You do. The kids loved the special decorations you did for my ma's birthday party last summer, and you were a big help with our wedding decorations. Aggie has a way of making a home warm and comfortable, but you put the sparkle in."

"See," Ev said. "That's what I mean. You're good at adding the special touches to make an occasion festive. We should all tell you that more often."

"We should," Mrs. Jones agreed, who stood beside Doro. "And you made cranberry relish. I know that will be tasty. You used your grandmother's recipe, didn't you?"

Doro nodded. "Fresh cranberries, apples, oranges, and walnuts." Getting the citrus fruit had not been easy or cheap, but it was a key ingredient.

"My mouth is watering," Wade said.

"Mine, too," Ev agreed.

Mrs. Jones smiled. "You'll love it." She turned to Doro. "Now, I could use you for a more mundane chore in the kitchen. Making whipped cream." She glanced at the men. "In a few minutes, we could use your help in getting dishes on buffet tables."

Everyone pitched in, which made quick work of the various tasks. By quarter to noon, every dish was ready to serve, and the plates and cutlery were in place, as well. Since diners were already arriving, Mrs. Jones removed her apron. "We'd like to get folks seated at tables as they arrive. Then, we'll have them go to the buffet table-by-table."

"We'll all help with that," Doro said before the rest of her group agreed. Before they went to man the two doors into the room, she turned to Ev. "Have you spoken with Coach Munroe?"

Ev nodded. "Tee and I ran into him yesterday. When I seconded Wade's invitation to sit with us, he gladly accepted the overture. Even though he can be cantankerous, Munroe would like to eat in peace. His words."

"Good," Doro murmured.

"With a little luck, Longley and Baylor won't shoot their mouths off. If they do, Wade and I will handle them, so don't worry. Just enjoy dinner," Ev said.

His smile eased her mind, if only a little. "I will," Doro assured him.

Their conversation was cut short by the arrival of more diners. Most offered friendly greetings, but Longley and Edie, who entered by Doro and Ev's door, pushed past without a glance. Baylor entered through a door on the other side, where Aggie and Wade were directing guests to tables. Doro briefly exchanged greetings with President Adams and the deans before directing them to a table near the front of the room.

When the crowd was settled, Doro and Ev made their way to the places assigned to them. Aggie, Wade, and Floyd Quartine were already seated.

After taking a place next to her best friend, Doro asked about Baylor.

"He glared at Wade and me when we welcomed him," Aggie replied. "What about Edie and Longley?"

Doro rolled her eyes. "They ignored us." She glanced to where the group sat with two others who lived in Wheaton Hall. "I hope they don't start trouble when Coach Munroe arrives. He'll have to walk right past their table, no matter which door he comes in."

"I wonder why he's late," Aggie said.

"Maybe working out some new plays for the team," Floyd put in. "Michaw College has won the big tournament three years in a row. I'd sure like to see them make it four."

"That'd be great," Doro agreed.

"It would," Ev added, "and you're probably right about Coach working on game plans. Tee and I ran into him yesterday. He mentioned wanting to add a couple new plays at today's practice."

"By the time every table goes to the buffet, he'll be here," Wade said. "Munroe likes good food as much as I do."

Ev chuckled. "Put me in that group."

The by-play made Doro smile. Ev was always hungry, and she often wondered how he stayed so lean. The same was true of Coach Munroe, who was well-known for his interest in food.

After everyone at her table had filled their plates and sat down, Doro looked around in case the coach had taken a place elsewhere, but there was no sign of him. However, Longley and Baylor stared daggers at her. Doro stared back before tackling her meal. Casual conversation ensued until Ev brought up Munroe again. "No sign of the coach."

"Mr. Munroe has been here for five years, and I've never known him to miss a campus dinner," Mrs. Jones observed. "I hope he's not ill. A lot of people have colds."

"That's true, but he's never been absent from a big meal in my memory, either," Doro added.

"If he's concerned about the tournament, he probably wanted to get more done before practice," Floyd said. "But he's missing a wonderful dinner."

"Which isn't like him," Mrs. Jones murmured. "I always worry when sickness spreads across campus. I suppose it's an after-effect of the Spanish flu epidemic. We lost a few folks in town and at the school."

Floyd patted her hand. "You have a kind heart, Violet, but Coach Munroe is a healthy young man. I'm sure he's fine."

"I'll stop by the fieldhouse later," Ev said. "Floyd is probably right about Coach working on game plans. Munroe mentioned the possibility of running late for the meal and joked about me making sure some was saved for him. I'll check after we eat, if he doesn't show up by then."

"Good idea," Mrs. Jones observed. "Please tell him that we have leftovers. Mrs. Fisher will be in her suite here until she leaves for her sister's place on Wednesday. She'll be happy to fix a big plate for him. In fact, there'll probably be enough for the entire team."

Ev nodded. "I'll let him know."

A moment later, Doro went to the dessert table with Ev, where they encountered Longley and Baylor. Both professors glared at them.

"Officer Mallow, you were smart to tell Munroe to stay away," Baylor said. "His presence would've spoiled dinner for some of us."

"That's for sure," Longley agreed. "Just seeing him gobble up food like he hasn't a care in the world is sickening. We have to observe it every morning at breakfast and often at dinner. Sometimes, even at lunch."

"And listen to him brag about his job and his team," his friend added.

Their snide remarks annoyed Doro. Although she was not a fan of Coach Munroe, she did not like hearing anyone denigrated. "Why do you two hate him so much? What has he ever done to you that's so terrible?"

Baylor sneered. "Belittle us for having brains and for not being athletic, like that's an important goal."

"Yep, every chance he gets," Longley agreed.

The memory of Munroe using *milquetoast* to describe the two professors came to mind, and Doro wondered if he used the term to their faces. Most likely. "That's mean, but can't you let it go?"

"Let it go," Baylor echoed. "We're losing our jobs. He's not and neither are you two." He jerked a thumb at Doro and at Ev. "The trustees would support either of you, but it's not like that for us. We don't have connections with the board, like you." He stared at Doro. "Didn't your father go to school with one of them? And teach two others?"

Denying facts was futile. Showing sympathy might help. "I'm sorry if some of them intervened," Doro said. Before she could say more, Baylor interrupted.

"Longley and I struggled to get through college and graduate school. Have you ever fought to keep a roof over your head, Professor Banyon?"

The question held Doro mute. She had not but what could she say?

"C'mon, Bay, let's get out of here," Longley said before stalking off with his buddy behind him.

After picking up two dessert plates with pie, Ev turned to Doro. "Let's go back to our table."

"Good idea," she murmured. On the way, Doro watched the professors and Edie Farrow leave.

"What happened when you were getting pie?" Aggie asked as soon as Doro and Ev sat down.

"Longley and Baylor were complaining about Coach Munroe again," Doro replied. "They're glad he's not here."

"That's unkind," Aggie said. "The coach is prickly. I ran afoul of him when one of his players was a problem in my class."

After a bite of pie, Doro responded. "I didn't know that."

"It was handled in short order, but I had to involve President Adams." Aggie smiled. "I don't want to spoil dinner by discussing it, but some of Munroe's players are arrogant."

"And he can be, too," her husband added as he stood. "I'm getting dessert."

Aggie smiled. "I'll go with you."

After the couple left the table, Doro turned to Ev. "At least there wasn't much of a squabble, and it was directed at us. I'm sorry for those people losing their jobs, but Longley and Baylor didn't need to get nasty because we have work."

Ev picked up his fork but did not begin eating dessert. "Try to put yourself in their shoes. They'll probably be eliminated on Wednesday, and you just got a big promotion. That has to be hard for them to take."

"I'm sympathetic," Doro murmured.

His gray gaze clouded. "I wasn't suggesting you aren't, but pitying people isn't the same as knowing how they feel. When you've struggled for everything, the thought of losing it is crushing." He ran the fork tines around the edge of his dessert plate. "Evidently, neither Longley nor Baylor was raised with many advantages, and they mentioned fighting to get their degrees. They shouldn't have been rude and mean, but I see their frame of reference."

Although he had not criticized her, his words stung. Her throat clogged with hurt, Doro laid down her fork because she could not swallow another bite.

Ev laid his hand on her arm. "I'm sorry. I shouldn't have said that. It was unjustified. You're such a caring, soft-hearted person. They shouldn't have gotten nasty with you."

"You didn't say anything wrong, and it is hard to put myself in someone else's shoes although I try."

"We all have that challenge," he assured her. Ev pointed at her pie. "You better eat that, because I can't stand to see it go to waste."

Doro snatched up her fork. "Don't worry. That won't happen," she said before digging in again.

After the entire group at the table helped clean up, it was nearly three o'clock, so the two young couples left. Once they got outside, Aggie and Wade headed toward town while Doro and Ev went to get Tee. They only made it partway to Maple Hall when two boys, basketball players, raced toward them shouting. "I wonder what's wrong," Doro said.

"Maybe they can't get into the fieldhouse. Coach could still be in his office charting plays," Ev observed. "I think practice was scheduled for three-thirty."

"You gotta come quick," the shorter redhead managed to choke out.

"Yep, hurry, Officer," the other young man said.

Both were breathless, which made understanding them hard. "Slow down, boys. What's wrong, Robert?" Doro asked the redhead.

"It's coach, Professor Banyon. When we got to the field-house, we found him on the floor of his office," Robert replied. He jerked a thumb at his buddy. "Artie and I were early, but a couple other guys came before we left. They're still in the building."

"Have you called Doc Silven?" Ev looked from one boy to the other.

"Coach doesn't need a doctor," Robert murmured.

Doro and Ev exchanged a long look. "What makes you say that?" she asked.

"He's dead, Professor."

Chapter Five

For endless moments, Doro grappled with the revelation. But was Robert right? Coach Munroe was young, only a few years older than Doro, and fit. The man often participated in his team's practices. Surely, he had not dropped over dead.

Ev asked the question in her mind. "Are you certain?"

Robert Windsor nodded. "My grandfather is a doctor. He taught me how to take somebody's pulse. Coach didn't have one." The boy swallowed hard. "Besides, there's blood on the floor, and he's all crumpled up right by his desk."

"You didn't touch the body, other than to take his pulse, did you?" Ev made the query to both boys.

"No, sir," Artie Rawlinson, his dark eyes filled with repressed tears, responded. "Can you come?"

"Of course." Ev glanced at Doro. "You're coming along, aren't you? I could use your expert help, as always."

"Certainly."

"Good," he replied, relief in his tone and expression.

Doro and Ev trailed the boys to the fieldhouse. The two-story red brick structure resembled other campus buildings with its white trim and ivy climbing the walls. Behind matching white columns adorning the front were four sets of double-doors. On game nights, they were unlocked to allow a free flow of attendees to come inside. At other times, the building played host to physical education classes and to the college coaches, who had offices there. When classes were in session, the place was filled with activity. Not so now. Their footsteps clattered on the terrazzo floor, and the only light filtered through the dirt-streaked clerestory windows since no ceiling lamps or sconces were on. As they walked on in silence, the group passed several closed doors before arriving at one that stood ajar.

"This is Coach's office," Robert said in a quiet voice befitting a sickroom or a mortuary.

Ev let Doro precede him. After entering the room, they saw two more players, one dark-skinned and the other light, standing next to the body. Both had tears in their eyes. "You haven't touched anything, I hope," Ev said.

Both young men shook their heads. "We just waited to make sure no one else came in," Clyde Porter, the darker one, said. The boy glanced at Doro. "Are you here to investigate, Professor?"

"Officer Mallow and I were about to get Tee, so I came along." Doro offered a reassuring smile. The young man was a frequent visitor to the library, so she knew him well. "There may be nothing to investigate, Clyde."

"If you look behind Coach's desk, you'll see there probably is," the other boy, lean and lanky with almost colorless blonde hair, said.

Since the kid had been in Doro's mystery course, he was well-known to her. James Docket had expressed great interest in the books, so he had some familiarity with murders—at least fictional ones. Doro glanced at Ev who moved past the players.

"You fellows are right. We've got a case here." Before he crouched down, Ev gestured for Doro to join him.

Her hand went to her mouth as she gazed at the crumpled form and the blood on the floor beneath it. "Can you tell what happened?" Doro had her own suspicions.

"It appears to be a stab wound. There's a small slice in his neck." After rising to his feet, Ev looked around the group of boys. "Please get Constable Lammers. If he isn't at his mother's house, he's at home. Fetch Doc Silven, too, and don't tell anyone else what happened here. All right?"

"We'll keep quiet," James assured them.

The other three nodded.

"And please hurry," Doro added. After the boys took off without a backward glance, she shoved her hands into her coat pockets. Despite wearing gloves, her fingers felt like ice. "Coach must've been killed before noon, because he planned to be at the dinner around that time."

"True," Ev agreed, "and now, we know why he wasn't there."

"Unfortunately, we do." Doro looked around the cramped office. A desk lamp shed light on an array of papers. She focused her attention there. "He was working on plays, but there are two different scripts."

Ev bent over the desk. "There are. One probably belongs to the assistant coach."

Doro's brow furrowed. "Clint Spalling is working through the tournament. From what Stan Jackson said the other day, it sounded like Clint made up a lot of the plays. Maybe he and Munroe were working together on these."

"Maybe so, because I've gotten the idea that Clint's often involved in creating game plans." After another glance at Munroe, Ev gestured toward the door. "Let's stand on the other side of the room. I want Wade and Doc to see the things as we did, and I'd like to hear them coming. We can look for the murder weapon after they observe the scene. I don't want to disturb things."

"All right." When both of them were stationed near the door, Doro again looked back at the desk. "You've mentioned talking to Clint, and it sounds like you two chatted more than a couple of times."

"A few times."

When he did not continue, Doro asked a direct question. "Is there more to your conversations than you already said?" She figured there must be or Ev would not be shifting from one foot to the other while avoiding her scrutiny.

"A little more," he admitted before meeting her gaze. "As you know, Clint has been seeing Miss Jackson."

"I know, but I'm not well-acquainted with Miss Jackson. I know she rents a room from the Piersons, who are also relatively new to town." Reverend and Mrs. Pierson, a couple in their forties, had only been in Michaw for a handful of years. Doro knew them and liked them, but she missed the old pastor and his family. "This is her first year at the high school. Aggie and I welcomed her last summer. I said she could bring her classes to the library any time, since the one at the school is tiny and the town library isn't big, either."

"Did she take you up on the offer?"

Doro shook her head. "She thanked both of us but indicated there are plenty of materials at the school?"

"Are there?"

"If she sticks to the textbooks, I suppose so." Doro shrugged. "She seemed shy, so that may be part of the issue."

"Clint isn't reserved," Ev observed.

"No, he isn't. Sometimes, he acts like a kid himself."

A low laugh left Ev. "He's only twenty-five."

"That's not much younger than you and I, and we don't act like kids."

"I grew up fast after my dad died, and you were probably born mature." His lips twitched as he spoke the last phrase.

Since she knew Ev did not want sympathy about how hard he'd had things as a boy, Doro focused on his observation about her. "I played with dolls. Of course, I had the dolls being the students in my library. I wasn't content to use my little books, so I hauled them to my dad's den. I pulled all the books I could reach off the shelves and put my dolls next to them on the floor."

"I can visualize that," he said with a grin. "I wish I'd known you when you were a little girl."

"That would've been fun." She smiled. "It's fun just having a casual conversation, since that hasn't happened for days."

A moment of silence preceded his reply. "I've been busy and preoccupied. Sorry."

For several seconds, she searched his face. Although she wanted to pursue a deeper discussion of his recent withdrawal, Doro returned to the matters at hand. "Do you know why he and Stan Jackson weren't at today's dinner? Miss Jackson could've come with them." A niggling finger of doubt traced her spine. Stan Jackson had been angry at Munroe on behalf of his sister, and Clint Spalling was upset, as well. Where had the pair been this afternoon?

"All three often eat Sunday dinner with the Piersons."

The comment provided fresh revelations. "You know them much better than I do."

Ev leaned against the doorframe. "Remember, I make rounds several times a day, and I run into Clint fairly often. I'm also a big basketball fan. Occasionally, I see Stan in College Hall, since he cleans there."

"I like basketball," Doro said, fixing on the first part of Ev's statement.

"But you aren't out-and-about as much as I am. Clint seems to think of me like a big brother, so he's asked for advice a couple of times."

Doro's gaze went wide. More and more details were coming out about Ev's and Clint's friendship, which surprised her. What Ev said about being around the campus often was true. "You never mentioned talking with him a lot."

"I wasn't holding out on you," Ev replied. "Clint didn't want anyone to know about a couple of issues. One was what Stan mentioned on Monday. When his job was eliminated, Clint was upset. I told you that. But I didn't say how upset or that his main target was Coach Munroe."

"Target," Doro echoed. "In what way? Not a literal target."

Again, Ev's gaze moved away from Doro. "Clint shot his mouth off but took it all back."

Dismay filled Doro. "Did he threaten the coach?"

Ev let his head rest against the wall. "Clint said he wished Munroe would drop dead, but he didn't mean it. He took it back almost immediately."

Several seconds elapsed before Doro responded. "People say things like that without any intention of causing harm, but Coach Munroe is dead. Murdered."

Ev's nostrils flared with a sharp intake of breath. "Clint may have been at the Pierson house for dinner. Stan, too. Like I said, both of them often eat there on Sunday, so I'm not sure either one is a strong suspect."

Doro chewed on her lower lip. "Stan blamed Munroe for Clint not keeping his job, and Coach ranted about Clint being more interested in Miss Jackson than in the team."

With one hand, Ev massaged the back of his neck. "We've talked about that in the past, and we agreed we felt the same way. Putting a loved one ahead of a job doesn't mean people don't work hard and do well. You and I do. So do Aggie and Wade. Family first. Then, work. Besides, Munroe originally said it after the team lost a big game."

Surprise filled Doro. "I didn't know that. When?"

"After the game you missed," he murmured.

"So, he was using Clint as a scapegoat?"

"Clint believes that, and I think it's quite likely," Ev replied. "You know how Coach Munroe was. He berated Clint in front of people by accusing him of being blinded by love like some schoolboy."

"That's awful." Doro studied Ev's expression. "You sympathize with Clint."

"I understand how he feels. He's cares for Miss Jackson, and she cares for him. They want to court the appropriate length of time and go on to an engagement. He can't do that when he has to find a job elsewhere. Not being able to see her is breaking his heart. I'll feel the same way, if I have to leave here."

Alarm filled Doro. "Why would you have to leave? We both have jobs."

Ev ran a hand over his face. "Right now, we do. But no job is completely safe. I've already lost the part-time deputy position."

Her heart hammered hard. "Did President Adams say something about your campus job?"

His gaze moved to a point beyond Doro. "Not really."

The vague reply and his outward reaction made her think about Ev's conversation with his old boss. "Did you call Lowery asking about a job with him?"

His gaze slipped to her and away again. "I told you that we talk sometimes."

"You've been busy." Or so Ev had told her. "I assume Lowery is, too. I'm surprised you both have time to chat, especially when calls must go through several operators."

As his nostrils flared with a sharp intake of breath, Ev looked back at Doro. "The calls aren't frequent because there's no shortage of bootlegging operations for Lowery to investigate."

"Around here?" While Doro did not want Lowery haranguing Ev to return to the Bureau, or Ev inquiring about going back, she hated thinking locals were involved in rumrunning. Only a year-and-a-half earlier, a local bootlegger had been murdered, which had led to a tricky case—one where Ev had temporarily worked with the Bureau.

Confusion clouded his gray eyes. "Around Michaw, you mean?"

"Yes. I'm wondering if he's asking you for information or wanting you back at the Bureau."

A contemplative expression covered Ev's face. "He always wonders if anyone around here seems suspicious. More than a few students go to city speakeasies, but I don't have evidence of them running booze. Same with locals."

The response neither confirmed nor refuted her warring worries. Before Doro formed another remark, the sounds of footsteps in the corridor ended their discussion. Within moments, Wade and Doc approached them. Ev waved the pair inside while Doro led the way to Munroe's office. The four basketball players came in behind the men. "You got here quickly," she said. Too quickly considering she had not gotten to the bottom of Ev's call with Lowery.

"The boys picked Wade up at his mother's place, and Aggie called me while they drove over," Silven explained. "She plans to contact President Adams, too."

"I've got a vehicle," Artie said, "so, we all went together."

Doro smiled at the boy. "That was smart."

"It was," Wade agreed before focusing on Ev. "The group told us Coach Munroe was killed, maybe stabbed."

"That's right," Ev agreed. "It looks like he was working on plays, since papers are strewn across his desk. He's on the floor behind it, and the evidence would lead to a conclusion of stabbing."

Doro nodded. "The wound is most likely from a sharp instrument."

"If you both believe that, you're most likely right," Wade observed.

"We didn't search for a weapon, since Ev wanted you to see the scene just like we did," Doro put in.

"That'll help," Wade said.

With one hand, Ev gestured toward the open door. "Go in and see what you think."

After Wade and Doc entered the office, Ev turned to the four boys. "Stick around here for a little while. We might have more questions for you."

"Sure," Robert replied. "We can go inside the gym and sit on the bleachers."

"The perfect place," Doro said. The group, their steps as slow as men four times their age, walked down the corridor. When they disappeared from view, she looked at Ev. "This has to be hard on them. Finding their coach murdered in his office only a few days before their big tournament. President Adams will be upset, too. He's had so much to handle over the last few months, what with enrollment falling. Now this."

"There's been a lot on him since last spring," Wade said,

Doro nodded. During the college's Founder's Day celebration, a priceless book had been stolen, and a visitor had died. That had led to Doro, Ev, Aggie, and Wade cracking another case, but more importantly to her, Ev had proposed at the conclusion. She smiled at the memory.

His gaze narrowed on her. "I didn't figure you looked back on those few days with a positive bent."

Her grin intensified. "A few minutes of that long weekend were memorable in a terrific way."

Before Ev replied, Wade's voice broke into their discussion. "Can you two come in here?"

"Let's go." Ev let her precede him.

Wade faced them. "You already said Munroe planned to work on new plays for the team, and that's backed up by the evidence."

"It is," Ev agreed. "I'm sure you noticed the two different handwriting styles."

"I did, but Munroe wasn't planning to meet anyone, was he?" the constable asked.

Ev shook his head. "Not to my knowledge. He was here ahead of today's practice, from what we know."

"We talked to several players, and they came to the fieldhouse around the same time," Doro added.

"Someone else wrote on these papers," Silven said. "Someone who was helping create a game plan."

Wade scratched his head. "He might work on plays with the team captain but more likely with his assistant coach."

Next to Doro, tension radiated from Ev. A glance at him revealed a set jaw. Despite Ev's friendship with the assistant coach, he would tell Wade everything, but moments passed before he did.

After giving a thumbnail sketch about the entire situation, Ev finished with, "I'll talk with Clint Spalling after we wrap up here."

"All right," Wade said. "When will the rest of the team be here?"

Doro looked at her watch. "Practice was supposed to be soon, I think."

"At three-thirty, from what Munroe told me," Ev said.

"I'll stick around," Wade said. "I'd like you here, too, Ev."

"I can stay as the campus security officer," Ev replied.

Wade tapped Ev's shoulder. "You'll be my deputy again soon. For this case, let's say you're working in that capacity on a temporary basis. Not that you don't have enough to do on campus,"

Wade said before stepping behind the desk where Silven knelt on the floor. "What do you think, Doc?"

Silven got to his feet. "It looks like Coach died almost immediately since the wound is to the carotid artery. It's small and shallow, but lethal."

"At least he didn't suffer," Doro murmured.

"No, he didn't," Doc agreed as he looked from Doro to Ev. "Obviously, the weapon wasn't laying out when you two got here."

"I'm afraid not. We can look around, but maybe we should wait until we get fingerprints. With players in-and-out of here, I'm afraid there are already plenty," Ev replied.

Wade folded his arms across his chest. "I was at Ma's place, so I didn't have our fingerprinting kit handy. Aggie's picking it up and bringing it. She'll have to go back to our house for the extra keys and on to the office, so it'll be a bit."

"Great," Ev said. "Let's wait until we get prints to really dig around. No sense in making more."

"I agree," Wade said.

As Doc again looked at the victim, he made a suggestion. "I'd like to get the body back to my office for a better examination than I can do here."

"I'll help you take Coach to your vehicle," Wade said.

"Thanks," the physician replied.

As was typical for moving a dead body, Doc had brought a stretcher and blanket. After he and Wade fetched it, Ev helped them lift Coach Munroe and walked out with the pair of men. Doro stood by the main door to the fieldhouse. While she waited, Doro leaned against the wall. The discussion with the players had not provided any clear direction. Hopefully, more information would arise when they met with the group because the last thing the campus needed was an unsolved murder.

Chapter Six

E ven before the two lawmen got back, one more basket-ball player arrived. Doro recognized him as a student from her mystery novel course. "Hello, Mike," she said.

Mike Vassal was black-haired and blue-eyed. The boy, who stood just under six-feet, watched Doc pull out of the parking lot before responding. "What's going on Professor Banyon? Several guys were coming over early to practice their foul shots. I hope they weren't messing around and getting hurt. We're already down to seven players." His gaze filled with anxiety.

The team usually fielded twelve, but a few players had left school due to financial problems. "No, none of them is hurt," she replied. While she was speaking, Ev and Wade returned.

"What happened that you're here?" Mike asked. His gaze narrowed on Ev.

A long breath escaped the security officer. "There's some bad news."

"Professor Banyon said none of the guys is hurt," Mike responded.

"She's right. None of your teammates is injured, but your coach is." Ev stopped for a moment before finishing in a softer tone. "I'm sorry to say he's dead."

Silence reverberated in the chilly November air. When Mike spoke, his voice sounded thin and thready. "That can't be. Coach isn't old."

Sympathy squeezed hard on Doro's heart. Losing someone, especially someone young and healthy, was hard to comprehend. Munroe, in his early thirties, should have had many more years ahead of him.

Mike blinked fast but moisture still escaped his eyes. With the back of a hand, he wiped it away. "How? Why?"

Wade took over the explanation. "I'm sorry. I know you all loved Coach Munroe," the constable said.

Doro wondered if that was true or if it was simply how things appeared. She had thought the coach and his assistant got along well. "I've had a few players in my classes. You're one, Mike, and you liked Coach."

"Most of us did," Mike said. "But he could be tough. Not saying that's not necessary sometimes."

A glance at Ev and Wade revealed they felt the same tension she did. Because she knew the boy, Doro went ahead. "But not every player liked him."

Mike shook his head. "You can ask any of the fellas, and they'll say the same. Vince Brownlee and Coach have been at odds for weeks. Not that I'm accusing Vince. I'm not. They've argued a few times. If Vince wasn't such a good player, and we weren't already shorthanded, I think Coach would've thrown him off the team."

The observations troubled Doro. "What did they argue about?"

A moment preceded Mike's response. "Vince and Dale Krowl broke training rules a few times by going into Toledo. Mostly before the season started, but it's still against the rules."

"They visited speakeasies, I suppose," Ev put in.

"Yes, sir," Mike said. "They got caught sneaking into the dormitory way after midnight. More than once, Coach let them go with a warning, but he yelled loud enough to be heard way down the hall in the fieldhouse. If he'd benched both of them, we wouldn't have extra guys. Playing a whole game with no subs would be tough, not to mention we'd be shorthanded if someone fouled out."

"How long ago were Vince and Dale first caught?" Doro asked.

"About six weeks ago," Mike replied. "They got caught for the third time Friday night. Yesterday at practice, Coach said they'd be gone as soon as he had two more players. He and Vince got into a shouting match in the gym. Vince was upset because his dad would be furious if he got cut from the team. He gets tuition money from some big donors because he's such a good player. Without that, Vince couldn't stay in school."

"Basketball has always been big at the college, and the team's had great success for years," Doro observed. That was why some alumni had pooled funds to help top-notch athletes with tuition. Usually, the boys appreciated the support. Occasionally, one was like Vince—thinking he could flaunt the rules because he was a star.

"But Vince wouldn't hurt Coach Munroe," Mike insisted. "You should talk to Professor Longley. He hates Coach and sports."

Ev's forehead furrowed. "What makes you say that?"

Doro repressed a smile. Ev was digging for clues without giving too much away.

The young man's mouth quirked. "I'm in Longley's literature class, and he's railed about the college spending money on athletics more than once. He's given me and Artie trouble about getting out of class on Fridays, if we have road games. It's school policy to allow that, but Longley makes a stink every time. Baylor is the same way. I have him for math, and he has attendance as part of the grade. Coach talked to him more than once about not penalizing me for missing a few Fridays. Approved absences shouldn't be taken into consideration, but Baylor disagrees."

"Do you know how their discussions went?" Ev inquired.

Mike grimaced. "Last season, Coach had to get President Adams involved. That made Baylor even madder. I wasn't in his class but a couple other guys were. This fall, he let me know I better not miss any classes other than on road trip Fridays."

As Doro listened, she realized the campus grapevine had not carried these tales, probably because financial issues had taken top billing. "So, things have gotten worse in the last few weeks?"

Mike nodded. "Longley got a head of steam going after word circulated that jobs were being cut due to enrollment dropping. Same with Baylor."

After a moment, Ev said, "Let's go inside. Most of the team should already be in the gym. Constable Lammers and I will want to speak with each of you individually."

The boy walked ahead of Doro and Ev. When Mike was out of earshot, she paused and Ev stopped beside her. "It has to be after the scheduled time for practice. Vince and Dale aren't here yet, which bothers me."

"Me, too," Ev agreed. "If they don't show up soon, Wade or I will go looking for them. Until then, let's see what else we can learn from the others. I don't want to pose too many questions to the entire group, but a few shouldn't hurt."

She let a moment pass before making another observation. "Clint isn't here, either, and I'd expect the assistant coach to arrive early."

Ev's jaw tightened. "So would I, but something might've kept him. Sometimes, Reverend Pierson has congregants stop by, which could've delayed dinner. Clint says that's happened in the past."

"Maybe so." As she went with Ev to the gymnasium, Doro reviewed their current information. Despite great success as a coach, Roscoe Munroe had made more than one enemy. Which one had killed him remained to be seen, but hopefully, not for long.

When Doro and Ev entered the silent room, they found the team seated in the bleachers. Moments later, Wade and President Adams walked in. All eyes went to them, so Doro and Ev stepped aside and let the university administrator take center stage.

"You all know the sad news already. I can't believe what happened right in this building, but Constable Lammers promises that the killer will be found and brought to justice. I know he and Officer Mallow will work long and hard until that happens." Adams nodded at Doro. "Professor Banyon will be part of the effort. All of you know she's a fine amateur sleuth, so answer her questions, too."

Since Doro knew most of the boys, she saw few pitfalls. Only Vince Brownlee came to mind as someone who might not cooperate with her. The thought was not fully formed when the young man in question sauntered into the gym.

"Why hasn't practice started?" Vince asked, as his blue gaze skittered over his teammates. Tall with strawberry blonde hair, he was not only the team captain, he was the star center.

Doro thought that position fit him perfectly because the kid loved being the center of attention, which was the primary reason he had dropped her class the previous fall. Vince had showed off every chance he got. In fact, he made chances, and that was where they had clashed.

"Sit down, Mr. Brownlee." President Adams turned to Dale, who stood several inches shorter than his buddy. "You, too, Mr. Krowl." Dale immediately went to the bleachers and took a seat. Vince moved more slowly. When he reached his teammates, he made a point of nodding at almost all of them. After finally sitting down, he leaned back on the bleachers with his long legs thrust forward and his rangy arms spread out.

"So, what's going on?" Vince asked.

President Adams cleared his throat before providing the basic fact that Coach Munroe was dead, probably murdered. Vince shrugged dismissively, while Dale had no outward reaction.

Before the administrator could say more, Assistant Coach Clint Spalling strode across the gymnasium. "I saw Doc Silven, and he told me what happened. I can't believe it." All color was gone from the man's face, making his almost black eyes stand out more than usual.

A snort left Vince. "Why not? You and Munroe were at odds more often than he and I were. The man ruffled plenty of feathers on this campus, so him getting knocked off is hardly shocking."

Gasps left many of his teammates. James who was seated nearby, swiveled toward Vince. "Coach let you get away with a lot, Brownlee. Too much, but that doesn't mean some of us didn't respect him. Or that we don't mourn his loss." His young face was taut with anger and grief.

Vince sneered. "You've been cozying up to him for two years, but you're still the back-up center. You always will be, since you get stuck in the key. You can't guard anyone your height or taller, either. Not sure how you even made the team, except your folks donate to the road trip fund. Guess they'd stop if you got cut."

Color suffused James' pale face as he jumped to his feet. "Why you sap."

"Sit down, Mr. Docket," President Adams said, but his voice was not as stern as when he had spoken to Vince. "Now is the time for you boys to pull together, not go after each other. I expect much better from all of you, and I expect it now."

After taking his seat again, James nodded. "Yes, sir."

Vince said nothing but gave a slight nod.

President Adams gestured toward Ev and Wade. "Please let the team know what you expect as your investigation progresses. I'll back you up completely."

"Ev, since you're the campus security officer, why don't you start?" Wade asked.

"All right," Ev replied before focusing on the team. "You all know what happened. We need your complete cooperation as we investigate. I can't stress enough how important that is. Being forthright and honest is just as critical. We want to find Coach Munroe's killer as soon as possible. Your assistance will make that happen faster. Constable Lammers, Professor Banyon, and I will talk with each of you individually. Then, we'll want you to keep quiet about the case for now. Gossip will only make solving it harder. Do you all understand?" His gaze rippled over each young man before resting on Vince.

As Doro watched, she saw acquiescence on most of the faces. Only Vince and Dale looked askance. Vince's reaction did not surprise her, and Dale was his buddy in rule-breaking, which did not make them killers. It did make them possible impediments.

"Good," Wade said. "I'd like to conduct the interviews in the constable's office. Please head there now. Since we don't want you discussing the murder until after we talk with you, I'll walk with one group and President Adams will go with the other."

"What about you, Officer Mallow?" Clint asked.

Ev smiled at the assistant coach. "Professor Lammers will be here with our fingerprinting kit shortly. After I get the prints in Munroe's office, I'll be along."

The assistant coach's expression froze. "We've all been in his office, so how will that help?"

"We may ask you, all the players, and anyone else who's been there to provide prints eventually. If we turn up some that don't match any of you, we'll definitely look carefully at that person," Ev replied. "That can wait a while. First, we need more information to come up with suspects."

As she listened, Doro realized the prints might not help solve the case.

"So, you'll fingerprint all suspects?" James asked.

Ev nodded at the boy. "We will. Right now, we're only gathering facts. Fingerprinting will come when we identify some solid suspects."

"That makes sense," James murmured.

"Any questions?" Wade asked.

"I've got one," Clyde said. "We heard Coach was stabbed. Why not take fingerprints from the weapon?"

"We would if we found one," Ev replied. "We surmise it was a sharp instrument with a point and a narrow blade. No such implement was immediately visible, but we'll check more closely after getting the prints.'

"Like a pocket knife?" one of the boys asked.

Wade shook his head. "Doc Silven thinks it had a longer blade than that."

"Maybe a letter opener?" Clyde Porter voiced the question.

"Possibly," Wade replied.

James pushed forward on the bleacher. "Coach had a beautiful brass one. Real sharp with a five-inch blade and an ornate tip. His wife gave it to him their last Christmas together. He always had it on his desk. One day, I stopped by and he'd accidentally cut his palm with it. A lot of blood. Coach said he was lucky it didn't slice his wrist instead."

"We didn't see it, but I'll look more when I go back," Ev said. "Was the cut long enough to need stitches?"

"Maybe," James said. "I'm not sure. Coach didn't show me the actual wound."

When no one spoke, Wade continued. "Thanks. I'll call Doc and see if he had to stitch Munroe's hand. Now, the rest of us will head to my office."

The boys scampered out of the bleachers and on to the gym floor where they formed two groups. Clint joined them. "Our ball boy, Horace MacPherson, should be here any minute, so he can join the three of us, if that's all right."

"Sure," Ev agreed. "If he doesn't show up soon, we'll have to find him."

"Horace has his own timetable," Vince said.

"He does," Dale agreed.

Clyde shook his head. "A lot of times, Horace gets here early and goes to see Coach. Then, he ends up running errands. That's what makes him late to practice."

"That's true," Clint agreed. "Munroe had Horace doing a lot for him."

Since he was a local boy, Doro had known Horace MacPherson all his life. The twenty-year-old loved basketball and had worked with the team for years. Because he learned slowly, Horace made it through twelve years of school with a lot of help from his parents and much understanding from his teachers. Always eager to please, he often ran errands for folks. In her experience, Horace was prompt and proficient. "I know him, and that's true. If someone asks him to do an errand or chore, he always does. He enjoys helping out." Both Vince and Dale glowered at her. Doro stared back. Vince had only been in her class for a day, but he had been a nuisance. Dale made it through the entire term, but he was unenthusiastic at best. Finally, the two players turned their attention elsewhere. As silly as it might be, Doro felt like she had won a skirmish.

"All right," Ev said. "Maybe he'll come while we're getting fingerprints. We'll talk with him, too."

"The rest of us will head out," Wade said. "Aggie should be here any time with the kit."

Ev nodded. "We'll watch for her at the main door."

Doro and Ev let the two groups go ahead of them. When the players, assistant coach, Wade, and Adams were out of the building and well on their way, Ev stopped outside the entrance.

The chilly breeze made Doro glad she had not taken her coat off. "We learned quite a bit already."

After leaning against the brick building, Ev folded his arms over his waist. "We have. I know you didn't bring a notepad, but there should be one with the fingerprinting kit. Will you jot everything down?"

"Sure. That way, we can all go over the information after the interviews."

"Exactly," Ev agreed with a slight smile. "Aggie can help, too, if she doesn't have to watch the children."

Her voice broke in. "I don't. They're with my mother-in-law, my sister-in-law, and their cousins, so I won't be missed."

Doro grinned at her friend. "It's good you have some time to yourself." Since classes ended. Aggie had been with Wade's three children almost all the time they weren't in school. While she loved them and vice-versa, it was a big change going from a spinster professor to a wife with three youngsters. Doro wasn't sure she would have made the transition as easily.

After handing the kit to Ev, Aggie shrugged. "I enjoy being with them. They're well-behaved and a lot of fun."

"Plus, they love you dearly. That's obvious to anyone who sees you with them." Doro was happy for her friend, who had been alone since her parents died and her brother stayed in France after the war.

A wide smile lit Aggie's face. "And I love them. I'm a lucky woman." She winked at Doro. "You and Ev won't have a ready-made family, but you can create your own. In fact, a married couple is a family, albeit a small one."

Heat scorched Doro's cheeks. As modern as she was, the discussion of conceiving a family proved embarrassing. A sidelong glance at Ev revealed he felt much the same way. Red suddenly smudged his face.

"I'll get those fingerprints," he murmured.

Before he got away, Doro plucked at his coat sleeve. "Is there a notepad, so I can get what we know already down?"

Aggie reached into her pocketbook. "I brought a blank one for you."

"Terrific," Doro replied before turning back to Ev. "Do you want help collecting the prints?"

"It's a one-person job, as you know," he replied.

The memory of their first case made Doro smile. After a rocky start, during which Ev had put her on his suspect list, the pair had worked together to catch a killer. Part of their investigation had involved taking fingerprints, a fascinating and new process to Doro at the time. First, she had watched Ev. Then, he had let her do it herself. "It is," she agreed, "and you're more skilled at it than I am."

One of his shoulders lifted in a half-shrug. "I have more experience, which is why it goes faster for me, but you did a good job."

"I remember the two of you getting prints from the president's office a couple of years ago," Aggie said. "It sounded like an intriguing process."

"Why don't the both of you come along? You can watch and do some of them yourself. Whoever isn't taking prints can make notes," Ev said.

"What a wonderful idea," Doro replied.

He winked at her. "Every amateur sleuth needs to be proficient at fingerprinting. You were well on your way, but we haven't had an occasion to do it recently."

"Aggie and I can both practice," Doro said.

Her best friend put two hands up, palms out. "I'll watch the two of you for a while. I don't want to mess anything up."

After the group arrived at Coach Munroe's office. Ev waved the two young women inside. "I'm guessing we'll find plenty of prints, but it's worth taking them," Ev said before setting to work. "Same with looking for that letter opener. After we get the prints, we can dig around."

Both young women watched as he brushed a fine powder over the desk. Almost immediately, some of it stuck to the surface in patterns.

"You can see the prints already," Aggie said. "Doro told me about the process two years ago, but seeing it is amazing."

"That's only the start," Doro told her friend.

While the two girls watched, Ev pressed tape to the desk surface and carefully rubbed it out until each piece held a print. Then, he pressed the tape to the special cards tucked into the kit. He worked methodically for fifteen minutes, both on the desk and on the chair arms. "The ones on the chair match many on the desk, so they must belong to Coach Munroe. A fair number of others on the desk match one another, which could indicate they belong to Clint. I'll try for a few on the desk lamp, the wall switch, and the file cabinet. Then, you two can do a few more from the desk."

Aggie, who had taken a chair next to Doro, perched on the edge. "How exciting."

Anticipation rose inside Doro, too. How many amateur sleuths got to take fingerprints? Not many was her guess. But how many were engaged to a lawman? When Ev got to the doorknob, he paused to study the image. "Did you find something different?" she asked.

"Looks that way," he replied before crossing back to the desk and putting the tape to a clean card. For a long moment, Ev studied the impression. "This one isn't like the others. It stands out. It may not mean anything, but we'll definitely keep it safe and sound until we find some solid suspects. Now, you two can take prints."

Doro gathered some fingerprints, and Aggie did more. After they finished, the group searched the desk, the file cabinets, as well as Munroe's coat pockets. No trace of the letter opener surfaced.

"The killer must've taken it with him," Doro said, as the trio walked to the constable's office.

"Which was smart," Aggie added.

A harsh breath left Ev. "It was, but finding it would've been a big help."

"Would we want a case to be solved so easily?" Doro asked in a lighthearted tone. "We wouldn't get to conduct interviews, collect evidence, and chase clues then."

Ev chuckled. "No, we could sit back and relax."

"Pshaw," Doro insisted. "Cracking a case after deep detective work is satisfying."

"And exhausting," her best friend put in.

"You two sound like old fogeys," Doro said. "Come on, let's get to the constable's office before you need your naps."

Ev offered an arm to each of the two young women. "Hold on in case this old fellow requires support."

"Gladly." Doro clasped his arm, because now that she had him, she would not let him go.

Chapter Seven

A few minutes later, they entered the office where all seven basketball players were seated at the battered table by the woodstove. Wade stood behind the counter while Clint and President Adams sat at what had been Ev's desk for more than two years. A twinge of regret twisted Doro's heart. How did seeing the office after losing his post make Ev feel? His stoic expression gave no clue.

Both the assistant coach and the college administrator stood to relinquish their seats to the two young women. After thanking them, Aggie turned to Wade. "I can make fresh coffee. How about if Doro and I get a tin of cookies out? The boys are probably hungry."

Several of the players quickly agreed, which had Doro repressing a chuckle. She noticed Wade and Ev rolling their eyes. Because she thought they might nix the idea, Doro commented. "Even though some of us had a big meal, it's been a while.

Cookies and coffee wouldn't hurt anyone." Not that she wanted another bite.

"Sure. Get the cookies," Wade agreed.

Doro and Aggie went into the little back room but kept the door open, so they did not miss a word.

At the same time, Ev took the fingerprinting kit to Wade. "One print stands out as different from the others I got. We searched but didn't find the letter opener."

"Interesting. Yep, this one is definitely unique. A lot of others match one another." Wade said as he glanced through the cards. After setting them aside, he continued. "I spoke with Doc for a minute. Coach Munroe's hand needed a few stitches after his other wound from it. Like today's wound, it was shallow, but the blade had to be very sharp. Doc had forgotten until he got the body laid out in his office. He planned to call us about it."

"Good to know," Ev murmured. "It has to be really sharp."

Wade nodded.

Doro put a tin of cookies on the table. When the boys thanked her, she nodded but her attention was on the men at the counter. As their exchange continued, their voices lowered. Doro gestured to Aggie that they should move closer. Sitting at Ev's old desk accomplished that.

Clint, who had joined the lawmen, spoke. "One set probably belongs to me. Coach and I worked on plays yesterday."

"But you weren't with him today." Wade made it a statement, not a question.

The assistant coach shoved his hands into his pants pockets. "No, sir, I wasn't. Coach Munroe had practice scheduled for this afternoon. All week, he told me that I didn't need to be at the fieldhouse until just before it started. Yesterday afternoon, he changed his mind, and he said we needed to work this morning. We could take a break for the campus dinner and get back at it, but I already had plans to eat with the Piersons, and Coach knew that. I still met with him this morning."

"Was he upset when you went ahead with your plans?" Wade asked.

Tension stiffened Clint's spine. "Yep, but that's nothing new. He'd been getting testier and testier these last few weeks." He glanced at Adams. "After my job got cut, he worried about the college doing away with the basketball program. He figured a win at this week's tournament could make a difference. Not for me, but for the team."

A glum expression blanketed the administrator's face. "We didn't want to eliminate your position, but the college has to cut expenses until enrollment is up again."

"I know," Clint murmured.

As she listened, Doro felt increasingly sad and upset. So many people, through no fault of their own, were hurt by the current economic issues.

Ev leaned against the counter. "Did you and Munroe both draw up plays yesterday?"

"Yep. And again this morning, like I said. I spent two hours working with him. He sometimes designed some and asked for my perspective. Other times, he had me do them. This week, I created a few myself and presented them to him. He drew all over my plans." Clint's jaw tightened. "He might've used them anyhow, but I wouldn't have gotten credit."

Doro could not abide people stealing ideas from their underlings. No wonder the assistant was at odds with his head coach. Although she understood the animosity, Doro felt increasing anxiety. Could Clint have arrived early, argued with Munroe, and attacked him? The possibility seemed all too real. Her attention strayed to the table where most of the players were busy eating cookies and drinking coffee. Only two were focused on the conversation at the counter. One, Dale, looked away when his gaze met Doro's. The other, Vince, smirked at her.

"Young Mr. Brownlee is full of himself," Aggie whispered. "He was in one of my classes last year. Did the bare minimum to pass, fell asleep periodically, and muttered under his breath when he was awake. I've never had a student be so obnoxious or disrespectful. I spoke with him more than once before reporting his attitude and behavior to the athletic director, who talked to Munroe. A little improvement happened after that, but a lot of smirking and snoozing continued until President Adams interceded."

"That makes me glad he dropped my course," Doro said.

"Lucky you," Aggie murmured.

The conversation among the men continued, but only to set a plan for interviews. "I wish I had a separate office," Wade said, "but we could use our storeroom to interview the boys one at a time."

"That's our best option." Ev addressed Adams. "Would you stay out here, sir? I'd like for Doro to take notes, but Aggie might be good enough to be with you and the boys while they wait."

"Of course," the president replied. He smiled at Aggie. "I'd be pleased to have you here, Professor Lammers."

Aggie's new name, even after four months, still sounded strange to Doro. How long would it take her to get used to being Doro Mallow? And exactly when would her name change occur? Cracking the case took top priority, but a serious talk with Ev would follow. Doro did not want to be engaged for years. She wanted to know where she and Ev stood.

"I'm happy to help in any way," Aggie said.

"Then, let's get started interviewing the team," Wade put in.

Doro pulled the notepad out of her pocketbook. "I'm ready."

Ev winked at her. "Not a surprise, since you're always sleuthing."

Doro, with a grin, responded in her usual way. "Not always. But as often as possible."

❦

Before calling the first player, Ev and Wade rearranged the ten-foot by twelve-foot storeroom. First, they moved several crates out of the way. Then, they carried four chairs in.

"There's plenty of space," Doro observed as she scanned the area.

"But no desk or table for your notepad," Ev replied.

"I've worked without that plenty of times. It's a little awkward, but I'll manage," she said.

"Then, we're ready to start?" Wade asked.

Doro nodded. "Let me jot down all the names, so we can check them off as we go." She wrote down several before asking a question. "Are you planning to question Clint last?"

The two men exchanged a glance before both agreeing. "That seems best."

After grabbing a pencil from her bag, Doro jotted down names. "Horace isn't here yet. We'll want to talk to him."

Ev put one hand to his forehead. "Like Clint said, Horace could be running errands for Munroe. I've seen him do that, and he always asks if I have any tasks for him. Someone else could've enlisted his services, too."

As she thought about the young man, Doro could only agree. "Quite likely. He does odd jobs for various townsfolk, which earns him a little pocket money. He does favors for free, as well. When he was in high school, all the coaches let him help. He's not coordinated enough to play sports, but he loves them."

"He does," Wade agreed, "and it's good of the college to let him work with the team. If he doesn't show up soon, I'll call his house. His folks may not know a practice was scheduled for today, since the team doesn't usually work out on Sunday. Horace might've gotten confused himself."

To Doro, that seemed unlikely. Horace MacPherson's life revolved around his work with the teams. While he might be running errands, for Munroe or someone else, he would not forget a practice. With effort, she focused on listing the interviewees already present. "I put Dale Krowl at the top."

"Any special reason?" Ev asked.

Doro shook her head. "No. He was in my mystery novel course this term, so he came to my mind right off. After him,

I have Clyde, Artie, Robert, Mike, James, Vince, and Coach Spalling. I figured we could fit Horace in whenever he gets here. I hate to make him wait, because he'd get nervous."

"I agree," Wade said. "He isn't a suspect, and he'll be upset. As cranky as Munroe could be, he was patient with Horace from what I know."

"He was," Doro agreed.

Wade nodded. "Then, we'll ask Horace a few questions to see if he was near the fieldhouse earlier, and that's it."

"Fine with me," Ev agreed before turning toward Doro. "But do you have any reason for the order of interviews?"

"Not really, except for making Vince the last player to talk to us," she said. "Letting him stew seems like a good plan."

"You know everyone except Clint better than Wade and I do. Any insights to share before we begin?" Ev asked.

For a moment, she rolled the pencil between her palms. "Robert and Artie were clearly shocked when they came to tell us about Coach. Also, they've both sung his praises long before now, especially when they were in my class."

"You know them very well," Wade put in.

"I do," Doro replied. "I don't see them as suspects."

"You have great judgment so, unless some evidence points to one of them, we'll keep their interviews short. Any others stick out as similar to Robert and Artie?" Ev asked.

"Clyde and James were serious students, and they also seemed to like and respect Coach Munroe," Doro said.

"Then, we'll keep their questioning short. If any of the four reveal something troubling, we can always change our tactics." Ev turned to Wade. "Doro and I talked to Mike Vassel for a few minutes while we were waiting for you and Doc. We can recap it later for you."

"You don't want to talk with him again?" Wade inquired.

"I think we should, if only to keep up appearances for the other players." Doro tapped the pencil against her notepad. "Like the other four I mentioned, he doesn't have a strong motive."

"I agree," Ev said, "and he was forthright with us. Again, unless something arises to change it, we shouldn't need to speak with him for long."

"Sounds fine to me. I'll get Dale," Wade said before returning in only moments. The constable gestured to the chair across from Ev. "Take a seat, son." After the boy did, Wade settled beside the player.

"I don't know anything about what happened in Coach's office," Dale began. "I wasn't there today, but I have been in the office a few times this term."

The last comment made Doro wonder if he was providing an excuse for his fingerprints being present. Did he need an explanation?

"We're not saying you or any of your teammates were there today, but we need information to give us background," Ev explained.

"That's right," Wade agreed. "For starters, are you aware of anyone having a beef with Coach Munroe?"

Dale's hazel gaze moved to the floor. "I dunno."

Both lawmen focused on Doro, who nodded. "You've never heard your coach argue with any of your teammates or anyone else?" she asked.

The boy shifted on the hard chair before looking at Doro. "Coach can get stirred up when guys are late to practice or if they break training rules."

"Understandable," Doro said. "Any other times?"

Dale shrugged. "He and Coach Spalling have words occasionally."

"What do you mean?" Doro asked. "Heated arguments or mild disagreements?"

The boy glanced at the two lawmen before looking back at Doro. "Before Coach Spalling lost his job, it wasn't so bad. Since then, both of them are on edge a lot. I get it. My pa is out of work because his company closed. He and my ma yell more." Dale ran one hand over his face. "I was glad to come back to school in September, just to get away from them. I graduate in May, so I can get my degree. With luck, I'll get a job right off. Then, I'll help my folks and little sisters. They're only eight and nine, so they can't pitch in like I can. Sometimes, I wonder if I should quit school and get a job now, but both Ma and Pa want me to finish."

"You're doing the right thing," Ev told Dale. "Getting your degree should help you get a decent job, even now."

Some of the tension left Dale's face. "That's what my folks say."

"You plan to become a teacher, right?" Doro asked.

Dale nodded. "Yes, ma'am."

"You'll find a position," she assured him. "There will always be schools and students. Your father was an accountant with a construction company, wasn't he?"

"Yep. They haven't gotten any new projects for almost a year. When they wrapped up the last of the ongoing ones, the business shut down," Dale replied.

"I'm sorry to hear that," Doro murmured. While Dale was likely to find work after graduation, some students might not. With effort, she got back to business. "So, the two coaches have been at odds."

A sigh escaped Dale. "They weren't ever real close, but the two have argued more lately. I get that Coach Spalling is mad about getting canned. The truth is, he did more coaching than Munroe. He was always early to practice, and he'd stay late with guys who wanted to work on their defensive moves or foul shooting. He encouraged all of us. Munroe barked orders and got mad if you misunderstood or messed up."

"Did he criticize you?" Doro asked.

"Not much." Dale grinned. "I'm a good forward, maybe the best in our league. I don't make a lot of mistakes on the court."

Doro smiled in return. "I can't disagree because I've seen you play. I'm glad Coach Munroe appreciated your skills."

The young man's good humor faded. "He never praised me much, but Coach Spalling did. He was good about finding something positive in all of us. Munroe played favorites."

The comments interested Doro. "Who were his favorites?"

"Rob and James were his best buddies," Dale responded. "They hung out in his office a lot."

Ev chimed in. "Coach Munroe never found fault with them?"

Dale shook his head. "Nope. They could do no wrong."

After scribbling more notes, Doro paused. Dale had not mentioned getting into trouble after going to Toledo speakeasies. She decided to approach the issue in an indirect manner. "Did they break the rules and not get disciplined?"

The young player clasped his hands together until his knuckles showed white. "They followed Munroe's rules like they were law."

"Did everyone?" Ev asked.

A glance at the young man told Doro that he was thinking about the speakeasy forays. Would Dale crack and admit his wrongdoings?

"You know the old saying. *Boys will be boys*," Dale replied.

Doro gritted her teeth to keep from blurting out a curt retort. How she hated that adage. Within moments, Ev and Wade filled in admirably.

"Funny that no one ever says *girls will be girls*," the constable said.

"Yeah, it is," Ev agreed.

Dale chortled. "You were young not so long ago, Officer Mallow. Surely, you remember what it was like."

Ev's gray eyes took on a frosty edge. "After my dad died, my boyhood did, too, so, I didn't have time to break rules. I needed to help my mother keep a roof over our heads and food on the table."

The boy's expression went blank. "Yeah, well, a little fun doesn't hurt anyone."

Long moments of silence permeated the room. Doro glanced from Ev to Wade, but both men were focused on Dale, who started to scrape his feet on the floor. Letting him stew seemed like a fine idea, so she waited.

Dale cleared his throat. "Can I go?"

"Not yet," Wade replied. "We have some interesting information about you and your buddy Vince."

Surprise flared in Dale's gaze. "It's probably not true."

Ev smiled. "You don't know what it is."

"I know some of my teammates gossip about Vince and me cuz we're the best players," Dale said.

"If it's false gossip, you can tell us. Just remember that getting caught coming in late is recorded," Ev said. "Munroe isn't the only one who had rules. The college does, too."

A bright flush stained Dale's cheeks. "We didn't hurt anybody by going into the city."

"You could've hurt yourselves," Wade pointed out.

"We just went to speakeasies." Dale looked around the group. "I bet all of you have been in them."

Doro pressed her lips together. A year ago last summer, she had gone to one looking for Ev, who had disappeared while undercover investigating bootleggers. Determined to find him, she had enlisted Aggie and Wade to help. While visiting a speakeasy had been fascinating, and productive since they found Ev, Doro was not going again. The memory of a shootout between rival gangs, with Ev in the line of fire, was enough to keep her away.

Ev leaned forward. "As a Prohibition agent, I was in a few. Twice, I got shot."

The reminder made Doro's mouth go dry as she looked at Ev. He was fine and should stay that way as long as he was the campus security officer, which was a safe job. Far safer than being a Prohibition agent.

"We aren't coppers," Dale protested.

"Civilians get caught in the crossfire between gangs and between gangsters and lawmen," Wade said. "You're lucky that didn't happen to you. Besides, you knew Coach's rules, and you broke them. That considered, it's no surprise he didn't cater to you and Vince. Not benching you for breaking rules seems like enough leniency."

Dale hung his head. "I suppose." After a moment, he scanned the group. "Neither of us hurt him."

"Why were you late to practice?" Ev asked.

Color flamed in Dale's square face. "We were goofing off is all. No witnesses. I guess we liked seeing Coach fume when we weren't on time. I know it's foolish, but Coach Munroe got after Vince sometimes. He knew Vince has to keep his special scholarship to stay in school, but Coach wouldn't promise that'd happen. He held it over Vince's head, trying to keep him in line."

"Trying to keep him in line, but not succeeding," Wade suggested.

One of Dale's shoulders lifted and fell. "Vince is our best player and the top one in our league. Nobody at any position is better, including me, and I'm good. Coach Munroe should've appreciated that, but he liked to boss guys around. Mostly the ones who didn't put him on a pedestal."

"Munroe was a darn good player himself," Wade pointed out. "He was on two teams that won the AAU championship."

The American Athletic Union held an annual tournament where teams from schools, businesses, and clubs competed. Being on a winning team was a significant accomplishment. Doro wondered if the players truly appreciated their coach's prowess.

"Yeah, and he told us a bunch of times," Dale muttered.

The information did not surprise Doro who had found Munroe to be an insufferable boor. She did not discount his talent or achievement, but tooting his own horn was obnoxious. When neither Ev nor Wade defended the man, she figured they agreed.

"Thanks, Dale," the constable said. "You're free to go, but tell your buddies to hang on. We'll get the next one in a couple of minutes."

Dale nodded and hurried out.

After the door closed behind him, Doro slumped back in her chair. "I wasn't aware of the dynamics around the basketball program until this afternoon, but I'm not surprised. Coach Munroe wasn't a warm person in my experience."

A snort of laughter left Wade. "Or in anyone else's experience, as far I know. The man rarely engaged in a conversation where he didn't mention his college and amateur ball accolades or the successes of his teams at Michaw College." He shook his head. "I shouldn't disrespect the dead."

"As investigators, we have to view victims through an impartial lens," Ev observed.

"That we do," Wade agreed. "Do you want to keep following your list?"

Ev addressed Doro. "What do you think?"

She twirled her pencil in her fingers. "You two can choose, but I'd still like to make Vince wait a while."

The grin lifting Ev's lips also glittered in his gaze. "Punishing the kid a little?"

"Not really," she replied. "If he gets in-and-out before most of the others, he'll hang around and harangue them. He already started at the fieldhouse, and I don't think we should give him more opportunity."

"A good point," Wade said.

"Yep, so let's make him wait and talk to Clyde next, like you have down," Ev said. When the others agreed, he stood up.

Before Ev stepped out of the room, Doro offered a reminder. "Remember how shaken Clyde was."

Ev grasped the edge of the door. "Thanks for jogging my memory." He went on by revealing the boy's teary reaction to Wade.

"Understandable, but Dale didn't mention him as being a favorite," Wade observed.

"He didn't," Doro agreed. "Dale didn't tell us about going to speakeasies with Vince before being confronted about it, either. He's a nice enough kid, but he wasn't particularly forthright."

A sliver of silence cut into the conversation before Ev responded. "And he wasn't happy to admit he and Brownlee got in trouble."

"That's another reason to let Vince stew," Wade said.

"Then, I'll get Clyde," Ev said.

Within moments, the player and the officer entered the storeroom. Ev gestured to the seat that Dale had vacated. "Sit down and relax."

Doro immediately noted why Ev added the last word. Tension rolled off Clyde in waves. "We only want some background information that might help us identify suspects, Clyde," she said. "I know you liked Coach Munroe."

The boy nodded. "Yes, ma'am. He was real good to me. I'm not the best player on the team, but Coach gave me credit for always practicing hard. When my skills improved, he praised my work."

Not having seen, or heard about, that side of Munroe, Doro felt surprised. No wonder Clyde had shed tears. But Dale had not mentioned this teammate as a coach's favorite. "This part might be uncomfortable for you, but we need a better picture of Coach Munroe."

Clyde's deep brown eyes went wide. "You come to all our home games, so I figured you knew Coach real good. You both work for the college, too."

"I've only spoken to him occasionally," Doro replied. His negative remarks about women being professors had kept her from pursuing in-depth conversations. According to Munroe, hearth and home should be a lady's only domain.

Clyde looked at the lawmen. "You know...knew Coach, didn't you?"

Wade shook his head. "Only in passing."

"I've talked to him a few times, but I can't say we were well-acquainted," Ev said. "That's where you can help. We want to know a little more about who might have gotten into an argument with him. Did he have disagreements with others often?"

The young man braced his elbows on his knees and leaned forward. "He and Coach Spalling got into it a few times lately." Clyde went on with the same story Dale had told. "I don't blame either of them. It's hard not knowing what'll happen. Money gets tight when folks are out of work. My dad still has his job, but who knows for how long?"

"You're getting financial help, aren't you?" Doro inquired.

"Yes, Professor. My folks couldn't afford to send me to college without it." A slight smile played across his lips. "I was the best player on my high school team, and I was all-city three years running. Of course, it was a small city."

"I've seen you play," Doro said, "and you're an asset to the team."

Clyde's slight smile turned into a grin. "Thank you."

"It's true," Ev added. "You only need more seasoning to be the best player."

The pleasure drained from his expression. "Coach Munroe was fighting for me to stay in school. Now, that he's gone maybe the team will be eliminated..." Clyde's voice trailed off. "Even if it isn't, Artie and I might be the first to go with a different coach. Lots of colleges have only white players. Maybe another coach will want that, too."

Doro's heart constricted. "President Adams won't let someone new keep you two from playing," she said with complete certainty. The administrator was fair-minded, and he insisted his faculty and coaches were the same way. Despite Munroe's other faults, he evidently was. Color did not matter at Michaw College, which was one of the great things about the school.

"I agree with Professor Banyon. You and Artie aren't going to be cut, if the team continues," Ev said. "You're excellent players and fine young men. That's what counts, and those qualities are appreciated here."

Relief filled Clyde's dark eyes as he smiled again. "Good. I love school, and I want to be a teacher." He looked at Doro. "I loved Professor Darwine's classes. I didn't think I'd care for poetry, but she made it real interesting." Clyde glanced at Wade. "She was my teacher before she married you. I know she's Professor Lammers now."

The constable nodded. "She is, but you can call her by her maiden name."

Clyde smiled before again meeting Doro's gaze. "I knew your course would be great, Professor Banyon, and I looked forward to taking it. It was even better than I figured it'd be."

Doro would have taken more pleasure in the compliment if she had felt certain about athletics continuing at the college. But there was little certainty now, and that affected young men like Clyde Porter. She hoped he could finish school. "Thank you. That means so much."

After winking at Doro, Ev addressed the young player. "Getting back to the case, can you tell us anything that might help? Did you ever hear anyone threaten Coach Munroe?"

Clyde chewed on his lower lip. "A couple of times, Vince said he wished Coach would die but not to his face. Just in front of the team."

The words confirmed what they had already heard. "How did the others react?" Doro asked.

"Dale laughed, and so did Mike but more like a nervous laugh. Mike didn't really seem to think it was funny. The rest of us didn't like hearing it. Rob spoke up, and so did James," Clyde replied.

After making more notes, Doro rolled the pencil between her hands. "You've been a big help."

"No more questions? I can go?" Clyde asked.

His eagerness was hardly a surprise. The whole situation had to be upsetting. "If Constable Lammers and Officer Mallow don't have any questions, I'd say you're free to leave," Doro replied.

Ev gave the same parameters to Clyde as he had to Dale. Then, he and Wade dismissed the young man. After Clyde left, he addressed Doro and Wade. "We've got some puzzle pieces to put together. Now, we need them confirmed."

"And we need more to fill in the blank spaces," Wade agreed.

"There are five more players to interview," Doro pointed out. "They may shine a light on the situation. Not that the killer couldn't have been someone not associated with the team. In fact, that seems just as likely to me."

"Longley and Baylor were both mentioned in passing. Having heard them argue with Munroe, I'd like to find out if any players know more," Ev said.

"We'll find out," Doro assured him. They had to because letting a murder go unsolved was not an option.

Chapter Eight

They did not discover much from the next four players, but all of them verified Clyde's assertions about Munroe being supportive to certain boys. They also agreed that the coach and his assistant had grown apart over the weeks since Clint's job was eliminated. The young men answered questions quickly and respectfully. The interview with Mike was the shortest, since he had already spoken in detail. He reaffirmed his original story.

When he left the room, Doro turned to the two lawmen. "His chuckling in the bleachers had to be from nerves."

"I agree," Ev said.

"It's a common reaction," Wade agreed. "We didn't get much new information, but I sure wish we had the letter opener."

Ev scratched his head. "Finding it would be useful. Of course, it's not likely since the murderer must've taken it along. Now, it could be any place."

"Yep," Wade agreed. "Plenty of woods around to bury it, and the creek going through town is another good place. Lots of other options, too. Hunting for it would be like searching for a needle in a haystack."

A rueful smile touched Doro's lips. "It would. And we aren't apt to secure a confession, either. The case is following familiar steps. As usual, we're gleaning bits and pieces of evidence and gathering them together. When we have more, a puzzle will take shape. Finally, the key parts will be revealed." Although Doro loved the process, she looked forward to the solution, and it never came too soon. "Before we interview Vince, I'd like to get a cup of coffee. How about you two?"

Ev stood and stretched. "Getting out of this chair would help me."

"Me, too," Wade agreed. "As great as dinner was, I wouldn't mind a cookie with my coffee."

"I hope some are left," Doro put in. "Young men eat a lot."

"So do older ones," Ev said as he patted his abdomen. "Despite having a great dinner and not being a kid, I'd love a couple of cookies."

Doro lightly tapped his arm. 'You're not much older than the players."

"I'm twenty-eight, which is a decade older than some of them," he pointed out.

A snort left Wade. "I'm old enough to be their father."

After laying a hand on the constable's sleeve, Doro smiled. "You're the perfect age, according to Aggie." The fifteen-year gap between her best friend and the town constable had been an impediment to them courting. At least Wade had hesitated for that reason. Aggie had never cared.

He grinned. "She's the one who's perfect and not just in age. I'm a lucky man." Wade tapped his friend's shoulder. "So are you."

When Ev said nothing, Doro glanced at him. His jaw was tight, but why? Usually, he mentioned how lucky he was. But not now. She swallowed hard over a rising tide of emotion. Something was wrong. What could it be? Despite her focus on the case, that question remained at the back of Doro's mind.

"I am," Ev murmured after a long pause. "Let's get Vince and finish these interviews."

"First, I'm stretching my legs and getting a cookie," Wade replied.

As soon as the trio stepped into the main office, Vince got up. "I can't sit around waiting all day."

A frown darkened Wade's face. "You can sit for as long as necessary, so get back in the chair." The firm voice and stark wording were from Constable Lammers, not the amiable husband, father, son, friend, and neighbor of every day.

Vince's jaw dropped. "We've got a game coming up Friday. We gotta practice."

"Whoa," President Adams said. "I haven't decided whether or not the team will go to the tournament."

"Not go? We have to be there," Vince insisted.

Clint gestured for Vince to sit down. "Coach Munroe just died. We need to show some respect."

A snort left Vince. "Like you have for the last few weeks? You two got into more than one yelling match, and you told him the team would struggle without you because you're the one who's created most of our plays and game plans. Now, we should believe you're grieving?"

Color surged into Clint's face. "This isn't the time to discuss old issues."

"Right," Vince muttered.

"Sit down, Mr. Brownlee," President Adams repeated.

After several moments, Vince did, but the sullen expression remained on his face.

"We wanted to get coffee and cookies, if any are left," Wade said.

Aggie, who was sitting at Ev's old desk, rose with a smile. "I saved a few cookies, and there's coffee in the flask. It should still be warm."

Wade returned her smile. "Even if it's cold, it'll give a boost of energy."

"What about you two?" Aggie asked Doro and Ev. "Coffee and cookies?"

"Sounds good," Ev replied.

Doro joined her friend at the sideboard on the back wall. "Just coffee for me, but let me help."

While Ev and Wade talked with President Adams and Clint, the two friends went about preparing refreshments. "You've spent a lot of time on interviews. I hope you've gotten some good clues," Aggie murmured.

"A few," Doro replied in the same soft tone as her friend. "We'll have plenty to discuss after we finish, but we need more information. A lot more."

"It's early in the investigation," Aggie pointed out.

"True," Doro agreed. "President Adams didn't say if he's set on the team not going to the tournament. Did he discuss it with Clint while we were in the other room?"

Aggie shifted to face Doro. "They talked about the tournament. Both feel torn, so I'm sure there will be further deliberation. It'll be a difficult decision."

"It will, and I'm not sure which way I'd decide." Respect for the dead was important, but so were the futures of the young men on the team.

"Me, either," Aggie said as she finished putting cookies on a plate. "If you bring two mugs, I'll take the dish and one mug."

After the two friends carried the refreshments to the desk, Ev stood to help Doro while Wade did the same with Aggie. When the entire group was settled, the constable spoke. "We were talking about Horace, who hasn't shown up. That seems odd, because he should've gone to the fieldhouse by now. Since it's locked, he can't get in and it's too cold to wait outside for long."

"I agree," Doro said. "Horace would go home, not stand around for a lengthy time. Even if he ran errands for someone, he wouldn't need this long. Besides, it's Sunday, so no businesses are open. The limits the number of errands he could do."

"Would you call his house, Aggie? After we start the next interview would work," Wade said.

"Of course," she replied. "I hope he's all right."

"There could be a simple explanation," Doro put in. But was there? Practice had been scheduled for three-thirty, a time that had passed over an hour ago.

"How long do I have to wait?" Vince called across the room.

Wade shot the kid a quelling glare. "We'll let you know when we're ready to interview you."

The constable's strong response made Doro smile. Wade was easy-going, but he could be firm when the occasion demanded strength, as it did now. Vince muttered under his breath before falling silent.

After a swallow of coffee and a bite of cookie, Ev looked at Clint. "Is Brownlee always so full of himself?"

The assistant coach released a pent-up breath. "He's a great player. He knows it and uses it, which sometimes got on Coach Munroe's nerves. Mine, too."

"I can understand why," Doro observed. "He was in my class for one day before dropping it. I wasn't sorry to see him go. He clowned around the entire time. A real nuisance."

Aggie leaned forward. "He stayed in my class for the whole term, only because it was required. Throttling his outbursts was an ongoing issue."

"He's like that with almost every professor," President Adams put in. "It had nothing to do with you personally, as we discussed at the time."

"I appreciated your support," Aggie said.

Adams grinned, which made him look more like a student than a senior administrator. "That's part of my job, and I'm happy to stand behind fine professors like you. I'm sorry when you have to put up with antics from students. It's inexcusable."

After expressing her thanks, Aggie turned to her husband. "Doro mentioned going over everything you've learned after you talk with the entire group. I'll let your mother know after calling Horace's house. The children were having fun with their cousins, so they won't miss us."

Wade chuckled. "I'm sure they won't. When that group gets together, they don't want it to end."

President Adams pulled out his pocket watch. "I can stay another hour. Then, I need to work on my reports for the Board of Trustees meeting on Wednesday. Mrs. Jones will type it all up tomorrow and mimeograph copies on Tuesday. It's a major task, so I want to give her plenty of time."

Doro's stomach knotted as she considered what the administrator would have to relay to the trustees about the school's finances. Although her job seemed secure, others would not be so lucky.

"It won't take long to question Vince. I can stop by your office tomorrow and bring you up to date," Ev said.

"I'd appreciate that," the administrator said.

After draining his coffee cup and finishing off two cookies, Wade got to his feet. "Let's interview Brownlee."

Ev's response was to stand up and hold Doro's chair.

"I'll be here when you finish," Clint said.

"Good. We'll have a few questions for you." Wade gestured toward the storeroom. "Vince, wait out here for a minute."

Again, Vince grumbled. "Why did I have to be the last player questioned?"

Wade shrugged. "The luck of the draw."

Doro repressed a chuckle. There had been no draw, only a decision to make the obnoxious boy wait until the end.

After stepping into the storeroom ahead of the two lawmen, Doro picked up her paper and pencil. "What's the strategy for talking with Vince?"

"Since he dropped your class, you don't know him well," Ev suggested.

"No, I don't," she agreed. "Certainly not like I know some of the others."

"Then, maybe Wade and I should ask most of the questions," Ev suggested.

Doro nodded. "It'd probably be best. One day of him in my class and he made it clear that women should be wives and mothers, not professors."

A snort left Wade. "That's the main reason Aggie had trouble with him. She hated to go to President Adams, but the coach and athletic director didn't help her much."

Doro was surprised Aggie had not told her about the problems, which had evidently started around the time her friend and the constable became engaged. Aggie had probably leaned on Wade.

"He may have more if he's involved in Munroe's murder," Ev muttered.

"Time will tell," Wade said.

Ev rubbed his temple. "Since Vince is apt to be the least cooperative, how about if you and I take turns questioning him, Wade?"

The constable grinned. "Sort of back-and-forth to keep him off-guard."

Ev chuckled. "That's a good plan." His amusement fled. "I still hate to think one of Munroe's players is the killer."

"We all do, but only a couple are serious suspects. Or have you changed your mind since talking to some of them?" Doro asked.

After a shake of his head, Ev responded. "As far as I can see, you were right about most of them having no motive."

"I agree," Wade put in. "We may turn up more clues when we talk to Longley and Baylor."

"They had some rough words with Munroe the other day. It's also interesting that he characterized their treatment as harassment." She thought back to the previous Monday. "When we saw him with the two of them in College Hall, Munroe accused them of hounding him."

"That was how he framed the issues," Ev agreed. "Like I've told you, the three of them have argued at meals a few times. Even though Munroe came across as arrogant, Baylor or Longley usually started the arguments."

Vince, strutting into the storeroom, ended their discussion. "I hope this won't take long."

Wade gestured to the empty chair. "Sit down."

The tallest of the players, Vince folded himself into the chair before shifting around. "Did you get the most uncomfortable seating available?"

With effort, Doro repressed a grin. Maybe the boy would answer questions more quickly than she figured, if only to escape.

"Not many fellows are over six-feet tall," Ev pointed out.

Vince glanced from one lawman to the other. "I've got both of you by a few inches."

"You do," Ev agreed. "I'm six-foot even, and the constable is a bit shorter. You must be six-three or six-four."

"Six-three."

"From the games that Doro and I have seen you're taller than many centers." Ev continued in a conversational tone.

"Only a couple of guys in our league are my height," Vince agreed.

"But you're the top scorer," Ev added.

A grin lit Vince's face. "Yep."

After a quick glance at Wade, Ev again focused on the player. "Since you're so good, most of the plays revolve around you."

"You get the ball to the player who can put up points," Vince replied.

Wade jumped into the conversation. "How did your team-mates feel about that?"

"They know I'm the best player in the league, and they rely on me to score," Vince replied.

"None of them is jealous?" Ev asked.

A harrumph left Vince. "So, what if they are? Even though I'm more talented, some guys could work harder."

"Did Coach Munroe agree?" Wade inquired.

"He got after a couple of them," Vince replied. "Rob's got good moves, but he could make more effort. His folks have money, so he's not relying on help from donors. Same with James. Resting on their laurels is what Coach Spalling calls it."

The mention of the assistant coach riveted Doro's attention on the center. She knew Ev and Wade would ask pertinent, probing questions, and she was ready to take more notes.

Ev posed the next question. "Did you get along better with Spalling than with Munroe?"

"Spalling wasn't as overbearing. He got what it's like to be young. He didn't brag on himself all the time, either." Vince shook his head. "Coach Munroe not only told us about his exploits over and over, he had a bunch of old plaques and trophies all over this office."

"If you end up with a lot of trophies, you won't display them?" Out of the corner of her eye, Doro saw Ev bite his lower lip—undoubtedly to repress a laugh. Vince Brownlee was hardly the humble type.

"Sure, but not old stuff from years ago," the player replied.

"Coach Munroe played in the college and amateur ranks less than fifteen years ago," Wade pointed out.

"Right. A long time," Vince said.

Wade pressed his fingers to his forehead before getting back to the case. "What about Munroe's interactions with other players? Did anyone argue with him or get special treatment?"

"Rob was in his good graces, and so was James. They did whatever Munroe told them."

"What about players having run-ins with him?" Ev asked. "Other than you and Dale."

Vince's spine straightened as his gaze went wide. "We didn't really have run-ins."

"But you got caught out after curfew, and Munroe wasn't happy when he discovered you two went to speakeasies in Toledo," Ev said.

After Vince shifted in his chair, he shrugged. "It wasn't serious."

The lawmen allowed a period of silence to develop before Wade spoke. "He told you to tow the line or risk losing your financial support, didn't he?"

Dull color rose in Vince's thin face. "My folks can't pay for my college tuition. I need outside money to stay in school."

"Which Munroe knew," Ev put in.

"Sure," Vince muttered.

"And he held it over your head," Ev suggested. "Didn't he warn you not to mess up again, or you'd be off the team? Wouldn't that mean being out of school?"

The center's blue gaze glittered with some repressed emotion. "I was his best player. He wouldn't have let me get away."

Ev shrugged. "But you couldn't be sure."

"I didn't kill him," Vince shot back. "If you want to find someone at odds with Munroe, look at Spalling or his custodian buddy. I overheard the two of them talking about how Coach ought to be the one to go, not Spalling. Or Baylor and Longley. They give all of us trouble cuz we're athletes. Last year, Coach had to go to Adams about the two of them."

"How did the professors bother you guys?" Ev asked.

Doro knew he was seeing if Vince's story was like his teammates' version. And it was.

"Penalizing us for being out of class on travel days. Marking our work down. Harder to do in math, but easy to find fault in an essay," the boy replied.

While jotting down the information, Doro considered it carefully. He was right about subjective grading, but most English courses had set criteria. Vince had named her primary suspects, but was he accurate? Or was he creating a smokescreen?

Chapter Nine

Over the next ten minutes, Ev and Wade asked more questions but got no new information, so they let Vince go. The group went into the office area as the front door slammed shut behind the player.

Aggie studied Doro, Ev, and Wade. "You all look exhausted."

Doro sank into a chair by the big table. "We've never interviewed so many people in a row."

"True, but we needed to get them on record before they compared stories," Wade pointed out.

"We did," Ev agreed as he glanced around the office. "Where's Clint?"

Aggie put her hand to her throat. "I called Horace's home and found out he left for practice on time. His folks thought he was there all this time. When I told them what happened to Coach Munroe, they were worried sick. His father and a neighbor headed out to look for him. Clint went, too. I know you want to talk to him, but I couldn't see making him stay here when Horace can't be found. It'll be dark soon."

Wade laid a hand on her arm. "You were right to have Clint help." His attention went to Ev. "You and I should join them."

"Absolutely," Ev agreed. "We can leave right off."

"I can go along," Doro put in.

Ev's gaze ran over her. "You're still in your high heels. Stay here with Aggie and call a few people who could pitch in. Ask them to set out as soon as possible and check back here in an hour, if they don't find him. Wade and I will come then, too. If necessary, we'll get better organized and go out again."

"If Horace is found, his mother will call here," Aggie said. "We'll get word out by calling around town. With the darkness, searchers will use flashlights. I'll call around town and ask folks to put their porch lamps on. When Horace is safe, I can spread the word to turn them off, so that can be a sign to the searchers to head home."

"That's a great plan," Doro concurred.

"It sure is," Wade agreed.

"Yep. Good thinking, Aggie," Ev said before asking, "Did his father have any ideas about where Horace might've gone?"

"Mr. MacPherson said Horace would never miss practice. In fact, he almost always goes early, but sometimes, he goes through the park, so they planned to start there thinking he might've fallen and gotten injured. Even though most of the snow from a few days ago melted, there may be some in the wooded areas. Slipping is possible. Plus, there's rough terrain on two sides," Aggie said.

Dismay hit Doro hard as her mind spun out other ideas. "It's possible he fell and injured himself, but what if Horace got to the fieldhouse early and saw the killer?"

"That's what I wonder," Aggie said. "I'm not sure it occurred to his father, and I didn't want to scare him more."

"You were wise not to suggest the idea," her husband said. "We didn't see any sign of Horace when we were in and around the fieldhouse. Ev and I searched the building before I headed back here. Not the offices, although we tried the doors. They were locked."

"There was no sign of anyone," Ev agreed. "I didn't look again after we took fingerprints, but you and I made a good search, Wade."

"If Horace saw something, he might've run off," Doro suggested. "It would jolt him, even if he only came across the body. He's hidden in the past. Once on Halloween, some other kids scared him by jumping out and hollering. Horace hid in a shed behind a house on Oak Street for a couple of hours."

"How old was he at the time?" Ev asked.

"Fifteen, but he's always been small for his age," Doro replied. "Shy, too, and you know he's a little slow."

A reassuring smile touched Ev's lips. "I know, but he's a good kid. We talk from time-to-time. Any other incidents of him hiding?"

"A couple times when he was younger," Wade put in.

Doro nodded. "Since the Halloween episode, other kids in town have acted better."

"They should," Ev observed.

"I hope it's just that Horace is hiding," Aggie murmured.

Doro linked arms with her friend. "So do I." Unfortunately, other possibilities existed, and some were troubling.

"We'll scour the campus and town for the kid," Ev said.

"Let's start at the park. At the very least, we might run into the searchers and set a strategy." Wade glanced at the women. "If you get more volunteers, ask them to spread out across town. Since it's Sunday, no businesses are open, so he won't be at one of them. The grade school and high school are closed, too. No activities, either."

"Before leaving, Clint called Reverend Pierson. He went to look in the church right away but called back to say he didn't see Horace. He's joining the search, too, and he'll ask a couple of neighbors to canvas that side of town with him," Aggie added.

"Good," Wade said.

Aggie chewed on her lower lip. "Maybe I should've interrupted the last interview."

"It was only fifteen minutes difference, Ag," her husband said. "Besides, a few people are looking right now. And we'll get more. Horace will be home safe and soon."

Doro hoped Wade was right, but where had the boy gone on a Sunday? Or had he been taken? She and Aggie discussed those questions after the men left.

"Horace's life has revolved around the team for a couple of years," Doro observed. "If he saw Coach Munroe dead on the floor, he would've been traumatized."

"I agree, which means he could've taken off in any direction," Aggie murmured, "although you'd think he would have gone home by now."

Doro wrapped her arms around her waist. "If he caught sight of the killer, Horace might've been worried the person saw him, too. If so, he wouldn't want to put his family in danger. When his mother had influenza last year, he was distraught."

"I remember, and you're right. I'm going to make more calls," Aggie said as she went to the telephone.

"While you're doing that, I'll knock on doors down the street. That way you won't have to call all of them. Ask the operator to spread the word whenever she connects other calls, too."

"I will."

After slipping into her winter coat, Doro donned her gloves and a hat before heading into the twilight. A shiver rippled through her when a cold blast of wind blew down Main Street, and she hoped Horace was some place safe and warm.

※

When Ev and Wade returned an hour later, the young women jumped to their feet. One look at Ev telegraphed the bad news. "You didn't find Horace." Doro could not keep the dismay out of her voice.

He ran one hand over his fatigue-lined face before pulling Tee out of his jacket. "No. We didn't even run across anyone who saw Horace after he left his own street." When he put the little dog down, she ran to Doro, who fussed over her.

"I picked her up on the way back, since she's been alone for a few hours. She did her business, despite the rain, but I had to put her under my coat and carry her most of the way," Ev said. "She refused to walk far after getting wet."

"Smart girl," Doro murmured as she held Tee who snuggled close.

"I'll get the old blanket out of the storeroom," Aggie said. "Then, she can rest."

In small groups, the other searchers entered the office, so Tee did not lie down. Instead, she greeted everyone. Their weary expressions turned to smiles as the men took turns petting her, and Tee maintained her enthusiasm with all of them. Unfortunately, each group gave the same bad news: no one had seen any trace of Horace. Although his father thanked them individually, he looked bereft. Doro wished she could say something to lift his spirits, but what? As Doro observed the group, she noted they were all damp around the edges and many were shivering. "I'm sorry we don't have more seats around the stove," she said.

"That's all right," Wade told her before focusing on the men. "Before you all head home for something to eat, some dry clothes, and slickers, let's go over what parts of town need to be covered and split into groups again."

General assent rumbled through the room. Within a few minutes, a fresh strategy was set, and the searchers left with the agreement to regroup in an hour at various locations. They would report back to the constable's office later. Everyone agreed to look for Horace until they found him.

As the men exited, chilly air rushed into the office. So did the sound of icy rain. "It's pouring," Doro observed.

A sigh escaped Ev. "The steady drizzle turned to sleet about a half-hour ago."

"No wonder everyone was cold and wet," Aggie said.

Although November often brought chilly, wet weather, a clear night would have been preferable for searching. And for a boy who might be hiding in fear.

"Come and sit by the stove," Aggie urged.

After the men hung up their coats and hats, they settled at the big table near the fire. "Thanks for adding more wood," Wade said as he put his hands toward the stove. "I didn't realize how cold I was until we got inside."

"Me, either," Ev agreed. The shudder that rippled through him put an exclamation point on the statement. "I sure hope Horace found a place out of the elements." The others concurred.

"You both need a meal along with a change of clothes," Aggie suggested.

Her husband nodded. "I'll call Ma and see if she can make some sandwiches. You two could help most by staying here. We need a headquarters, and this is it." He released a long, low breath. "Maybe Ma can keep the kids overnight. There's no school this week."

"I already spoke with her," Aggie said. "She's delighted to have all of her grandchildren spend the night, since her boarders are gone. When she heard what was happening, she sent two of the kids over with baskets. There's leftover fried chicken and biscuits, along with apple pie that they had for dinner. She tucked cookies in. Doro and I ate, but there's plenty left for the two of you. We'll keep coffee going, as well. A couple of ladies will bring more sweets, so we'll have snacks for everyone later."

A weary smile curved Wade's lips. "Sounds terrific."

"It sure does," Ev added.

After the women laid food on the table and their men dug in, Doro and Aggie sat down.

"Are there many places left to look?" Doro asked.

Ev shook his head. "Some nooks and crannies. Sheds and garages. And a few houses are empty since the owners left town for work elsewhere."

"Horace wouldn't break into a home," Doro said.

"Probably not," Wade agreed, "but he could be hiding on a back porch or in a garage."

A weary sigh escaped Ev. "If Horace is tucked into a dry niche, he had to hear us, but he may be too scared to come out."

"He'd go to his father, I'm sure," Aggie said.

"Maybe, but Mr. MacPherson couldn't be everywhere although he tried. The man moved from one group to another tirelessly," Wade replied. "Mrs. MacPherson came out for a while, too, but she's fighting a bad cold, so her husband insisted she go back inside."

"That was wise," Doro observed. "Getting wet won't help her get better."

"Is anyone with her?" Aggie asked.

Between bites, Wade replied. "Mrs. Pierson and a couple of neighbor ladies."

"Good," Doro said. "She has to be worried sick."

An uneasy silence fell while Ev and Wade continued their makeshift meal. After a few moments, Aggie made a suggestion. "Why don't Doro and I get clothes for you two? You're almost the same size, so Ev could wear something of yours, Wade. Then, you can take a little more time to rest and warm up."

Her husband chuckled. "I'm a little shorter and a few pounds heavier, but Ev is welcome to anything I have. I told him to change when he got Tee."

"I didn't waste time doing that," Ev said. "Besides, she was eager to get out."

When Doro studied Ev more closely, she saw exhaustion lining his face. Going back to his room for dry apparel would only use up more of his flagging energy, so borrowing clothes was better. "A belt will help. As for the short length, you won't get the cuffs in icy puddles that may form."

Ev grinned. "Good points. Although it's probably ungallant to send you two out in the sleet, I'd love to sit here a while longer."

"You could never be ungallant," Doro assured him. "Besides, we'll borrow the rain slickers, and there are a couple of umbrellas in the storeroom. That way, we'll stay toasty and dry."

"Our house is nearby, so we won't be out long," Aggie added.

Within moments, the two friends set off for the Lammers home, leaving their men to relax and restore themselves for the coming ordeal. As they walked through the silent town, Doro considered the possibility of finding young Horace soon. And she wondered if he was missing voluntarily, or if something more sinister was afoot.

Chapter Ten

Within twenty minutes, Doro and Aggie returned to the constable's office to find not only Ev and Wade, but Clint, President Adams, and several basketball players. Doro noted that Vince and Dale were not in the group. She wondered why. Before the young women even got the rain slickers off, little Tee darted toward Doro, who scooped her up. "Hi, sweetie."

"She's been snoozing," Ev said.

Doro ruffled the dog's soft fur. "You deserve that," she said before setting Tee down. Almost immediately, the pup made her rounds, getting attention from everyone in the room. After being petted and fussed over, she returned to her makeshift bed, curled up, and dozed off. Doro, weary to the bone, envied her.

When the door opened again, Violet Jones and Floyd Quartine stepped inside. Doro knew Tee was tuckered out because the little dog only lifted her head an inch before conking out again. Since Violet and Floyd were two of Tee's favorite people, the dog had to be exhausted.

"I telephoned these two about our dilemma," Adams explained. "Mrs. Jones volunteered to call some professors and other employees in hope of getting more searchers."

After laying her umbrella and coat aside, the secretary turned to the group. "About a dozen agreed to come out. Several demurred, citing that they may be coming down with something." A harrumph left her. "Coming down with wanting to stay in a warm room, most likely."

Doro repressed a chuckle. "Twelve more people will help," she observed before addressing Ev. "Here are the dry clothes."

He and Wade expressed their thanks before taking turns changing in the storeroom. When Ev returned, Doro bit back a chuckle. Wade's pants fell above Ev's ankles, which made him look like a schoolboy who was outgrowing his clothes. Since he was always immaculately dressed, the sight was incongruous and amusing.

"Don't laugh at me," he murmured in her ear.

"Never," Doro replied, but a chuckle escaped her. Before she could say more, Ev spoke again.

"And don't say you're laughing with me, because I'm not laughing." While that was true, merriment sparkled in his silver gaze. "Even if I look ridiculous, it feels good to have dry clothes on."

"You could never look ridiculous," Doro whispered. Far from it. The man was too handsome for her peace of mind. For a moment, a period of silent connection vibrated between them. Reassured, Doro was about to step forward, but Ev stepped back.

His gaze scanned the room. "A crowd is gathering."

She followed his gaze. "Yes. Which is good." For the search, but not for what she had been considering. Doro cleared her throat. "I took the advice we gave you and borrowed something from Aggie while we were at her house. This is more comfortable than my good dress and shoes." The knee-length wool skirt and matching pullover sweater felt good.

His attention returned to her. "We have the same discrepancies since you have a couple more inches and a few less pounds than Aggie."

"At least the two of us wear the same size shoes," Doro pointed out, gesturing to the brown ones on her feet. "High heels are only good for special occasions. These Oxfords are giving my feet a rest."

Ev laughed again. "I love your party shoes."

Warmth crept into Doro's cheeks, but she appreciated the observation. Usually, Ev was generous with his compliments. Over the past week, they had been few-and-far-between. But so had casual conversation. "Let's join the others."

"We better," he agreed.

Before Ev started forward, Doro scanned the assembled group. "I see a number of professors, but not Longley or Baylor."

After scrutinizing the assembly, Ev concurred. "Neither do I. Maybe they're among those who didn't want to leave a toasty room."

"I'll ask Mrs. Jones after the searchers go out again." When Ev's brow furrowed, Doro continued. "Just curious."

Fresh amusement filled his gaze. "Of course, you are."

❦

Fifteen minutes later, the men headed out again. After that, waiting proved tedious, and fending off sleep when nothing happened was not easy. To pass the time, Doro, Aggie, and Mrs. Jones took turns making coffee and tending to search parties who returned periodically to get out of what had turned into a steady wintry mix. Tee greeted each group, got plenty of attention, and rested between visits. Doro wished she could relax as easily as the sweet pup.

After one small group returned to the fray, Mrs. Jones sighed. "At least it isn't snowing, although it may yet. I'm worried for Horace. He's rather frail, and he has to be cold unless he somehow found his way into an unlocked building."

"That's not impossible. Many folks don't secure their businesses or homes, even when they're away," Aggie replied.

"President Adams had all the doors on campus checked already, and none was open," Doro pointed out. "They even walked through the fieldhouse in case Horace never left there. But he would've heard us earlier, so that seems unlikely. Because Ev often chats with him, Horace would know his voice."

"It seems like he would, but if he's scared..." Aggie's voice trailed off.

Mrs. Jones braced her elbows on the table and steepled her fingers. "All the campus buildings have some nooks and crannies, but the fieldhouse may have more than the others." Her forehead furrowed as if she was trying to recall something.

Doro sat up straighter. "I know the campus pretty well, but I wasn't aware of that."

A smile brightened the secretary's face. "Many years ago, when my husband first took a job here, one of the coaches brought his dog to the fieldhouse on a Saturday. Since no one else was around, he didn't keep his pet in his own office, and she took the opportunity to tour the building. I'm not sure exactly where she was found, but it took time to locate her. The coach said she'd gotten in a little niche on the top floor, which was only an attic for storage. It hasn't been used for years, though. Not since an annex was added for equipment."

"How would someone get up there?" Doro asked.

Mrs. Jones answered after a moment's hesitation. "It's been a long time since I thought about that place. The regular staircase was taken out when the storage area was moved. Even though the attic isn't used much, a pull-down stairway was put in. I've heard the attic ceiling is very low, so any adult would need to scrunch over. That's why items aren't kept there any longer," Mrs. Jones replied.

"Horace spends a lot of time in the fieldhouse, so he might've seen the hatch," Doro suggested. "It's visible from the floor, right?"

Mrs. Jones tapped her fingers together. "It was, and the ceiling is low in that particular corridor. If my memory serves me, there was a rope to pull the attic door open."

"I wonder if it's still there," Doro murmured. "I can't picture it."

"You wouldn't see it in the normal course of things. The corridor is narrow, and the door to it is set behind a row of lockers," Mrs. Jones said. "You'd have to go back there to see the door."

"At the south side of the building?" Doro asked.

"Yes," the secretary replied.

"I wasn't aware of a hallway behind the lockers, but I know where they are," Doro said. "Even if Horace couldn't pull the stairway down, he might be hiding back there. He would've heard people calling, but he might be too scared to come out."

Aggie nodded. "Maybe so. We should check, but how will we get into the building? Ev locked up when we left after doing the fingerprints, and he must still have the keys on him, since the searchers checked there."

Mrs. Jones reached for her pocketbook. "President Adams gave me his set of keys to all the buildings. He was with the group that used them earlier. Since they went through the building, he didn't want to carry them with him when he went out again."

When the secretary pulled out a ring filled with keys, Doro understood why the college administrator did not want them in his pocket. "Here you go, girls."

As Aggie accepted the ring, Doro jumped to her feet. "Let's take Tee along. Horace loves her and vice-versa, so she might draw him out, if we can get close enough to let him know it's just the two of us and her."

"I've seen the two of them together when Ev takes Tee on his rounds, and I agree," Mrs. Jones said. "The dog would be a lure for Horace."

"Do you mind waiting here by yourself while we check the fieldhouse?" Doro asked.

"Not at all, but you two be careful. There's a killer around somewhere," the secretary warned, "and you're well-known as amateur sleuths."

Aggie grinned. "Doro is the real sleuth. I'm her sidekick."

Mrs. Jones' lips moved, but they did not quite form a smile. "All the same, be cautious."

"We have Tee, and she's a good watch dog," Doro assured the older woman. In response, Tee woofed.

"We'll be fine," Aggie agreed.

"Bundle up. It's cold, and I won't be surprised if the freezing rain changes to snow soon," the secretary advised.

"There are two extra slickers, so Aggie and I will put them over our coats. I can tuck Tee inside until we get to the field-house," Doro said.

The two young women and the little dog headed outside. Normally, Tee loved to walk but, as soon as the icy precipitation hit her, the pup let Doro slip her under the rain gear.

"All I can see is Tee's nose," Aggie said with a laugh.

"She hates rain," Doro murmured, "and I'm not fond of it, either. Sleet is worse."

"The gusty wind and cold temperatures don't help," Aggie murmured.

The young women rushed on. As they reached the campus, they encountered several searchers. Doro's boss was among them. Former boss, she reminded herself.

"You two should be inside. We've got plenty of help to search. Just no luck yet," Floyd Quartine said.

"We're heading to the park again," one of the men told the retiring library director. "We'll go on ahead."

"I'll catch up," Floyd promised.

After the other three men went on, Doro shared their plan. "Do you know anything about the attic?"

"I've actually seen the hatch, but I've never been up the stairs. There used to be a hook on a long shaft stored on the wall back that way," Quartine said. "Horace might've seen it, if it's still there. It's an unusually long set of steps. If you go up, be cautious. It looks wobbly."

"We will," Doro put in. "In any case, we'll take a look, but Horace could be in the hidden corridor."

"Maybe I should come with you," the man observed.

"We'll be fine. Tee will alert us to anything odd," Doro assured him. "Besides, if you don't rejoin your group, they'll wonder what happened."

A moment of quiet preceded his acquiescence. "All right, but don't take any chances."

"We never do," Doro assured him.

"Hmm, not sure I agree with that," he murmured. "I'll meet my group, and we'll circle back to the fieldhouse, just to ease my mind."

Since Doro knew arguing would not budge the man, she nodded. "With luck, we'll have Horace with us."

"That would be wonderful. See you shortly," Quartine said.

Although the precipitation was not as heavy as earlier, the two friends hurried on. When they got to the fieldhouse, Doro pulled out the keys and unlocked the door. Complete darkness surrounded them as they stepped inside.

Aggie moved her flashlight beam around until it fell on a wall switch. She quickly flipped it into the on position. A series of overheads lamps came on. "That's better."

"It sure is," Doro agreed. With one hand, she freed Tee and placed her on the floor. The little dog wagged her tail wildly. "She's ready to search."

"Or just stretch her legs," Aggie observed.

"That, too," Doro said with a laugh.

The little group headed toward the northwest corner of the building where a narrow corridor branched out from the main one. Again, Aggie shone her flashlight around until the beam illuminated a switchplate. Doro turned it on, but only scattered sconces lit up.

"If no one comes back here often, the bulbs probably don't get replaced regularly," Aggie commented.

"Evidently not," Doro said as she continued on. Within moments, Tee woofed and pulled forward. After walking another twenty feet, Doro stopped. "The ladder is down."

"Maybe we should wait for help," Aggie said.

Doro shifted from one foot to the other. "What if Horace is up there and too afraid to come back down?" When Tee put her front paws on the first step, Doro scooped up the little dog. "You can't go up these open stairs. Aggie will hold you."

After Doro held Tee out, Aggie took the pup. "Be careful. Not only are the stairs rickety, we can't be sure what's up there."

Well aware of the possibilities, Doro took a deep breath before switching on her flashlight. After Tee whined, she patted the little dog's head. "It's all right, girl." Tee's response was to push forward. "I can't carry you up, and I don't want you falling through the open steps. I'd like to take you, but it wouldn't be safe." Having canine backup seemed like a wonderful idea. Any backup did. But going on alone was the only viable option. With effort, Doro schooled her thoughts. The killer had to be long-gone. If anyone was in the attic, it was poor Horace. And maybe some critters. "I won't be long." With that, Doro started climbing.

"We'll be right here," Aggie assured her.

Any reassurance was welcome, but Doro made no reply. Instead, she carefully ascended the stairs. With each footfall, the boards groaned. Even the handrail creaked when Doro grasped it. The higher she went, the darker it got. Only the thin beam from her torch provided illumination. When Doro reached the top, a musty smell invaded her nostrils, and she exhaled sharply. As she stepped on to the attic floor, something brushed her face. With one hand, she swatted at it. Relief filled her when she realized it was a cobweb, but relief was short-lived. Cobwebs meant spiders. Although not afraid of them, Doro preferred to avoid contact with insects and other possible attic inhabitants. She did not take time to enumerate the possibilities.

After composing herself, she shone the light around the interior. Although the first pass revealed nothing, the second illuminated a slumped form. A human one. Without fore-thought, Doro—heart pounding in her ears—rushed for-ward, dropped to her knees, and focused the beam. Horace's smudged face came into view. When his eyelashes fluttered open, Doro gasped with relief. "Horace, are you all right?"

A garbled response left him.

Suddenly, Doro noted the young man was bound and gagged. Her first action was to yank the handkerchief out of his mouth. "Are you hurt?"

"No." The single word came out in a weak, wobbly voice.

A wave of empathy crashed over Doro when she saw streaks on his dirty face. The poor kid had been crying, and who could blame him? "Let me get you untied. Aggie, Professor Lammers, is waiting for us downstairs. So is Tee."

That evoked a smile. "I heard her and you two. I heard others a while back, but they didn't come to get me, and I couldn't call out."

"They didn't know about the attic. Neither did I until Mrs. Jones told us." As she spoke, Doro pulled out a pocketknife, one that Aggie had gotten out of Wade's desk drawer before they left the constable's office. Her friend had suggested they might need it to jimmy a lock. Instead, Doro used it to cut the ropes. When she finished, she sat back on her haunches. "Rest a few moments before trying to stand up. I want to tell Aggie I found you, but I'm only going as far as the ladder. All right?"

"Sure," Horace replied, although his voice was still tremulous.

Doro hurried to the opening and called to her friend. "I found him. He seems okay, but I want to take it easy coming down the steps. He's been tied up, probably for a few hours."

"Maybe I should get a few men to help," Aggie called back.

"No, I want to get Horace out of here."

Those words were barely out when a male voice reached her. "Doro, it's Floyd. I came back to check on you girls. On the way, I ran into Ev and a few others. He'll be along in a couple of minutes."

The news was a double-edged sword. Ev's strength would be useful in ensuring Horace's safe descent, but he would not be happy she and Aggie went searching on their own. "Let me know when he's here." With that, she scrambled back to Horace. "Officer Mallow is coming, and he can help you get down the ladder. After all this time being stuck here, you're probably stiff."

"I like Officer Mallow," Horace said. "He's always nice."

Warmth spread through Doro. Not everyone took time with Horace, who often had trouble carrying on a conversation. Being the team ball boy helped him, and so did people like Ev who interacted with Horace like he was any average young man. Privately, Doro thought he was above average with his caring, kindness, loyalty, and diligence. "He's a nice man."

Although the flashlight did not dispel all the darkness, Horace's grin was clear. "You must think so, cuz you're gonna marry him."

"I do think so," she replied. Doro had no opportunity to say more because her fiancé's voice interrupted.

"Doro, I'm coming up," Ev hollered. Within moments, he entered the attic. His own flashlight focused on her and Horace. "Are you all right, son?"

"Yes, sir." Horace's voice sounded stronger.

"Good." Ev crossed to where Doro crouched on the floor beside Horace. "What about you?"

Did his tone sound chillier? Because Doro knew he would not chastise her in front of the kid, she took the opportunity to defend her actions, albeit furtively. "Just fine. After Mrs. Jones told us about this attic, Aggie and I decided to check it out. We weren't sure when any of you men would be back, and we didn't want Horace stuck in here any longer. If he was here. Which he was." When she realized she was babbling, Doro paused. "He was bound and gagged, so he couldn't holler when he heard voices earlier."

"I see." A note of amusement crept into his voice. After kneeling down, Ev addressed Horace. "How about if Professor Banyon and I help you stand up?"

"I'm not a baby," the young man said.

"Of course not," Ev agreed. "But you've been tied up in an uncomfortable position for a few hours. When I was a copper in Detroit, we found a burly boxer who had been in a similar circumstance for the same amount of time. He insisted on standing up alone and fell flat on his face. I'd rather not see that again, so how about a little help?"

A moment passed before Horace replied. "Okay."

Although Doro was not sure Ev's story was true, it worked. She gripped the boy's right arm while Ev took the left one. "Ready?" she asked.

"Yes, ma'am," Horace responded.

Within moments, the decision to help him proved correct because Horace wobbled before righting himself. "Take it slow and easy," Ev said. "There's no rush."

"I wanna get outta here," Horace said, his voice strained.

"We'll do that now," Ev replied. "Let's head to the ladder."

Neither Doro nor Ev released their hold on the kid, which proved wise because Horace leaned heavily on them. When they reached the opening, Ev slid his arm around the young man's back.

Doro looked at Ev for some sign of what to do next. Allowing Horace to descend on his own might not be wise. What if, in his weakened conditioned, he fell? Not wanting to voice the thought in front of Horace, she focused on Ev. "We need to be careful going down. It's such a narrow ladder. Rickety, too."

"You're right."

His immediate agreement let Doro know he understood her concern, but Ev had probably already considered Horace's physical condition and emotional state. "Maybe you should go down first and Horace can follow. Then, I'll come."

Ev glanced from her to the kid, who had not come all the way to the floor's edge. "Why don't you go ahead? We'll wait until you're all the way down. How does that sound, Horace?"

The young man, eyes wide, gazed at Ev. "It's a long way." Fear underscored each word.

"Did you walk up or did someone carry you?" Ev asked.

"I got carried, I guess," Horace replied.

Doro and Ev exchanged puzzled glances. "What do you mean? Aren't you sure how you got up here?" she asked.

"I got conked on the head," Horace replied.

Dismay flashed through Doro. If he had been an average twenty-year-old, she would have scolded him for not saying so immediately. But he was a special young man. "Do you have a headache?"

"Not exactly. Just a sore spot." His fingers went to the lower right side of his head.

"Is it all right if I touch it? I won't press down," Doro assured him.

"Sure."

With the utmost care, she gently laid her hand where his had been. "You've got a goose egg. Are you dizzy?"

"Maybe a little," Horace said. "Someone did it when I went in Coach's office. Coach was on the floor. He must not be all right because he didn't help me."

Doro swallowed hard. "You're right. He would have if he could have."

"Something bad happened, didn't it?" Horace asked in a trembling voice.

Ev patted Horace on the back. "It did. Whoever hit you also hurt Coach Munroe."

"Real bad?" Horace's voice was rough and raspy.

For a moment, Doro met Ev's troubled gaze. Withholding the truth would not do any good, especially since they would have to question Horace soon. Hiding the facts would be impossible then. "I'm so sorry, but Coach Munroe is dead."

With one hand, Horace wiped his eyes. "I knew he wasn't all right because he wouldn't have let the man take me off."

"No, he wouldn't," Doro agreed. She cleared her throat. "Let's get you out of here."

"Yes, please," Horace murmured.

Ev ran one hand over his face. "All right. Here's what I think is best for all of us. We'll let Doro go down first. Then, you and I will take the steps one at a time together. I'll put an arm around your waist. You can put both hands over that arm. With my other hand, I'll hold the hand rail. We'll go real slow, and we can stop and rest any time. How does that sound?"

To Doro, it sounded dangerous and not only for Horace. If the kid got nervous and resisted or moved wrong, he could send both of them tumbling down. Since she had no better solution, she simply agreed. "I'll go ahead." After reaching the bottom, Doro crossed her fingers.

"I heard Ev's plan," Aggie murmured. "It may be the only way to get Horace down, but it seems dodgy."

"I agree on both counts," Doro whispered.

Floyd patted her on the back. "I'll stand on one side, if you two will take the other. We can be guard rails."

After the young women agreed, Aggie put Tee down. Doro gave the dog a pat on the head. "Be a good girl and stay." She put emphasis on the last word. Tee immediately sat down. "Good girl."

While Ev and Horace descended the ladder, Doro kept both hands near the rail. For what seemed like an eternity, but was probably only five minutes, she riveted her attention on them. Twice, Horace stumbled and Ev—grappling with the impact—faltered but did not fall. Finally, the pair was on the floor. Relief slackened Doro's body. They were safe.

When Tee danced merrily around Ev and Horace, the boy dropped to his knees. "Thanks for finding me." In response, the little dog licked his face.

Ev turned to Doro. "Tee played doggie detective again?"

"More or less," she agreed. "When we came over this way, Tee got animated. She must've sensed Horace was up there."

After sinking to his haunches, Ev petted the dog, too. "Good girl." Tee took a brief moment to lick his hand before resuming her ministrations to Horace. When footsteps sounded in the narrow corridor, Ev stood up.

"Let's go out to where it's better lit," Floyd suggested.

The little group reached the main corridor about the time Wade, Horace's father, and Doc Silven reached them. Mr. MacPherson opened his arms, and Horace went into them. "Thank heavens you're all right. What happened?"

When the young man did not answer, Doro provided an explanation. "I'm glad you're here, Doc, since the bump should be checked."

"I was out searching with Mr. MacPherson when Ev said he was headed this way." Silven turned to Horace. "Can I take a look?"

"Sure," the boy replied.

After a cursory examination, Doc stepped back and held up his thumb. "How many do you see?"

Horace giggled. "One."

"That's good," the physician said. "I'd like to look you over a little better, but we can do it at your house. Your mother is anxious for you to get home."

"She sure is," MacPherson agreed. "The other men in our group went to tell her."

A watery smile lit Horace's face. "Maybe I can have an extra piece of cake. Ma said only one after dinner."

His father laughed. "I'm pretty sure you can have as much cake as you want."

Horace beamed. "Let's go home."

Mr. MacPherson turned to Ev. "I suppose you want to talk with him."

"We'll need to do that but not until Doc examines him more carefully. But if we could ask a couple of questions now, we might learn something important," Ev said. "Horace knows what happened to Munroe."

Horace's father hesitated before nodding. "If Doc says it's all right."

"A couple of questions. Then, he should get home," Silven said.

Ev knelt in front of the boy. "You got hit on the head, but do you recall anything before that?"

"It could help us find Coach Munroe's killer," Doro murmured, as she sank next to Ev.

Horace glanced from one to the other before turning his attention to Tee. "Coach's door was open. I could see it from a ways away, so I started whistling the fight song. He always liked that."

"Was the door wide open?" Doro asked.

"Pretty much," Horace replied. "I went right in and didn't see him." His forehead furrowed. "There was someone behind the door. I thought maybe Coach was getting a book off the shelf. I was gonna say something...but I got hit. I sorta woke up when the man shoved a cloth in my mouth. At least it didn't stink." He looked at his father. "It smelled like you and Officer Mallow, too."

The comment had both men gasping, but Doro recalled Ev's aftershave. "It smelled like sandalwood. I caught a whiff of the gag myself."

"That's a popular scent," Wade put in.

"It is," Silven agreed, "but I don't use it."

"Nor do I," Floyd added.

"You gave us a good clue, Horace," Doro said.

He grinned. "Good, but can I go home? My head hurts. Cake would help."

Everyone chuckled before Doro replied. "Of course."

"I'll call the constable's office as soon as Horace is up to talking more," Silven assured him.

Doro picked up Tee, who was still licking the boy's face. "Come on, girl. Your buddy has to go."

"When you come to talk, will you bring her?" Horace asked. "I like Tee, and she likes me."

"She sure does," Ev agreed, "so, we'll bring her, if it's all right with your dad."

"Of course," Mr. MacPherson said. "My wife and I are fond of her, too. We love dogs in our house."

"Then, Tee will be with us," Doro assured him.

With that, Silven, MacPherson, Floyd, and Ev got the boy to his feet. He wobbled less than he had coming down the ladder. "We brought my vehicle, since my house was on our way here," Silven said. The physician had been among the searchers.

"We'll make sure you get there without incident," Ev put in.

"I'd appreciate it," Horace's father replied. "Ride along with us, Mr. Quartine. Your place is on our way."

"I want to escort Violet home," Floyd said.

"We can drop you off at the station," Doc Silven offered.

After Quartine accepted, the men saw the boy safely into the car. Doro and Aggie, with Tee in tow, followed after them. Ev walked behind the trio. After the vehicle pulled away, Ev faced Doro. She put one hand up. "I know what you're going to say."

His dark brows rose. "Do you?"

"Tee could probably stretch her legs, so I'll just walk her over there." Aggie gestured to a line of boxwoods thirty feet away.

"Coward," Doro murmured.

The lilt of laughter followed Aggie as she and the dog headed away.

Doro watched them go until Ev caught her hand in his. Reluctantly, she turned back to him. "It wasn't much of a risk."

He pressed his lips together until a grin erupted. "I agree."

Her jaw dropped. "You do?"

"We'd already been through the fieldhouse, and the killer wasn't likely to stay long anyhow. They seldom do. Him being here hours later, especially when he left a victim..." Ev shook his head. "Not very apt to happen."

"True."

"I'm just glad Mrs. Jones thought of the old attic access. It's not something anyone else mentioned. I wish they had because we could've gotten Horace much sooner."

"From what she said, it hasn't been used in decades. Her husband told her about it many years ago, but she never actually went back there herself, and she'd forgotten about the place."

Ev's forehead furrowed. "Which makes me wonder how the killer knew about it."

Doro chewed on her lower lip. "I wonder the exact same thing, and I also wonder what other men in town use sandalwood aftershave or soap."

"Like Wade said, it's popular but plenty of fellows don't use scent at all. Not that I take note."

"I don't always, either." After his detachment over the past week, Doro hesitated to admit she noticed sandalwood because of him. Instead, she said, "But I'll think about it and ask Aggie and Mrs. Jones if she noticed it on any of the players."

"Good idea. At least it might narrow the field."

"That would help."

"We should get to the constable's office," Ev said.

When he started to turn away, Doro grabbed his sleeve. "Wait a minute. Aggie has Tee, which gives us a few minutes to talk."

A bleak expression descended on his features. "We need to solve this case."

"It'll only take a short time. Please don't brush me off again."

His gaze widened. "I wouldn't brush you off."

"But you have. Repeatedly. I know the depression is hard on everyone, and you must be fretting about your job. If you are, can't you at least tell me? We're a couple, and we should share our concerns. Not hide them from one another."

He looked at a point over her shoulder. "The uncertainty is getting to me, and I'm sorry if I've been standoffish. I don't mean to be. I just don't want to spoil your happiness over your promotion with my fears. Or ruin the holiday."

"You're the most fearless man I know. How many times have you faced down criminals?"

A rueful smile tugged at one corner of his mouth. "More than a few."

Relief spread through Doro. Seeing him look happy was a tonic. "So, you can face anything, and so can I. Remember that."

When he met her gaze again, his expression grew solemn. "I'll try."

Since that was a concession of sorts, Doro let the subject drop. Finding Munroe's killer and Horace's abductor was of utmost importance. She and Ev could settle any lingering issues later.

Chapter Eleven

As Doro, Ev, and Aggie walked back to the constable's office, the wintry mix changed to snow. Ev offered an arm to each woman, which helped them traverse the increasingly slippery walkways. When they entered the building, Doro breathed a sigh of relief. Being out of the elements felt wonderful.

Wade came from behind the counter to help Aggie with her coat, while Ev did the same for Doro. While the group removed their outerwear, Mrs. Jones poured three mugs of coffee. "Have something hot to drink," she urged the trio.

"I'll help you carry the coffee, ma'am," Wade put in. "The rest of you sit by the fire. I've been back for a few minutes, so I've warmed up."

Doro gratefully wrapped her hands around the mug as she took a seat near the stove, while Aggie followed suit. After hanging up his coat, Ev helped Mrs. Jones with her chair before sitting down himself. Wade joined the group.

"As soon as word got to me that you girls found Horace, I headed back here. We've been letting the searchers know the boy is all right," Wade said. "Most of the town was involved in one way or another. People are happy to turn off their porch lights to signal his safe return."

"I'm happy about people pitching in," Doro murmured. She loved her home town, and neighbors helping each other was a big reason why.

"It's such a relief that Horace is safe," Mrs. Jones put in.

"If you hadn't remembered the old attic, we wouldn't have found him," Doro said.

A slight smile moved the secretary's lips. "I'm glad I thought of it tonight. Other old hands would've heard about the murder and Horace being lost by tomorrow morning. Not that a lot of them are left, but a handful are. I'm sure some of them are familiar with the trap door and all."

"The poor kid was shaken up," Aggie said, "and I don't blame him."

Wade braced his forearms on the table. "I hope he can provide some clues."

"He offered one," Doro replied before mentioning the sandalwood scent on the gag. "Does anyone recall a player or someone else wearing that scent?"

"Wade doesn't use it," Aggie observed.

"Ag, I hope you weren't considering me a suspect," her husband said.

She grinned. "Of course not. I don't often notice scents on other men, but Professor Longley must use a lot of shaving soap or aftershave in the morning, because I've smelled it on him."

"He came to see President Adams early on Friday morning, and you're right. The smell of sandalwood was quite strong," Mrs. Jones put in.

Doro pulled out her notepad and jotted the information down. "Anyone else?"

"Vince Brownlee's mother works in a department store. I recall him saying that in my class when one of the other fellows teased him about wanting to attract girls. Two moved away from him with their noses pinched, and one said sandalwood reminded her of her father, who also used far too much," Aggie said.

"I believe Clint Spalling also had some on," Mrs. Jones said.

After getting that information down, Doro studied her list. "Others may, too, but we could move these three near the top."

"Did Horace say anything else?" Wade asked.

Ev reviewed the only other details. "Doc will look him over and call if we can question Horace tonight."

"That's best," Wade said. "But frustrating."

"It is," Doro agreed. "There are other avenues to follow. Like talking more with Clint. I thought he was with one of you."

Ev nodded. "He was in my group of searchers. When Floyd found us and told me I was needed at the fieldhouse, I asked Clint to come here, so we could go over details about the case when I got back. That was maybe thirty minutes ago."

A frown furrowed Mrs. Jones's forehead. "He hasn't been back."

Uneasiness filled Doro. "Maybe he went home to put on dry clothes."

Following a glance at his wristwatch, Ev stood up. "No one's manning the Maple Hall front desk any more, since so many residents have already moved out. That means calling is out. I'll go over and see if he's there."

"Where else would he be?" Aggie asked. "It's not like he'd leave town. That would only make him look guilty, and I don't think he is."

Ev retook his seat. "I agree with you Aggie. Clint isn't a strong suspect in my mind. On top of that, he has good reason to stay in Michaw as long as possible."

Wade grinned. "I've heard he is stepping out with Miss Jackson, the high school English teacher."

"It's more like they're courting," Doro observed before revealing what Stan Jackson had told them.

"Clint had already shared much the same with me," Ev put in. "Since she, her brother, and Clint ate with the Piersons today, he has a solid alibi."

Aggie leaned forward in her chair. "That's good, but Stan Jackson wouldn't have been with them. I saw him on Friday, and he was planning to go away this weekend."

Doro turned to Ev. "Didn't Clint tell you that Stan was going to dinner with him and Miss Jackson?"

"That was the plan," Ev replied. "Obviously, plans changed."

"Maybe they changed for Clint, too," Doro observed.

"You're suspicious of him," Aggie suggested.

Since she knew the statement was actually a question, Doro nodded. "From what several players said, he and Coach Munroe were often at odds. The animosity worsened after Clint was told he'll be out of a job after the tournament."

"Being terminated, even when it's due to financial strain and not professional failing, is hard," Ev said.

Because Doro knew he was expressing his own feelings, she clasped his hand under the table. When Ev did not immediately return the gesture, anxiety coursed through her. The last thing she wanted was to be at odds over an investigation. Although sleuthing was her passion, he was her love. "I'm lucky not to be affected, but I understand why others are so upset," she said. When Ev squeezed her hand, Doro's shoulders slumped with relief.

"I feel terrible when they come in the office," Mrs. Jones said. "There's nothing President Adams can do, which disturbs him. These are difficult times."

"Do you expect a lot more jobs to be cut after the board meeting on Wednesday?" Aggie asked.

Mrs. Jones looked at Ev before focusing on Aggie. "I'm not sure. I hope not."

When Ev released her hand, Doro reluctantly let him go. She wished she could do or say something reassuring. They had only lost his part-time deputy constable's salary, although neither of them would be paid while the college was closed, but they would survive for six weeks. After all, she would not pay rent at her grandmother's home, and Ev could stay in the garage apartment for a time. When classes resumed, they could return to almost normal. The front door opening interrupted her reverie.

After walking in, Clint glanced around the table. "I hope I'm not interrupting anything."

Ev was the first to reply. "Not at all. Join us."

"Yes, please do," Doro added.

Clint hung his coat on one of the hooks by the door and sauntered across the room. He glanced around the table and headed toward an empty chair next to Ev. As he passed her, Doro caught the scent of sandalwood. She did not want to make an issue in front of Spalling, but she tucked the knowledge into the back of her mind.

After sitting down, Clint spoke again. "Sorry I didn't come straight here after you went to the fieldhouse, Ev, but I got two soaked feet walking through a puddle that I didn't see. I went to my room, got dry shoes, and put warmer clothes on. It's snowing now."

"Would you like coffee?" Mrs. Jones asked.

"No, ma'am, but thank you. Just being inside where it's warm is terrific," he replied. "I understand not keeping the heat turned up, because of the need to save money."

"If it's too cold, let President Adams know," Mrs. Jones said. "We don't want you freezing."

"Maybe you could take an empty suite with a fireplace," Ev suggested. "There are a couple of open ones now."

Clint shook his head. "I'll be moving out shortly."

Several moments of silence passed before Wade made an observation. "Maybe not. If the college decides to let the team play this weekend, you'd become the head coach."

Because she kept her attention on Clint, Doro noted his lips moving. For a brief time, she thought he was going to smile. Then, he shook his head.

"I'm not sure playing in the tournament is the right thing to do," the young coach murmured.

"Leave it up to President Adams," Mrs. Jones said. "He's calling several of the trustees first thing tomorrow to get their perspectives. Since he planned to speak with Coach Munroe's sister tonight, he'll get the family's view, as well."

"I didn't know Coach had family," Doro said.

"Just his sister and her children. His brother-in-law, who was evidently his best friend, died during the first wave of influenza," the secretary replied. "Tragically, his wife and young son died in the second outbreak. That was before he came to Michaw."

Although Doro had heard rumors about Munroe losing his family to the flu, she had never known for sure that they were true. Hearing Mrs. Jones confirm the fact provided understanding about the coach. No wonder he could be terse and touchy at times. Losing three people close to him had to take a toll.

"He never told me any of that," Clint said.

After the rest of the group agreed that his situation came as news to them, Mrs. Jones sighed. "He was a private man. I know he could be difficult, but when he told me about losing three relatives in such a short time, there were tears in his eyes. He got embarrassed, so I assured him I wouldn't tell a soul. Coach Munroe appreciated that." She hesitated for a moment before continuing. "He confided that he wished he'd spent more time with his wife and child, but basketball took precedence too often. When he hired you, Clint, he was relieved that you didn't have a sweetheart. He didn't want to see another young woman take a back seat to basketball."

Tension tightened Clint's jaw. "Me courting a girl was one of the first things he asked about."

Mrs. Jones nodded. "I'm not surprised. It was very much on his mind that the job of assistant would be time-consuming. He was an assistant when he first married and when their child was born. In fact, he was on a scouting trip the day of the birth. Coach felt terrible about that. His wife and baby were home from the hospital before he got back."

"I wish I had known," Clint murmured.

"We seldom know as much about people as we think, even when we see them every day," the secretary observed. "We all keep things to ourselves, especially heartaches."

For long moments, silence filled the room. During that time, Doro considered Mrs. Jones' life, which now revolved around her job. Mrs. Jones had no close family left, which was why Gramma Rose invited her for every holiday. "You're coming on Thanksgiving, aren't you?" As soon as the question was out, Doro realized how absurd it sounded in the context of their current conversation. Heat flamed in her cheeks. "After today's campus dinner, I just wondered. You could ride with Ev and me."

After giving Doro a puzzled glance, Ev agreed. "We can pick you up around noon."

Faint color rose in Mrs. Jones' face. "Rose invited Mr. Quartine, so we'll come together."

Out of the corner of her eye, Doro saw Aggie grin and repressed one herself. While she felt pleased for the older couple, Doro knew both would prefer privacy, not questions or comments. "It'll be lovely to have more people."

"Thank you," the secretary replied. "We're looking forward to it."

Doro looked at her best friend. "We'll miss you, but I'm happy you're spending the holiday with your new family."

Aggie's smile intensified. "So am I."

"We'll see you on Sunday," Wade said to Doro.

She glanced at Clint. "You're welcome to join us. We're celebrating my promotion."

"Thanks, but I've been having Sunday dinner with the Piersons," the assistant coach replied.

"And Miss Jackson," Wade put in.

"That's what you did today, right?" Doro asked. "Along with her brother." Would the last comment promote Clint to reveal the truth about where Stan was over the weekend?

"Stan went to visit a friend in the city this weekend, but he usually goes with us," Clint replied.

"Ev and I chatted with him on Monday. He's upset about you losing your job, and he said his sister is distraught," Doro put in. "It's understandable since you moving would interfere with the courtship."

"It's a tough position to be in," Ev added. "These are trying times for plenty of us, but you and Miss Jackson could still court."

Several seconds of silence passed before Clint replied. "We aren't courting. We're married."

Chapter Twelve

Doro stared at him in stunned disbelief. When she glanced around the table, she saw the others felt exactly the same way. "Why are you hiding your marriage? Miss Jackson could've gotten her job as a wife. You being her husband would have had no effect at all." Unlike some towns, Michaw schools employed married women. Doro's mother had once been one of them years ago.

Clint swallowed convulsively. "You heard Mrs. Jones. Coach Munroe didn't want a married man as his assistant. Before I got hired, he asked if I had a sweetheart. He didn't admit to losing his family and all, but he made it clear the job came first, so he didn't want anyone who might get distracted. The way he said it, I knew I couldn't tell him the truth."

"You were married then?" Ev suggested.

"No. We were engaged." After folding his hands on the table, Clint focused his attention on them. "I told Coach that I wasn't courting anyone, because I wanted the job. Michaw has one of the best basketball programs in the state. Being an assistant here is a stepping stone to a job of my own. At least it was until my position was eliminated. Even worse, some other colleges are disbanding their sports teams, so finding something elsewhere won't be easy."

Sympathy filled Doro, but so did curiosity. "Do the Piersons know you're married?"

Clint's nostrils flared with a sharp intake of breath. "We told them earlier today. As hard as it is to admit it to all of you, that was harder. They've been very good to Bonnie."

The others around the table exchanged a series of surprised expressions before Ev found his voice. "I'm guessing your marital status was part of what made you uneasy with Coach Munroe. You had to fret about him finding out."

The other man nodded. "I didn't want him to know about Bonnie and me, because he would've fired me. We went ahead and pretended to step out. Well, we pretended we weren't married, just stepping out because the athletic director's children have Bonnie as a teacher. The love her and sang her praises at home. One day in early September, he saw me talking with Bonnie and said not to worry about Coach if we planned to start seeing one another. He'd intervene because his children didn't always behave in school, but they did for Bonnie."

The admission reminded Doro of what she had heard a few days earlier. "Coach Munroe wouldn't go against the athletic director."

"Not over Bonnie and me stepping out," Clint replied. "But being married. That was too much. Besides, I doubt if the director would've liked us lying."

Mrs. Jones folded her hands in her lap. "Maybe not. I can't be sure, but Coach Munroe's insistence on having an assistant who wasn't engaged or married came from his grief and regret. Not only did he fault himself for being away so much, Coach Munroe shouldered the blame for his wife and child getting influenza. Several of his players came down with it on a road trip, and he became ill himself. His case was mild, but his family's illnesses weren't."

Clint ran one hand over his face. "I didn't know. Not when I took the job and not when I lost it. Not until you told us."

"You've been here for over a year, but Miss Jackson only came this fall," Aggie observed.

"There was no teaching job for her a year ago. During that time, I went to the city whenever I could, but she had Stan to look out for her. When I heard the local high school needed an English teacher, I made a special trip to tell her. We were all happy and relieved, especially when Stan got a custodial job. It took him down a couple of pegs, but he didn't mind. Whatever was good for Bonnie was what he did." A harsh breath left Clint. "Being an assistant here for another season would've given me enough experience to nab a head coaching job. Then, the crash happened last fall. Some schools dropped athletics in the spring, but I still had hope. Now, that's gone." He bowed his head.

Wade drummed his fingers on the table. "As far as I know, the college planned to keep Munroe on."

"That's the case," Mrs. Jones put in.

"Then, with Coach Munroe dead, you can probably stay on." Although Doro's attention was on Clint, she felt Ev stiffen beside her.

The color drained from Clint's face. "I didn't kill him."

"I didn't say you did." Although she watched him carefully, Doro could not tell if he was shocked by her observations or worried about being a suspect.

As the assistant coach's jaw worked, he looked to Ev. "You wanted to talk with me. Is it because you think I'm guilty?"

"We only want to know if you heard anyone argue with Coach," Ev replied.

"Or threaten him," Wade added.

The front door opening again interrupted. This time, Floyd Quartine stepped inside. Instead of removing his coat, he walked immediately to the table. "Sorry to interrupt. I didn't want Silven to drop me off first and delay getting Horace home and checked, so I went with the group. A couple of neighbors were still there. One brought me here." He looked at Mrs. Jones. "The snow is getting worse, so I wanted to take you home, Violet. My vehicle is still out front."

"It is late," the secretary said as she got to her feet. "Unless Floyd and I can be of help, we'll leave you to your work."

After the group wished the older couple a good night, Mrs. Jones and Mr. Quartine left. Doro was about to comment on their relationship, but Wade spoke first.

"Aggie, would you take notes? Clint may know something of interest, and we should jot it down," her husband said.

"Of course." Aggie got the notepad from his desk and put pen to paper.

Wade turned to Clint. "Do you know of anyone who might've had it in for the coach?"

"Coach could be tough with the players. He got after Vince and Dale a few times," Clint replied.

"Because they broke the rules," Ev put in.

Clint nodded. "It was wrong of them, so I don't blame him for chastising them. I just thought it should've been in private."

"Did you tell him that?" Doro asked.

"I did," Clint replied. "It was another point of disagreement, and he made it clear that my opinion wasn't welcome. He didn't like being second-guessed."

Ev leaned back in his chair. "Vince and Dale were probably upset at being embarrassed in front of their teammates."

"Sure," Clint replied. "Who wouldn't be? Not only that, Munroe was loud enough for anyone in a thirty-foot radius to hear him."

"Did any of the others have run-ins with Munroe?" Ev asked.

A shrug moved Clint's shoulders. "At one time or another, he yelled at all of them, but none held a grudge. And none would've attacked him."

"Yet someone did," Wade observed. "Anyone outside the team come to mind?"

Clint scratched his head. "A couple of professors who think they're losing their jobs made snide remarks when Coach and I were at the diner last week, but not just about him. They don't think schools need sports. Plus, they've given most of our players trouble."

"What are their names?" Wade asked.

Although she could guess, Doro remained silent and waited.

"Baylor and Longley," Clint replied. "They think they're better than dumb athletes, coaches included."

Aggie looked up from the notepad. "Did they use those words?"

"Yep, they did. That got Coach Munroe real mad," Clint replied. "Me, too. Longley is a crumb. I don't know Baylor as much."

Doro broke her silence. "How do you know Professor Longley, other than both of you being on campus?"

Clint's jaw worked. "In September, he asked Bonnie to step out with him several times. She refused, of course, but he wouldn't take no for an answer until Reverend Pierson interceded." A rueful smile touched his mouth. "I'd been calling on her, and the pastor liked me. Of course, Bonnie made it clear she welcomed my visits."

Although Spalling remained a suspect, sympathy filled Doro. How sad for the young couple to have to hide their marriage. Could resentment toward Coach Munroe have led to an argument between him and Clint? She had already witnessed Longley's and Baylor's antipathy, but would they—together or separately—confront and kill the man? Despite plenty of bits and pieces, the puzzle was far from taking shape. Did the missing parts represent more secrets? She glanced at Ev and wondered if he was withholding something from her. Although the tension between them had eased, it was not gone. But that had nothing to do with the case.

"It's understandable that you'd be upset with Longley, but how nasty was he to the coach?" Wade inquired.

"Like I said, both professors railed about useless sports and how coaches don't know much worthwhile. They made it clear both Munroe and I should be fired before they are." Clint paused for a deep breath. "Coach told them if they were half as good at their jobs as he was at his, maybe they wouldn't get canned."

"How did they respond?" Ev asked.

Clint's lips flattened. "Baylor said Coach would get what was coming to him, and Longley agreed."

Since the comment was similar to what Doro and Ev had heard from the professors, she glanced at her fiancé, who sat up straight and leaned forward. "And this was a week or so ago."

"About ten days," Clint replied. "Those two didn't even know they'd be fired. They still don't. Not for sure."

When the ringing of the telephone interrupted, Wade went to answer.

Listening to his side of the conversation, Doro knew Doc Silven was on the line. Gleaning other details proved to be impossible, but Wade's expression when he returned was not hard to read. His revelation backed her supposition.

"Doc wants Horace to get rest tonight. He might have a concussion, so we need to postpone our interview until morning," the constable said.

"We don't want to push the boy," Ev said.

"Certainly not," Aggie agreed.

"Of course not," Doro added. "Besides, we could all use some rest."

"I sure could," Clint put in. "Is it all right for me to leave?"

"Just one more question," Wade said. "Were you at the Pierson place all afternoon until coming to practice?"

Clint licked his lips. "Almost all afternoon, although Bonnie and I took a ride. We need some time alone together, and Sunday is usually when we can have that."

"I understand." Wade laid his hand on Aggie's forearm. "Every moment with your wife is treasured."

"Yes, sir. It sure is," Clint agreed.

Envy squeezed Doro's heart, but she kept her comments about the case. "When will her brother be back?"

"Maybe Tuesday." Clint folded his hands in his lap and stared at them. "He got told on Friday that his job will be cut after the Board of Trustees meet. He went to Toledo to look for another position."

As Doro noted the information, she formed another question. "When did he leave?"

"Friday after work," Clint replied. "He was eager to find something as soon as possible, and he has a friend whose employer was hiring a couple of weeks ago. Stan didn't want to leave Michaw because he and Bonnie are close. Not having a job changed his mind."

"Understandable." Despite being out of town when the murder occurred, Stan needed to be interviewed. He might have additional insight into who had argued with Munroe. She followed up with another query. "Does he clean in the fieldhouse?"

After a puzzled look, Clint shook his head. "Not unless there's some special need. He's got full charge of cleaning College Hall and the boys' dormitory, which is plenty of work."

"I'm sure it is," Aggie put in.

With no further questions on tap, the young coach donned his jacket and left.

As soon as the door shut behind him, Wade looked around the table. "It is late, and we all have to be tired, but I'd like to discuss what we know so far. Maybe Horace will give us the smoking gun in the morning. Maybe he won't."

Doro braced her forearms on the table. "If he knew something solid, I think he would've said so right off. I've known him all his life, and Horace is usually impulsive. He blurts things out without being asked and without thinking."

Wade rubbed his chin. "I've known him that long, too, although you've been around him more since I was gone so much when I worked on the railroad. What you say is my experience, too. We may be able to get some general observations from him, but if Horace saw the killer, he would've announced the person's name almost as soon as you found him. Even after being conked on the head and held in the attic, he would've identified the person—if he knew who it was."

"We know he didn't see anyone clearly," Doro said. "The scent of sandalwood is a clue, but not an especially good one since a few suspects wear it."

Ev slumped back in the chair and laced his fingers behind his head. "With that in mind, going over what we currently know is a good idea." He glanced from Aggie to Doro. "If you two agree."

"I can manage for another hour," Aggie said.

"I'm fine," was Doro's answer.

A smile tugged at one corner of Ev's mouth. "You'd say you were even if it wasn't true."

Although Doro put one hand up, her voice held a note of amusement. "Don't say I'm always sleuthing."

"I won't," he promised with a wink. "But I'll be thinking it."

Aggie and Wade laughed and, after a moment of mock severity, Doro did before turning to an important clue. "Did anyone else notice Clint was wearing sandalwood? We discussed that before, but it seemed stronger just now. Or maybe it was on my mind, so I took special note."

"My nose isn't that good," Wade admitted.

"I definitely smelled it, and it was evident," Aggie said.

"Yep, he uses sandalwood," Ev put in. "But remember, it's common."

Doro wrinkled her nose. "I remember. However, it's an important point."

"So, we'll eliminate men who don't use that scent?" Wade asked.

"That seems best to me," Doro said. "The handkerchief smelled of it, so we can assume the killer often, if not always, wears it."

The others agreed before going on to review other evidence. An hour later, Aggie pushed the notepad to Doro. "Maybe you'll make up the suspect list. Writer's cramp is kicking in."

Wade massaged her hand. "We can't have that."

A niggling finger of jealousy traced Doro's spine. Ideally, in six weeks, she and Ev would be married and such intimacies would no longer be considered improper. But now it seemed like their wedding would not be until spring.

Aggie smiled at her husband before looking at her best friend. "We've gone over everything. Horace's mention of sandalwood, the probable weapon, your interviews with the players, Coach Munroe's run-ins with a few people. Besides all that, how Carson Longley and Edie Farrow acted when you saw them earlier today was interesting. I don't know her well, but she took my old apartment in Wheaton Hall, so you must run into her, Doro."

"Occasionally, but she has little to say to me." Doro grimaced. "Evidently, she reveals English department business to Longley. Otherwise, she wouldn't have known about my tenure being granted early. Or about the number of courses being cut for next term."

"They're obviously smitten," Aggie said, "but that's no excuse for her giving out information before the chairman does."

"I agree," Doro said. "Edie and Longley were both upset over basketball being put ahead of academics in terms of money cuts. It's understandable, but..." Her voice trailed off.

"What we've witnessed among Longley, Baylor, and Coach Munroe is concerning," Wade added. "Longley uses sandalwood, but what about Baylor?"

No one in the group knew for sure. "I never noticed it on him," Doro said, "but let's keep them both in the running."

Ev nodded. "The number of confrontations between those two and Munroe can't be discounted. Job loss is enough to upset anyone, but Longley and Baylor have crossed the line on more than a few occasions."

Doro tapped her pencil against the notepad. "Longley has the stronger motive because he's courting Edie. Losing his position will put physical distance between them. Of course, she was upset, too."

"Evidently when Miss Jackson—Mrs. Spalling—turned him down repeatedly, Longley moved on," Ev said.

"And quickly," Aggie observed. "I saw him with Miss Farrow in late September."

"Aggie, you, and Longley are in the same department. Is he snappish with fellow professors?" Ev asked.

Aggie shrugged. "He flatters the tenured male professors endlessly. He's less pleasant to the women, even to the two of us who are tenured."

"That doesn't surprise me," Doro murmured.

"He's full of himself," Ev observed. "In my experience, Baylor is arrogant, too."

"I agree with Doro that Longley has a more powerful motive," Wade said. "Love is a potent force, and a man will go to great lengths for his lady."

"He will," Ev agreed.

For a moment, Doro pondered their assertions both personally and in light of the case. Only a few months earlier, Ev had said he would die for her—a vow that had magnified her love for him. As she scanned his profile, Doro again wondered about his suggestion to postpone their wedding. How did that mesh with his heartfelt exclamation from last spring?

Aggie's voice intruded on her reflection. "Munroe wasn't directly responsible for Longley and Baylor losing their jobs, and he had no power to have them reinstated." Aggie paused for a moment. "The same is true for Clint."

"Maybe not quite as true," her husband said. "Munroe could've fought for Clint's job. Evidently, he didn't."

"Should we compile a suspect list now?" Doro asked.

"Yes, let's do that before we call it a day," Wade replied.

After Aggie and Ev agreed, Doro flipped back through the notepad. "We've heard from several people that Vince and Dale were angry at Coach Munroe and wished him dead."

"Their confrontations with the man are clues," Ev said.

"Agreed," Wade chipped in.

"I'd go along with that," Aggie said.

"Where should we rank them? Vince and Dale could've been benched or kicked off the team, and they realize it." Doro looked around the group. When everyone agreed the two players went near the middle, she started a fresh sheet of paper. "We also have Longley, Baylor, and Clint."

"Longley should be near the top. A motive for Baylor is murkier," Ev said. "I'm sorry to say it, but Clint should be also be at the top."

"Absolutely," Wade said. "He lied to get the job, and he would've gotten fired if Munroe had found out. Of course, his position was eliminated anyhow. Munroe not fighting for his assistant seems odd, but they clashed a lot."

"Munroe not backing Clint may be part of the reason that the assistant coach slot was eliminated," Aggie said. "Basketball is big at Michaw, and some of the trustees might've agreed to keep the assistant coach if the head coach had taken up for him."

"That seems likely," Doro agreed.

Wade nodded "The college has always had a good team. Under Coach Munroe, it's become great. Not only do the trustees and alumni support the program, so does the town. Plenty of folks would like to see it continue, just as it is. Munroe would've had people in his corner, if he had supported Spalling."

"I agree," Aggie put in. "I've heard a few professors express concern about the program going downhill without an assistant."

"I have, too," Doro said. "President Adams probably knows more about the trustees' involvement. Like how much influence they exerted in keeping the basketball team."

"We can talk with him in the morning before going to the MacPherson house," Ev said.

"He'll be in the office early, but what about Carson Longley, Emory Baylor, and Edie Farrow? We need to interview all of them," Doro said.

Ev glanced at his wristwatch. "It's too late now."

"Morning is time enough," Wade said. "None of them is apt to leave town since they don't have vehicles."

"They all use the train station in Sylvania, so they'd need rides there. Getting one in the middle of night isn't likely," Doro added. "All this reminds me of Stan Jackson taking off. He was so angry with Coach Munroe on Monday. Maybe we should find out if he came home early. We've seen similar actions in past cases. Suspects appear to have alibis, but they don't when those alibis are checked."

"He'd be a suspect, if he was here," Ev said. "But a bunch of us were out a lot of last evening and part of the night looking for Horace. Stan rents Mrs. Collier's garage apartment. I walked behind her house when my group was on her street. No lights in the apartment, and only her vehicle sitting beside it. I went to the door, so she wasn't alarmed by people on her property. She confirmed Stan leaving on Friday afternoon. Plus, some snow had fallen by the time I got there, and there were no tire tracks."

"I see," Doro murmured. "Then, he's off the suspect list?"

"But I'd like to talk with him," Ev said. "He may have overheard something while doing his work."

"He could be an important witness, if he overheard comments in College Hall," Wade agreed.

Ev took Doro's hand. "We can double-check with Mrs. Collier, too. There's not a great place for him to hide his vehicle, if he returned early, but it won't hurt to cover the possibility."

"There's plenty to do tomorrow morning," Aggie said.

"Definitely," her husband said. "But we've got a strong start."

Doro scanned the list before turning it so the other three could see it. "Only two basketball players, Dale and Vince, but they don't rank high. Clint and Longley do. Then, Baylor with a chance Stan may be involved although that seems less likely."

Everyone agreed on the list.

When Aggie muffled a yawn, Wade slipped his arm around her shoulders. "I should get my wife home. I'm ready to turn in."

"I am, too," Ev said. "Doro and I will talk with President Adams as early as possible. Then, interview Longley and Baylor before talking to Horace."

"Good plan," Wade said before glancing at Doro. "Do you mind asking Edie to come here about nine o'clock? I'll get the two professors here before or after."

Doro chewed on her lower lip. "It might go better if we choose a different location for the professors and Edie. Longley and Baylor could be more cooperative in your office, Ev. As for Edie, I could speak with her alone before meeting Ev in College Hall."

"She might be more at ease in her apartment," Aggie said.

"Good idea," Wade concurred.

Ev was the last to agree. "She doesn't seem like she'd lash out, so it should be fine."

The veiled concern touched Doro. "It will be, and I can go to her place early. Even without classes in session, the secretaries are working through Wednesday."

Ev nodded. "None of us will get much rest, I'm afraid."

"It's like that with an investigation," Wade said.

"Always sleuthing for all of us," Ev observed with a smile.

As the others laughed, Doro caught Aggie's yawn and let her eyes close for a moment. "Right now, I'm happy to change my motto from always sleuthing to finally sleeping."

Chapter Thirteen

Monday morning dawned bright and cold. Doro looked out her window at the grass. Evidently, temperatures had risen overnight because the thin blanket of white was gone. While every season had its beauty, summer was her favorite. Starting the day was far more inviting when her nose was not cold upon waking up like now. With a sigh, she donned warm clothes before trying to make the bed. And it was trying because Tee was still burrowed beneath the covers. "Time to get up, little girl." The dog did not move. "All right. I'll be back before I meet Ev. Since you're going along then, we can wait to head outside." Tee lifted her head and wagged her tail before settling into the covers again. "You're a smart girl," Doro said with a laugh. The dog's response was a light snore.

When Doro got to Edie's apartment, she took a deep breath and knocked. Within a moment, the door swung open to reveal Edie clad in a straight skirt and high neck blouse. Since the top few buttons remained undone and the secretary was in her stocking feet, Doro realized she had interrupted Edie's morning routine. "I'm sorry to bother you, but I hoped we could talk for a few minutes."

Edie scowled. "You've never come to my door in the past. Why now?"

Doro cleared her throat. "I don't generally drop by my neighbors' apartments." Since Aggie had married, the statement was true. While Doro liked most of the women living in Wheaton Hall, she was busy with work, Tee, and Ev.

A harrumph left the other young woman. "Probably smart. As you can see, I'm getting ready for the office."

"Of course, but if we talk now, it would save you going to the constable's office later." Doro maintained a pleasant tone and let her assertion deliver the goods.

The secretary's expression went from angry to uneasy. "Why should I have to do that?"

"You were upset with Coach Munroe, and you left yesterday's dinner early. I'd like to find out more about that, so we can clear your name."

Edie wrapped her arms around her waist. "Surely, I'm not a suspect."

Not wanting to give away too much, Doro shrugged. "I can't give out information, but cooperating always makes someone look innocent." She did not continue by saying cooperation was far from a verdict of not guilty.

A harsh sigh left Edie. "All right. Come in, but I don't have long."

Doro followed the secretary across the familiar living room. While the furniture was the same as when Aggie had lived there, the place looked different. Her friend had made her home cozy and comfortable with handmade afghans and needlepoint pillows. Books had been stacked on shelves along with photographs. Edie's décor was less homey with a couple of small metal sculptures and postcards replacing the books, while art deco prints substituted for Aggie's watercolors on the walls. A bright fringed silk throw laid over one of the fireside chairs while an ashtray stood next to the other. Cigarette butts filled it and, when Doro took a seat, the odor of tobacco filled her nostrils. "I don't have much time, either," she said, whipping out her pad and pencil.

"Good, because I'm not a criminal."

"If we were certain about that, you'd be questioned in the constable's office."

Edie flushed. "I'll answer your questions, but I didn't hurt Munroe, and neither did Carson." The young woman's brief bravado ebbed as her voice wobbled. "I know that's why you're here. Your fiancé has been after Carson for being upset about the coach keeping his job. But wouldn't you be mad if your job was eliminated to keep sports going?"

The question disturbed Doro because she did not like any trustees using their influence to help certain people, but there was no solid proof some had, so she went on. "It's a difficult situation, and I understand why he's upset, but I need to get some information. What you say may help us eliminate Professor Longley as a suspect." When Edie nodded, Doro continued. "You and the professor left the holiday dinner before dessert was over. Where did you go?"

Color surged into her cheeks as she bowed her head. "That's private."

"You're aware that Coach Munroe was probably killed sometime around the dinner hour."

"But Carson didn't kill him," Edie insisted.

"Perhaps if you tell me where the two of you went and what you did, we could eliminate him as a suspect," Doro said. "It would help to know when he picked you up."

Edie's face went beet-red. "Carson came to Wheaton Hall shortly before eleven o'clock, and we walked around campus. I slipped out the back door. No one saw us, but we did. After dinner, we took a drive. A private drive."

Because Doro felt sorry for the girl, she softened her approach. "Did you see anyone on your way out of town? I presume you went for a ride in the country."

Edie licked her lips. "We did. A Sunday drive. We saw Miss Jackson and Coach Spalling, who were also heading out of town."

Dismay flickered through Doro. The assistant and his wife were supposed to be at lunch in the Pierson home. "About what time?"

One of Edie's slender shoulders lifted and fell in a half-shrug. "Maybe two o'clock. Or later. I'm not sure."

After jotting down a note, Doro wondered when the Spallings might have left the minister's home. She would find out later. "I see. When did you get back?"

Scarlet again surged into Edie's face. "About three-thirty, maybe closer to four. Carson dropped me at Wheaton Hall, and he went to his room."

"Did you see anyone when you returned to town?" Doro inquired.

"No. We came the back way," Edie replied.

Doro could guess why, but she saw no sense in embarrassing the girl more. While Longley was not in the clear, Edie was probably not involved—except perhaps to serve as an alibi. Would her beau be conniving enough to drag her into a murder plot, with his buddy Baylor as the killer while Longley covered up? Or was that too convoluted a plan?

"I don't know anything else, and I have to finish getting ready." Edie, who looked to be on the verge of tears, focused on Doro.

After a glance at her watch, Doro stood. "Thank you for your time." She was barely in the hallway when the door shut behind her. Needing to get Tee and meet Ev, Doro hurried on.

⁂

By the time she fetched Tee and got outside, Doro found Ev approaching Wheaton Hall. The little dog yipped and pulled forward.

A bright smile on his lips, Ev bent to pet the pup. "Good morning. Did you both sleep well?" he asked, looking at Doro.

"Well, but not long enough," Doro replied.

"I have the same issue," he murmured as he stood up.

After scanning his face, Doro asked, "When did you get up?" Quite a while ago was her guess. His eyes were bloodshot.

"A couple of hours ago," he admitted. "I woke up with my mind spinning."

"Thinking about the case?"

"That and some other things. Did you speak with Edith Farrow?"

As they walked on, Doro replied. "I did." She provided a summary of the conversation before posing a question. "What do you think?"

"It's good you talked to her alone. I'm not sure she would've admitted to spending a couple of hours with Longley if Wade and I had been present."

"I agree. She was clearly embarrassed and upset. It's hard to say for sure, but I don't think she's directly involved in the killing. With the time frame, it's not likely Longley was on the scene, either, although it's possible. She was rather vague about when they returned."

"True," Ev murmured. "Baylor has less motive, but I wouldn't rule him out. Plus, we need to confirm Miss Farrow's assertions. Maybe Clint and Miss Jackson saw Longley and her, as well."

"She's not Miss Jackson anymore," Doro pointed out.

"No, she isn't, and that stunned me," Ev admitted. "Clint made it clear they were smitten, but he never gave me a clue that they were already married."

After Tee finish sniffing, the little group moved forward. "Fear of losing his job kept them from admitting the truth, which is understandable. But a hard way to live."

"Yep," he agreed. "We need to check with the Piersons about Clint eating dinner with them, and going for a drive with his wife afterward."

"We might need to wait until we talk with Horace." Doro cast him a sidelong glance. "Did you arrange times to meet with Longley and Baylor?"

"I caught them at breakfast. Neither was friendly, but they agreed to be at my office in thirty minutes. We'll interview them individually, of course."

"Have you heard if Horace is up to seeing us today?"

"I spoke with his father a short time ago, and he'd like us to wait until ten o'clock to visit. His wife and Horace are still sleeping."

"They need rest. Being in the attic for a few hours had to be upsetting and exhausting, and I can only imagine how his mother felt all that time," Doro said. "I hope Horace has some clue for us."

"But you're not sure."

A soft sigh escaped her. "Like I said last night, he often blurts things out. Like he did about the gag smelling. He was distraught when I found him, so maybe he'll recall something else now."

"It's understandable. Being bound and gagged and left alone in the dark was a rough experience. The blow to his head with a possible concussion didn't help, so he may have something useful to share. In any case, we'll find out. At least Horace gave us one solid clue."

"Have you spoken with Wade this morning?"

"I did. He's not going with us, since we don't want to overwhelm the boy. Because the crime took place on campus, I have standing to conduct an official interview. Same with Longley and Baylor. Besides, Wade gave me temporary deputy status.

I'm not sure it'd hold up officially, since the town council didn't approve the step. Anyhow, we can go to the constable's office when we finish. Both Wade and Aggie will be there, so we can all decide how to proceed."

"Unless we get the crucial clue from someone," Doro murmured.

"Wouldn't that be nice?"

Doro sighed. "It sure would."

"President Adams is expecting us, but we'll talk in his office. Then, we can wait for the professors in mine."

"Great. We could leave Tee in the outer office with Mrs. Jones while we chat with him."

"Sounds fine."

Within moments, they were inside College Hall, where their footsteps echoed through the empty corridors. "I usually look forward to Christmas break, but having it start so early, especially under the current circumstances, isn't enjoyable."

"Nope, it isn't," Ev muttered.

When he said no more, Doro studied the tense set of his jaw. "It's hard to see colleagues lose their jobs."

They had taken another dozen steps when he responded. "Mostly, I'm interested in hearing how President Adams feels about some who are leaving. Especially Longley and Baylor."

Although the answer struck her as strange, Doro had no chance to reply because they had reached the office. Ev held the door while she stepped inside.

Mrs. Jones greeted them. "He's expecting you two."

"Wonderful," Doro replied. "May we leave Tee with you?"

"Of course," the secretary said. When she leaned over, the little dog rushed to be petted. "I'll enjoy the company. It's unnaturally quiet around here."

With Tee secured, Ev went to the inner door and tapped. "Doro and I are here, sir."

"Come in," the administrator called out. When the pair entered, he gestured to the two chairs across from his paper-strewn desk. "Please sit down. Sorry for the mess, but I'm still preparing for the meeting on Wednesday. I'm hoping to head off as many more cuts as possible." His gaze rested on Ev before again looking at his desk.

"We won't keep you, sir," Ev replied. "We're talking with Longley and Baylor shortly. Then, we're seeing Horace MacPherson at ten o'clock, but we had a few questions for you. And some information to share."

"Happy to help, if I can," Adams said.

After extracting pad and pencil from her pocketbook, Doro smiled. "We appreciate your cooperation."

"We certainly do," Ev agreed. "One thing we didn't have a chance to discuss yesterday was how Coach Munroe got along with others on campus."

The president's pleasant expression went blank. "He was hired when I was away from Michaw for a time. Munroe was an excellent coach. I can't argue with that, but he could be arrogant and overbearing. I heard from some players about the issue last year."

"How many complained?" Doro asked.

"Four. Two graduated, and two are still here. This year, two more got in trouble. Vince Brownlee and Dale Krowl ran afoul of Munroe," Adams replied. "Of course, they didn't tell me that they broke training. I spoke with Munroe at the time, and he didn't like being critiqued. He mentioned how important basketball is to the alumni, many of whom are big donors."

Doro's jaw dropped. "He said that to you?"

"He did," Adams confirmed. "I let him know that I don't bow to threats from anyone, and he backed off. I talked to other players later, and they reported him acting better."

"Have there been problems since then?" Doro asked.

Adams leaned back in his chair. "A couple of professors who are losing their jobs complained about him keeping his position. Evidently, the three of them have had harsh words more than once."

"I know who you mean. They all live in Maple Hall, so I've observed their quarrels. Plus, Doro and I heard one of their run-ins," Ev said.

"Did either Carson Longley or Emory Baylor threaten Coach Munroe?" Doro asked.

The president shook his head. "No. They just said his job should be cut because academics are more important than athletics. I value education tremendously or I wouldn't have become a professor and administrator, but sports add a lot to a campus. Basketball and baseball are both popular here, and cheering for the teams creates camaraderie. Now, we need that more than ever. I wish we could keep the schedule going through mid-December, but the tournament will be the last set of games until January."

"You're letting the team play?" Doro asked.

Adams folded his hands over his chest. "The final decision rests with the Board of Trustees, but I'm recommending that, so I've told Clint Spalling to go ahead with practices." His gaze flicked to Ev before settling on his desk. "My hope is that anyone who is let go will be rehired when conditions improve."

Again, Doro wondered when such an upturn might occur. Nothing indicated the economy would have a quick turnaround. "Ev and I feel fortunate." When her fiancé did not agree, she cast a sidelong glance at him, but he was studying his folded hands.

The silence lingered until Adams broke it. "You mentioned other interviews before seeing young Horace at ten o'clock. Perhaps, we should get on with your questions."

Although the silence ended, the tension did not. Doro pushed forward. "Of course. We understand Coach Munroe and Assistant Coach Spalling were sometimes at odds."

Adams released a pent-up breath. "As the college president, I have jurisdiction over athletics and academics, but I try not to intercede directly in either area unless necessary. We have competent deans, department chairs, and team coaches. I played baseball as an undergraduate, so I have some personal experience. Successful coaches need autonomy. I haven't always agreed with Munroe's rules, and I told him as much."

The cryptic answer evoked additional curiosity. "Did Spalling figure into any of those discussions?" Doro asked.

After a deep breath, the administrator answered. "When Munroe submitted Spalling's name as a candidate for the assistant's position, he revealed that part of his choice was due to Spalling being a bachelor. I found that odd and said so. The coach went on to say his rule was no courting, either. I told him Michaw has no such stipulation, and that we were moving to allow married women to work at the college." Adams smiled at Doro. "Which we've done since then."

"It's a wonderful step forward," she said, "but I suppose Coach Munroe didn't like it."

"No, he didn't," Adams confirmed. "He has no say in making hiring policies, and I told him the college wouldn't back him firing Spalling if the young man got a sweetheart. Later, I discussed it with our athletic director, and he agreed."

The last observation connected with what they had already learned. No wonder Clint had felt confident letting his supposed courtship of Bonnie Jackson surface. He had backing at the highest levels, which had to increase Munroe's antipathy. Doro quickly noted that information.

"How did Munroe respond?" Ev asked.

A frown darkened Adams' expression. "He said there are plenty of other reasons to fire an assistant. As it turned out, the college had to cut Spalling's job."

"Did Coach Munroe fight for him?" Doro asked.

Adams shook his head. "Not at all, and he indicated he'd hire someone else when the college rebounds."

Doro rolled the pencil between her palms. "Did Clint Spalling know?"

"I believe so," Adams replied. "And I'm sure he knew courting Miss Jackson was a big part of the reason. They didn't try to hide their relationship. That worsened the tension between Munroe and Spalling even though I prevailed upon Munroe not to fire Clint. Reverend Pierson did, too, as did our athletic director. But keeping Munroe from employing someone else later would have been tricky. College policy is to allow coaches to hire assistants."

Next to Doro, Ev drummed his fingers on the chair arms. "Last night, Clint told us that he and Miss Jackson are married and have been for over a year." Ev revealed the details.

A rueful smile touched Adams' mouth. "I didn't know, but I'm not surprised. I've seen them together, and they're smitten."

The administrator's comments gave Doro pause. President Adams was a widower. Her gaze strayed to the photograph sitting on the corner of his desk. A smiling young couple, clad in wedding finery looked out of the ornate frame.

Adams followed her gaze. "Caroline and I were childhood sweethearts." He looked from Doro to Ev. "As old as I am, I haven't forgotten what it's like to be young and in love."

Doro glanced at Ev, who had no outward reaction. "Then, you'd keep Clint on if the basketball program continues?"

"I surely would," the administrator replied.

Ev cleared his throat. "Getting back to the case. Clint knew Munroe suspected he was involved with Miss Jackson."

"He did," Adams agreed, "but I hate to think he's responsible for Munroe's death. Spalling is a fine young man, or so I've always thought. We need a coach to go with the team to this weekend's tournament, and I'm planning on it being him. If he's a serious suspect..."

"I'm sorry to say he is, but he's one of several," Ev replied. "We're hoping Horace can provide some detail to narrow the field or even pinpoint the killer."

"The boy's doing all right?" Adams asked.

"Well enough for us to talk with him this morning," Doro replied. "Doc wanted us to wait, since Horace was badly shaken when we found him. He might have a concussion, too."

"I heard your dog helped again," Adams said.

Ev grinned. "She sure did."

"Tee is turning into a doggie detective," Doro added. At that comment, Tee darted through the door between the inner and outer offices and woofed.

Mrs. Jones was right behind her. "Sorry. She heard her name and hurried off."

"That's all right," Adams said. "Just leave her here. Tee is more than welcome."

A short yip left the pup as she rushed behind the desk. Adams scooped her up. "You're a good girl." Tee's response was to wag her long, plumelike tail.

"She appreciates being acknowledged," Doro observed.

"I wish she knew who committed the crime," Adams said. "And could tell us. I don't like another suspicious death here."

"Neither do we, sir," Ev agreed. "We'll do our best to solve it quickly."

The administrator glanced from Ev to Doro. "You always do."

A thought in the back of her mind wiggled its way forward. "You know that Stan Jackson is Mrs. Spalling's brother."

"Of course," Adams said. "When he applied for a job here, he revealed the connection. In fact, Stan let me know she was the reason he wanted to move to Michaw. He took a step down when he accepted a job as a custodian. In Toledo, he was a bank teller."

"We heard he lost that job," Doro said.

Adams nodded. "He told me, which wasn't surprising since many banks have closed."

"He seems protective of his sister," Doro observed.

Adams' brow furrowed. "Is he a suspect?"

"No," Ev responded. "He's out-of-town. According to what he told Professor Lammers, he left Friday and won't be back until tomorrow."

"His supervisor asked about letting Stan have a couple of days off, and I approved it. There's not as much to do with no students on campus. Except for the basketball team," Adams said. "Anyhow, as far as I know, he is away."

"I was surprised he lost his job before the board meeting on Wednesday," Doro said.

Adams frowned. "Stan wasn't let go. I can't guarantee he won't be, but it hasn't happened yet."

Doro and Ev exchanged a troubled look before he addressed the administrator. "That's not what we've been told, so we'll look into the situation."

With a sigh, Adams put Tee down and leaned back in his chair. "You have your hands full again, but I'll help in any way I can."

"Thank you," Doro murmured. "Is there anything else we should know about Coach Munroe and any other difficulties?"

Adams braced his elbows on the chair arms. "You're aware of Munroe's run-ins with two players, two professors, and Spalling. I never heard him say anything about Stan Jackson, or the other way around. I don't know more, but if I hear something I'll pass it on immediately."

Doro tucked her pad and pencil in her bag and stood. "Thank you."

Ev rose beside her. "We appreciate your time."

"Best of luck to you. The sooner it's solved, the better," Adams observed.

"We agree." Doro paused for a moment. "Has Mrs. Jones talked to you about Coach Munroe's family?"

"He only has a sister left," the President said. "He lost his wife and child."

"He did, but there's more of a story, and it explains his thinking," Doro said.

A moment passed before Adams responded. "I'll speak with her today."

Chapter Fourteen

Doro and Ev decided to leave Tee with Mrs. Jones while they interviewed the professors. "Why don't you sit behind my desk?" he asked. "I'll sit in one of the chairs."

"You don't think Longley or Baylor will act out, do you?"

He shrugged. "They're on edge, so I'd rather not take a chance."

For a long moment, Doro considered his assertion. "I hope neither of them punches you."

A rueful grin tugged at one corner of his mouth. "I doubt that will happen, but I can fight back easier than you can."

Her gaze traveled to his jacket, but she saw no evidence of a gun. "You're not armed."

Ev shook his head. "You know I don't carry a weapon on campus. It isn't necessary. If Wade and I get to the place where we'll arrest someone, I'll be armed."

Although she disliked weapons, Doro sighed with relief. Coach Munroe had been stabbed, but the killer might have a gun. The memory of Ev collapsing after being shot outside a Toledo speakeasy would never disappear. "Good."

Before Ev could respond, someone banged on the door, and Carson Longley strode in. Doro slipped behind the desk and sat down, while her fiancé faced the newcomer.

Longley put his hands on his hips. "Edie was in tears when she called me after Professor Banyon grilled her. Why even question her? She did nothing wrong, and she knows nothing about Munroe's death." Longley glared at Doro. "You should know your place."

When Longley, took a step toward Doro, Ev blocked him. "Sit down."

For a moment, Longley turned his scowl on Ev. Then, he took a chair. "What's the meaning of all this? This morning when you woke me, I said I don't know anything, Mallow. You said you need information, but I'm guessing you want to charge someone with Munroe's murder. I didn't kill him, although that may not matter to you."

Ev's jaw tightened. "Of course it matters. We don't want innocent people in jail."

While she listened intently, Doro took a deep breath and nearly choked. The aroma of sandalwood was overpowering. Longley must have doused himself with it, because Ev's scent was much lighter. And far more appealing. "I spoke with Edie in her apartment, since I thought that would be less stressful for her. I'm sorry she was upset, but I didn't accuse her of the murder."

Although Longley looked dubious, he nodded. "All right. She's distraught about my job being eliminated. Now, this murder. It's hard for someone as sensitive as she is."

"I understand, but we still need to find out a few details," Doro replied.

"We do. First off, Professor Baylor, you, and Miss Farrow left dinner early yesterday. Why was that?" Ev posed the question.

"Bay and I were disgusted at being harangued. Several at our table asked both of us what we planned to do if we lose our jobs, which we know we will. We didn't care to keep discussing the subject," Longley responded. "Edie was with me, so of course, she left, too."

"Where did the three of you go?" Ev asked.

Doro gripped her pencil tighter as she waited to see if the professor would confirm Edie's story. A glance at Ev revealed that he was maintaining a bland countenance.

"Bay took a long walk," Longley replied.

When he failed to continue, Doro got specific. "What did you and Miss Farrow do?"

Pink tinged Longley's neck before moving into his face. "We wanted a chance to chat. We seldom have privacy on campus."

Again, the professor failed to provide a complete response. Doro did not want to ask again, so she looked to Ev who nodded.

"Where did you go?" Ev asked.

Longley ran one forefinger inside his shirt collar. "For a drive."

"I see," Ev murmured. "How long did you drive around?"

"Quite a while," the professor replied.

Ev leaned forward. "You didn't stop any place?"

The professor's Adams apple bobbed as he took several swallows. "Perhaps for a moment or two, but nothing untoward happened, and I don't want Edie's name tarnished."

His response relieved Doro who had feared less than honorable intentions on the professor's part. "We aren't suggesting any improprieties, and neither of us will reveal what you say here."

When Ev agreed, Longley exhaled sharply. "We spent a few minutes enjoying the view at one of the quarries."

Although Doro figured they saw little of the scenery and spent longer than a few minutes, she smiled. "Did you see anyone else there, going, or coming back?"

He bit hard on his lower lip. "We passed Coach Spalling and Miss Jackson, who were also heading out of town."

"What time was that?" Doro asked.

"Around one-thirty or a bit after. Maybe more like two o'clock. Not all that long after we left the dinner." The professor glanced around the table. "I know nothing more. It's true, I disliked Munroe, but I didn't kill him and I'm sure Bay didn't, either. If I can go, I'd like to see Edie. She was terribly upset by your interview, and I want to assure her that her reputation isn't in jeopardy."

"What about the time you picked Edie up?" Doro asked. "I was in the kitchen and front hall of Wheaton, but I didn't see the two of you until we met walking to the dinner."

Again, Longley flushed. "I went to the back door around ten-thirty, and we took a walk. We didn't see anyone until we ran into your group."

"I see," Doro murmured.

"Now, can I go?" Longley asked again.

When Ev looked her way, Doro nodded.

"It's all right with me, if you leave," Ev said, "but we may have more questions later."

After a slight incline of his head, the professor got to his feet and rushed out. Doro gazed after him with mixed feelings. "If the story about taking a drive pans out, he'll be in the clear. We know Clint met with Munroe most of the morning, and he didn't mention seeing Longley. Besides, at this point, I don't think the professor had anything to do with the murder. He seemed more worried about Edie."

"I agree," Ev said. "But I'm not sure about Baylor. A long walk? Maybe. Or maybe he just walked to the field house."

"My thoughts exactly," Doro said.

"He should be here in the next ten minutes," Ev observed. "Even though his apparent motive isn't strong, he was as angry with Munroe as Longley was."

Doro finished jotting down notes before taking a deep breath. Professor Baylor might hold the key to unlocking a solution because he might be the killer. Or maybe he would give away some detail that pinpointed the killer's identity.

※

When twenty minutes passed with no sign of Professor Baylor, Ev looked at his wristwatch for the fifth time in fifteen minutes. "We need to be at the MacPherson house in less than a quarter hour. Calling Maple Hall won't do any good, no one will be at the front desk."

"He doesn't have a vehicle of his own, does he?" Wade asked.

Ev shook his head. "He borrows his department chair's Auburn roadster at times."

Dismay pulled Doro's brows down. "Those have a push-button starter, so he doesn't need to ask for keys."

Ev ran a hand over his face. "I'll call Wade and ask him to dash to Maple Hall and check on Baylor. Then we can speak with Horace."

﹌

After talking with the constable, Ev ushered Doro out of his office. On their way to the MacPherson house, they picked up Tee, who pranced along but Ev fell silent. When he did not tuck her hand into the crook of his arm, as he usually did, Doro studied his profile. "You look gloomy. Are you worried we won't get the case solved quickly?"

His expression became puzzled. "What?"

Being distracted was unlike Ev. Usually, he showed single-mindedness during an investigation. "You seem lost in thought. I figured you were wondering if we can catch the killer in a timely manner. I know we just got thrown a curveball, but Baylor can't have gone far—if he's gone at all."

"Oh, yeah. I'm sure we will."

The response did little to explain his behavior. Perhaps, lack of sleep affected it. "Even though it seems like Stan Jackson is out of town, I'd like to see if his vehicle is at his boardinghouse. It's on our way and will only take a couple of minutes."

Ev cast a sidelong glance her way. "Sure. You were right about apparent alibis not always standing up, although I'm not convinced Stan's won't. Several people mentioned him leaving on Friday, and I saw no evidence being home last night."

"I just want to learn a little more, if we can, especially since he claimed to be losing his job. Why lie about that?" She sighed. "I don't think he returned to murder the coach, if he came back early at all. I just keep going back to last Monday when he was so upset with Munroe. Maybe he came back to ask the coach about trying to get Clint Spalling rehired. We've heard Stan is devoted to his sister, and he was mad at Munroe."

"If it was my sister in Mrs. Spalling's position, I'd be just as upset," Ev pointed out. "But we can ask, if it'll ease your mind."

"It will because his lie about losing his job also bothers me."

A moment passed before Ev responded. "When someone faces possible unemployment, he might look for a new job ahead of time. Especially when work is hard to find."

"That's a valid point, but I'll feel better if we check on his current whereabouts."

"Let's stop at the Collier place then," Ev said.

Doro smiled. "Good. It won't take long."

When they reached the white frame three-story home, Doro and Ev stopped by the driveway. "This path winds back past the garage, so some vehicles would be back there."

"If all the boarders were here, but most of them are students who left. Stan may be the only one living here at this point."

"True. I'm not sure. Let's knock on the door and ask if Mrs. Collier has seen him."

Doro headed to the front porch where she rapped on the door. Within a few moments, Mrs. Collier, a statuesque woman in her mid-sixties, answered. A smile wreathed her angular face. "Good morning. Please come in."

"We don't want to bother you," Doro said.

"No bother." She looked at Ev. "I heard you found Horace. I was sorry I couldn't go out and search myself."

Doro smiled at the older woman. "It was kind of you to send cake for the search parties. Everyone enjoyed it." After her neighbor had told the older woman about the hunt for Horace, Mrs. Collier had been among the ladies who sent treats to the constable's office.

"I sure did," Ev added.

The older woman flushed with pleasure. "I was happy to do it. Annie baked yesterday before she left for her sister's home for the holiday."

"How nice." Doro cleared her throat. "Not all of your boarders are gone, are they?"

"No, only the students. Professor Bannister is still here although he's visiting friends in the city until after Thanksgiving. He's been with me since my husband died a decade ago. Stan Jackson lives in the garage apartment, so I see little of him," the older woman replied. "Occasionally, he'll take a meal in the house, but not as much since the students are gone."

"Have you seen him this weekend?" Doro asked.

Her forehead furrowed. "I haven't, although I heard a vehicle early yesterday. I looked out, but it was still dark." She bit her lower lip. "I was a bit nervous and thought about calling the constable, but it was early."

"Wade wouldn't mind, ma'am," Ev put in. "If you don't feel safe, call him. He'll come over any time."

"I appreciate that, Officer Mallow," the woman said. "I was so sorry the town council eliminated your job. In these times, with bank robbers and bootleggers all over, we need more protection, not less."

"Budgets are tight," Ev said, "but Michaw is a safe place."

Mrs. Collier pursed her lips. "The murder makes one uneasy."

"Coach Munroe's death was probably personal, so no one else needs to fret," Ev said.

A little sigh escaped her. "Just terrible. I'm sorry for him but glad the rest of us can put our heads on our pillows and not agonize over a murderer coming after us," the woman replied. "Nonetheless, I'll be glad when Stan is back."

"You're sure the car you heard yesterday wasn't his?" Doro inquired.

"Even though I didn't see it at the time, Stan usually parks next to the garage. That spot is visible from my kitchen window, and no vehicle was there when I got up yesterday. None is there now, either," Mrs. Collier informed them.

"Who parks in the garage?" Doro asked.

"No one. I'm afraid I've let it get cluttered with old items. Stan's been working on getting it in better order, so he can park there over the winter, but it's a big job. I'm not sure how he's doing with it."

Ev looked at his wristwatch. "We need to go. Thank you, ma'am."

"Yes, thank you," Doro added.

"Come again any time," Mrs. Collier said as Doro and Ev descended the porch steps.

"Feel better?" Ev asked.

"I suppose, but let's peek in the garage before going to the MacPherson house."

"A good idea."

The pair walked back to the driveway and followed it to the garage. "Luckily, the snow melted. Otherwise, it'd be messy on this gravel."

"Yeah, but this surface doesn't reveal any tire tracks. That inch of snow would have," Ev pointed out.

"You're right," Doro agreed. "Maybe we'll find another clue, though. When they got to the side of the structure, Doro turned the knob on the door, which opened easily. One glance revealed a possible piece of evidence. "Stan has made space for an automobile."

Ev peeked over her shoulder. "He has. In fact, there's space for two vehicles. That doesn't mean he was here yesterday."

"No, but he could've parked inside if he was," Doro insisted.

Ev pulled on the brim of his cap. "You want him on the suspect list."

"You always say I have good insight and intuition. Besides, President Adams told us that Stan wasn't fired on Friday. I understand your point about looking for work ahead of a possible firing, but him lying is troubling to me."

"I can't dismiss Stan wanting to be prepared in case the worst happens. Or being a janitor might've bothered him. Besides, Clint lost his job, so maybe Stan figured on quitting if he found something better. Then, they could all move."

"Mrs. Spalling could keep her job. There are other married women teaching."

"But Clint wouldn't live off his wife, and if Stan is any kind of man, he wouldn't let his sister support all of them. It isn't done."

For a moment, Doro weighed Ev's words, which were true in her experience. Most men did not want to be supported by their women. "You could be right about his reasons for going to the city." After a last look at the garage, Ev walked outside. Doro followed. "So, you don't see him as a suspect?"

Ev ran a hand over his face. "The lying and his ability to park inside the garage give me pause. I'd rank him down with Brownlee and Krowl. Although there's no evidence Stan was in town when Munroe was killed, we can't be positive he wasn't. It's a good thing we came over here."

"We can discuss it more with Aggie and Wade. For now, we need to get to the MacPherson place."

As a response, Ev offered his arm and the pair, along with Tee, went on. When they reached the MacPherson home, a white-frame bungalow set on a quiet tree-lined street a few blocks from uptown, Doro and Ev ascended the porch steps. Before they could knock, the door swung open to reveal the lady of the house. Clad in a skirt that fell below her knees and a loose sweater, Mrs. MacPherson could have stepped out of the pre-war era. Her dark hair, swept into a neat chignon, added to her old-fashioned look.

"Good morning," she said, stepping back to allow them inside. "Please come in. Horace is waiting for you."

"I hope you don't mind us bringing Tee. We promised him we would," Doro said.

"Certainly not. We have two cats, and we love all pets here," the woman said. "Horace would love to have a dog, and we may get one now. If he hadn't been alone yesterday..." Her voice trailed off as she led them into the small parlor off the front hall.

Doro wanted to hug the woman, but the gesture would be far too familiar, so she offered a suggestion. "Unfortunately, there are always litters of puppies available. That's how we got Tee. Her mother was a stray, and Tee was one of several pups roaming around. Luckily, they all have homes. I'll keep my eye out for one that might be good with Horace."

The older woman's grim expression lightened. "Thank you."

"Tee," the boy called out as soon as he caught sight of the little dog, who responded by pulling hard on her leash.

"Let her go to him," his mother said. "She can't hurt anything. The cats have already hidden."

After Ev unclipped Tee's leash, she raced to Horace who sat near the fireplace with a blanket over him. The young man scooped the dog up, and she licked his face. Giggles escaped him.

"Sit down, and I'll bring coffee and cookies," Mrs. MacPherson said. "My husband went to the store, but he should be here shortly. Could you wait until then to question Horace?"

"Of course," Ev replied as he and Doro took seats on the sofa facing the grate.

"I'll be back shortly," the older woman said.

When his mother was gone, Doro focused on Horace. "How are you feeling?"

The boy kept petting Tee as he responded. "Got a headache, but it's not so bad as it was." His countenance brightened. "Ma and Pa agreed to let me get a dog. I hope Coach will let me bring it to practice." Abruptly, he frowned. "The new one. Will there be someone new? Will there be a team?"

His anxiety was not surprising, so Doro sought to ease his mind. "Coach Spalling is going with the team to this weekend's tournament. The school already decided to cancel the December games. In January, President Adams and the Board of Trustees will decide what to do about all athletics." At least Spalling would be going if he was cleared of murder, but Horace did not need to know that.

"Good," Horace murmured. "I like Coach Clint. He's real nice to me."

"Did Doc say if you can go with the team to the tournament?" Ev asked.

Mr. MacPherson entered the room and the conversation. "He told us that might be possible, but he won't make a firm decision until Wednesday."

"I'm lots better," Horace insisted.

His father smiled. "We're glad of that, but we'll follow Doc's advice."

A frown flattened Horace's lips. "All right."

As his mother entered the room, a big tray in her hands, Horace's father hurried to assist her. After the tray was on the low table in front of the sofa, Mrs. MacPherson poured coffee for everyone. "Help yourself to the cookies. They just came out of the oven." She handed her son a glass and a plate. "My cold is better, but I wore a mask like the ones from the influenza epidemic while I baked. I don't want anyone else getting sick."

"Sugar cookies are my best ones," Horace said before taking a big bite. "Can Tee have some?"

"Sure," Ev replied. "I always give her a taste."

The boy grinned before giving the dog more than a mere taste. Tee's plumelike tail wagged wildly.

As a chuckle rumbled out of Ev, Doro glanced at him. He looked more relaxed, which eased her mind. After consuming most of her coffee, she put her cup down and retrieved her writing supplies. Both of Horace's parents seemed to tense up, so she offered a smile. "We don't have many questions, and we'll stop whenever Horace wants to."

After finishing off one cookie, Ev added, "We will."

Horace put his glass aside and nodded. "I'm ready."

Ev offered a reassuring smile. "Why don't you tell us what happened when you went to the fieldhouse yesterday?"

While the young man kept petting Tee, he furrowed his forehead as if in deep concentration. Long moments passed before he responded. "The main doors were unlocked, like always. Coach Munroe knows I come early and shoot baskets before I put things in order. Sometimes, a couple of guys shoot with me."

Doro posed the next question. "Was anyone else there early?"

"Nope. I peeked into the gym before I went to Coach's office. I'm supposed to check," Horace said.

"So, you went straight to his office?" Doro suggested.

"I did." Horace licked his lips. "The door was open, but the office was sort of dark."

The answer made Doro pause. "There's no window in that room. Wasn't a lamp on?" Even though some of the information was not new, she wanted to put Horace at ease with a review.

"Just a small one," Horace replied. "I thought maybe he was behind the door where there's shelves. I'd been whistling and usually he whistles when I come in. He didn't, so I got worried and turned around. Someone was there, but I didn't even get out of the doorway and something hit me in the head."

Disappointment filled Doro because Horace hadn't had a chance to witness much of anything. Nevertheless, she jotted it down.

"Is that the last thing you remember before waking in the attic?" Ev inquired.

Horace bowed his head and concentrated on Tee. The silence expanded until Doro did not think he would reply. Finally, he did. "I was only half-asleep when the man carried me down the hall," Horace murmured. "He had that smell. Like Dad and you."

Doro gripped her pencil. "Do you recall anything else about him? Anything at all?"

Again, long moments passed before the young man answered. "He was strong, and he was wearing a wool coat because it scratched my face. I tried to lift my head to tell him, but it hurt, and I went back to sleep."

Although the observations were hardly smoking guns, Doro jotted them down. "When you say he was strong, do you mean because he carried you with no trouble?"

"Partly," Horace replied. "But he seemed big, but not real big." Since Horace was slight, his frame of reference might not be telling, and his inexact description failed to offer significant details.

"Did he sling you over his shoulders?" Ev inquired.

"Yep. Carried me up the ladder that way, too, I guess," Horace replied. "I didn't wake up again for a while. Then, I kept dozing off until Tee and Miss Banyon came. Mrs. Lammers, too. I heard talking and barking." A smile finally returned. "Tee's smart."

"She is," Doro agreed. "What time did you leave home to go to the fieldhouse?"

A puzzled expression covered Horace's face. "After Sunday dinner."

"It was almost two o'clock when he left, since we ate early to accommodate Horace going to practice," his mother put in. "Practice was scheduled for three-thirty, I think. He likes to go early."

"Did the man talk to you?" Doro wondered if a description of his voice was possible. If so, would it help?

"I woke up a little when he carried me up the ladder," Horace mumbled. "He said not to worry. He wouldn't drop me."

Doro and Ev exchanged a long look before he picked up the questioning. "Did you recognize the voice?"

"No. He sounded sick," Horace said.

Doro tapped the pencil on her notepad. "How do you mean? Was he hoarse?"

"Yep," the young man said.

Chances were good that the killer had disguised his voice, but it might be a clue. Unfortunately, not one of their suspects had been hoarse. While Doro had not figured on solving the case after Horace's interview, she had hoped for useful new evidence. Little had developed.

Ev got to his feet. "We appreciate your help, Horace. If you think of anything else, have one of your parents call the constable's office."

Mr. MacPherson stood. "We will."

After thanking Horace for his assistance and his mother for the refreshments, Doro walked out ahead of Ev, who scooped Tee up after she got a few more pats from her young friend. At the door, Mr. MacPherson shrugged. "I'm sorry he wasn't more help. Honestly, I figured he would've blurted out anything big when you found him, Professor Banyon. Like with the sandalwood smell."

"I thought the same," Doro agreed, "but we know the killer was a man." Not that they hadn't guessed as much.

"We did, and that could prove useful," Ev added.

After bidding the man goodbye, Doro, Ev, and Tee headed toward the constable's office. "What did you think about the killer sounding hoarse?"

"Probably the same as you. He was masking his voice."

"I'm afraid so, but that and what was said reveals some things. One, Horace would've probably recognized the voice and two, he reassured the boy, so the killer has talked with Horace in the past, and he has some conscience."

They walked a few more steps before Ev reacted. "Good points, but most of our suspects knew Horace well."

"That's true for all the players and Clint Spalling. Longley and Baylor must know Horace in passing, since almost everyone at the college does."

"Longley is bigger than Baylor, so I could see him carrying Horace over his shoulders," Ev observed. "Baylor seems too slight to achieve it."

"That's true, and so could Clint Spalling, or Vince, or Dale. And they aren't the only ones. Mrs. Spalling's brother Stan could, too, and he works at the college," Doro pointed out. "I might get further by talking to her. It could garner information about Clint and Stan. Since there's no school this week, I can go to the Pierson place. She must be there."

A pent-up breath escaped Ev. "You want to go alone?"

"She'd probably speak more freely woman-to-woman. Remember, she seemed shy when Aggie and I talked with her in August. Maybe chatting with one person would be easier for her. Besides, Reverend and Mrs. Pierson are apt to be around on a Monday."

"I suppose, but Mrs. Spalling may be too tense to talk since Clint is a suspect. He must've told her that."

"My plan is not to mention he's a suspect at all. I'll ask about Vince and Dale with the idea of seeing if Clint thinks one of them is guilty."

They covered another dozen feet before Ev acquiesced. "All right. You can get confirmation of when she and Clint went for a drive. More importantly, if you talk to her at the Pierson place, you'll be safe."

His concern touched Doro. "I will," she agreed. "I'll head that way now and come to the constable's office right afterward."

"Then, I'll take Tee with me. Mrs. Pierson is allergic to dogs."

"Poor woman." Doro petted Tee. "She's missing out on something wonderful."

In reply, the little dog woofed.

Chapter Fifteen

Doro covered the distance to the parsonage in a hurry, mostly to get out of the raw wind. While the overnight snow had melted, dampness hung in the air. She pulled her cloche more firmly over her hair. When she reached the two-story red brick home, Doro breathed a sigh of relief. Getting inside would be lovely, especially if there was a fire going. After knocking, she waited only a moment before Mrs. Pierson greeted her.

"Doro, how lovely to see you. Please come in and warm up for a moment."

As cold as she was, Doro did not hesitate. "It is brisk," she replied.

"I'm getting ready to host the ladies aid at noon, or I'd invite you into the parlor." The woman's apologetic tone and expression accentuated her words.

"That's all right. I came to see Miss Jackson."

"She isn't here. Even though school is closed for the week, she went in to work on some papers and things. I'm not sure exactly what."

Resignation and regret hit Doro hard. The high school was ten blocks in the direction from which she had come. "I'll catch up with her there."

"All right." The pastor's wife put her hand on the door edge.

Although Doro would have enjoyed a few more minutes of warmth, she could not hold up luncheon preparations too long. "I had another question."

"All right."

"Miss Jackson and Clint Spalling were here for dinner yesterday, weren't they?" When Mrs. Pierson did not immediately respond, Doro continued. "Did they take a drive after dinner yesterday? I'm not prying into their personal business, but they might have witnessed something important." According to Clint, the Piersons knew he and Miss Jackson were married, but Doro was not sure that was true.

A perplexed expression blanketed the woman's face. "Maybe you haven't heard, but they're married or so they told us yesterday. With that in mind, no harm was done by them going for a drive together. Usually, her brother rides along, but not yesterday."

Relief made Doro smile. At least one part of what Clint had said was true. "No harm at all. Just one more question. Was Stan Jackson here for dinner, too?"

Mrs. Pierson moved the door an inch toward Doro. "No, he went to Toledo looking for a job. He left here about fifteen minutes ago. He found a position and has to start tomorrow.

Not much time for a goodbye, but he wanted to tell his sister about the move." The woman's expression softened. "It'll be hard for her, because they're so close. But she has her husband."

Stan leaving so abruptly seemed odd, especially when he had not lost his position at the college. And he had lied about that. Something was amiss. Doro was not sure what, but she planned to find out before the custodian left town. "Can I use your telephone?"

"Of course."

With a shaking hand, Doro lifted the receiver, waited for the operator, and asked to be connected with the constable's office. Moments later, Colleen came on the line.

"Can I speak with Ev or Wade?" Doro asked the clerk. When she heard both lawmen had gone to question Professor Baylor, who was in his College Hall office, her heart sank. "Please call Mrs. Jones and ask her to send them to the high school as soon as possible. Have them meet me in the school office. It's important." After Colleen assured Doro that she would get the lawmen, Doro turned to the pastor's wife.

"Thank you. I'm sorry to be a bother, especially when you're getting ready for company."

"No bother, but I really must finish my preparations." As soon as Doro stepped on to the porch, the door shut behind her.

Surprise filled Doro. Evidently, the ladies aid luncheon ranked higher with the parson's wife than a murder case did. But maybe the woman's lack of concern was good because she would not tell all to her guests.

Although Stan was far from the only suspect who had a motive, he was the only one planning to leave town soon. That had Doro flying down the sidewalk.

As she headed toward the school, Doro secured her scarf more tightly around her neck and shoved her hands in her coat pockets. Her route took her parallel to Main Street, but she met no passersby. Few people would venture out on a such a blustery day. When she finally reached the high school, Doro breathed a sigh of relief because the front doors were unlocked. Since she did not know where the teacher's room was located, Doro stopped in the office.

"Doro, what brings you here?" Annabelle Dickerson, the school secretary, had been a classmate of Doro. While they had not been close friends, they had been friendly.

"I wanted to chat with Miss Jackson, and Mrs. Pierson said she was here."

"She is. Probably wanted to escape the ladies aid meeting at the parsonage." Annabelle rolled her eyes. "They used to only admit married ladies. Now, the group has diminished in numbers, and they're willing to take spinsters."

Although Miss Jackson was married, Doro kept the fact to herself. Instead, she focused on her old schoolmate. Annabelle had been engaged to a boy a few years ahead of them but, when the United States entered the Great War, he had been drafted. While he had survived the fighting, his mind had suffered from life in the trenches. Unsure what to say, Doro shifted from one foot to the other. "I've been asked about joining more than once. In fact, I was surprised Mrs. Pierson didn't bring it up today, but she was flustered with getting ready."

Annabelle grinned. "Don't worry. They'll be after you again, especially once you're married." Her attention went to Doro's left hand. "Pretty ring."

"Thank you," Doro replied. She could not help but look at her classmate's ring finger, where a small diamond still twinkled.

With reverence, Annabelle touched the jewelry. "Phillip seems better at times. Everyone says I'm foolish to wait after all these years, but I still love him. If the situation was reversed, I'd want him to visit me and harbor hope."

Tears stung Doro's eyes, but she blinked them back. "I don't think you're foolish at all. If Ev was in the same straits as Phillip, I'd do what you're doing." It was not a platitude. It was the truth.

A smile lit up Annabelle's features. "Thank you. That means a lot to me." Even though her voice wobbled, she sounded sincere. With the back of one hand, Annabelle swiped at her face. "Miss Jackson's room is 301."

"Mrs. Pierson thought Miss Jackson's brother was coming to see her. Has he been around?"

"I didn't see him, but one of the back doors is open. Some supplies are being delivered later. He could've come and gone that way." Annabelle frowned. "Bonnie told me about him losing his job on Friday, so I said how sorry I was. She said he was beside himself and upset over Clint losing his job, too. Being out of work will do that, but Stan was mad about some others keeping their positions. She worries about that."

Doro mentally reviewed Mrs. Pierson's revelations. What if Stan had planned to leave immediately after seeing his sibling? It had taken her ten minutes to walk to the school, which meant he had left the parsonage almost a half-hour ago. And he had driven. By now, he could be long gone. Dismay filled Doro. Mrs. Jones would have alerted Ev and Wade immediately, but her walk to Baylor's office would have taken a few minutes. If the two lawmen drove from the campus, they would need five minutes to reach the high school. But they were not here, so they must not have had a car on campus. Suddenly, Doro recalled Ev's statement that he would be armed when an arrest was possible. Since Wade did not usually carry a weapon, both of the lawmen would have retrieved their guns. Doing that would add time.

For several moments, Doro debated waiting for them. If she went upstairs, she could at least find out if Stan had left. If he hadn't, she would not confront him, but she could observe his actions and know which way he headed when he left. Set on an action, she again addressed Annabelle. "Ev and Wade will be here shortly. Send them to Miss Jackson's classroom, and tell them to be cautious." She hesitated before revealing the crux of her worry. If the man had not left, he might encounter Annabelle on his way, so she needed to be alert. "Stan may be involved in Coach Munroe's death. We can't let him sneak away and not know which way he goes."

Her eyes wide, Annabelle nodded. "Be careful, Doro."

"I doubt if Stan stayed around, if he's guilty. I'll just watch for him, not confront him."

As Doro sped to the top floor, she breathed in short gasps. When she got close to room 301, she slipped off her shoes and crept along the corridor to avoid being heard. Announcing her arrival could prove hazardous. When she drew close to the classroom, Doro heard voices—a man and a woman. Stan and Bonnie, no doubt. She pressed back against the hallway wall.

"It just happened. I didn't plan it," he said, his frustration obvious in his tone.

"Why did you go there at all?" the woman asked in a plaintive voice.

"He found out about you and Clint and threatened to reveal your marriage. I wanted to protect you."

On trembling legs, Doro tiptoed closer, but avoided standing in front of the door. If they did not see her, she could make a quick getaway.

"Instead of protecting me, you've made it worse. Now, Clint is being scrutinized," the woman said.

Doro held her breath and waited to hear more. Stan seemed more and more like the top suspect, but she wanted confirmation.

"I'm sorry," Stan said. "I didn't plan to hurt Munroe. I only wanted to scare him. He got furious and came at me, so I grabbed what was handy."

The tapping of heels on the classroom's hardwood floor echoed into the hallway, so Doro pushed herself flat against the lockers. When the sound passed the door and retreated, she released a pent-up breath. Whatever Miss Jackson, Mrs. Spalling, said in return was too hushed for Doro to hear, so she spun on her heel and hurried to the staircase. Unfortunately, Mr. Elliott, her high school history teacher, stepped out of room 307 just as Doro passed.

"Dorothea, how nice to see you," the man said in a voice that carried down the hall.

He had been slightly deaf a dozen years ago, so he had often nearly hollered during class. Evidently, his hearing was worse. Almost instantaneously, Stan Jackson appeared in the doorway of his sister's classroom.

"Mr. Elliott, get inside your room and lock the door." When he hesitated, Doro yelled. "Now. Right now." With Stan less than thirty feet away, Doro raced to the staircase. She was on the top step when Stan hollered at her.

"Hold on," he shouted.

Although Doro ran down the steps as quickly as her stocking feet would allow, her pursuer was fleeter of foot. Within moments, he was fifteen feet away and closing on her. Outrunning him was impossible, so Doro ducked into the office and locked the door.

"What's wrong?" Annabelle, still at her desk, called out.

"Telephone the college president's office again and see if Ev and Wade are on the way. Stan saw me in the hallway upstairs."

All color drained from the secretary's face, but she immediately picked up the candlestick base and ear piece. For what seemed like an eternity, but could have been no more than two minutes, Doro waited. Finally, she knew Annabelle was speaking with Mrs. Jones. After hanging up, the other woman stood. "She didn't find them right off. Evidently, they moved their meeting to a dean's office, but they left College Hall about five minutes ago. They got a ride to the constable's office to get guns and a vehicle. They should be here any minute. Mrs. Jones said to hide behind a desk and not let Stan in here."

Annabelle's words were barely out when pounding on the door ensued. Evidently, Stan had not immediately realized where she was. Now that he had, could he break down the door? Doro gestured to her former schoolmate. "Let's move this table against the door. It'll help a little."

Annabelle assisted, and the two young women hurried to huddle under a desk behind the counter. "I'm glad this door doesn't have glass. Most of the classroom doors do," the secretary said.

"That's lucky," Doro murmured although she wasn't sure how lucky because Stan kept beating on the wood surface.

"Is he armed?" Annabelle asked.

"I don't think so."

Mrs. Spalling's voice, muffled by the closed door, sounded from the hallway.

"I think she's urging him to give himself up."

"That'd be smart," Annabelle said.

Before Doro could agree, Stan shrieked at his sister. "I'm getting out of this town right now."

When heavy footsteps retreated down the hallway, Doro released a long, low breath and peeked over the desk. The table was still in place and the battering had ended. Now, she hoped the lawmen arrived before Stan got away. Pursuing him out of town could be dangerous. Although he had stabbed Munroe with a letter opener, the young man could have a gun. Maybe that was why he had gone to the city. She crept toward the door and shoved the table away.

"Be careful," Annabelle urged her.

"I will." When Doro opened the door a crack, she saw Mrs. Spalling bent over with her head in her hands. "Are you all right?"

After the teacher lifted her face, her tear-streaked cheeks became obvious. "Stan isn't a bad man. He's always been my protector. I just wish..." Her voice turned into broken sobs.

Annabelle rushed to her side. "Let's get you in the office." Although she said nothing, Mrs. Spalling let Annabelle assist her.

Knowing Ev and Wade would arrive momentarily, Doro rushed to the front doors and stepped outside. As a cold blast of air hit her, she wrapped her arms around her waist. The rear parking lot had a rough path which would take Stan out of town without passing the lawmen. If they did not come soon, Doro would head to the back of the school and do what she could to stop him.

Chapter Sixteen

Within moments, a vehicle pulled to a stop. Both he and Ev jumped out and raced to where Doro waited. Relief coursed through her.

"Mrs. Jones told us Stan Jackson is here," Wade said.

After a quick explanation, Doro finished with, "His sister is in the office, but he must've headed out back. He killed Coach Munroe, so I'm sure he'll try to get away."

"Let's each take a side," Wade told Ev. "Both the east and west hallways lead to the parking lot. We may not catch him if he parked there, but we can give it a try."

"I'm with you," Ev replied.

As he started toward the right, she called after him. "Be careful."

"Always," was his response.

Always being careful did not necessarily lead to always staying safe. Unsettled and anxious, Doro wanted to go with them, although she did not wish to be a distraction. Still, following at a distance was reasonable, so she hurried after Ev. By the time she got halfway down the east hallway, he was disappearing out the door. Doro picked up her speed. Within a few moments, she was on the back steps while Ev and Wade were covering the parking lot. Only three vehicles were there. As Doro scanned the area for some sign of Stan, she saw one of the automobiles start to move. Her heart kicked into overdrive because it was headed for Ev. "Watch out," she screamed.

Ev, whose back was to the car, turned toward her. As he did, he must have caught sight of the vehicle bearing down on him. Because the driver had not gotten it out of first gear, it was moving slowly. Ev jumped to the side, but the bumper caught him and he fell to the ground. Doro rushed to him while the car drove on until a shot rang out. One glance revealed Wade had aimed at a tire which was already going flat. When the vehicle slowed down, Stan jumped out and started to run away. Wade pursued him. Content that the situation was under control, Doro dropped to her knees next to Ev. "Are you all right?"

He pushed himself up. "Yeah. Just got the wind knocked out of me."

She narrowed her gaze on him. "The car hit you."

"The bumper grazed me. Nothing more."

Doro rolled her eyes. "Let's get you up then."

"I can stand on my own."

His petulant tone made him sound like an errant schoolboy. Doro bit her lip and stood back. When he grabbed at his hip, she repressed a grin. "Sore?"

"Only a little," he admitted, but his efforts to rise belied the assertion.

"Need some assistance?" she asked.

He grimaced. "Yeah. I want to help Wade, so I may need to lean on you at some point."

Although she did not see how Ev could catch up with the pursuit, Doro took his arm as he struggled to his feet. His first step wobbled, but Ev limped along the same path taken by Stan with Wade behind him. Doro walked beside Ev, who had pulled his gun.

By the time, they caught up, Wade had tackled the custodian from behind. "Get off me," Stan yelled.

"No way," Wade, nearly out of breath, heaved out.

Ev, his weapon pointed at Stan, stepped forward. "Don't move, Jackson. You're wanted in the murder of Coach Munroe."

"I didn't murder him," the custodian muttered. "Let me go."

"Not when you just ran off. We need to talk to you," Ev said.

While he pinned Stan down, Wade pulled a set of handcuffs out of his pocket. "Put your hands behind your back."

"No," Stan said.

Ev moved closer. "Do it now."

"You're not going to shoot me," Stan insisted. "You're a campus security officer, not a copper."

"I was a cop in Detroit. Then, I was a Prohibition agent. If you think you'd be the first man I ever shot, you're dead wrong." Ev emphasized *dead.*

While Doro knew Ev's background, the intensity in his voice and expression took her aback. She had often worried about him getting hurt, but knowing he had hurt others—albeit, crooks—sent a chill through her. Did she really know him? The last week, capped with his last assertion, made her wonder. Stan seemed just as uneasy, because he put his hands behind his back. Wade snapped the cuffs on and pulled the suspect to his feet.

Wade looked from Doro to Ev. "It looks like we caught another killer."

Ev re-holstered his gun. "We'll find out when we talk with him."

Doro had not had a chance to reveal what she overheard, which was powerful. That could wait until they arrived at the constable's station.

"Let's get him in the vehicle and take him to the office," Wade replied.

"Maybe I should bring it around back," Doro suggested as she studied Ev who was hobbling along.

Wade looked Ev up-and-down. "Good thing you have quick reflexes."

Ev glanced at Doro. "And a fiancé who issues timely warnings."

"You're a lucky man, just like me," the constable said.

"Let's get our suspect to the office," Ev put in.

As the little group made their way to the front of the school, Doro noted Ev's limp but said nothing until Mrs. Spalling descended the steps to stare at her brother.

"You've made matters even worse," she whispered.

Stan's dark lashes swept down to hide his clouded gaze. "I only wanted to protect you like our folks asked me to do."

Tears splashed down his sister's face. "I know." She focused on Wade. "He didn't mean to kill Munroe."

Ev and Wade looked at Doro.

"I heard enough to pin the murder on Stan," Doro said before turning to Mrs. Spalling. "Just contact your husband and come to the constable's office."

Annabelle, who had followed Miss Jackson out, gasped. "Husband?"

"It's a long story," Doro told her. "I'll explain later."

"All right," the secretary replied but her eyes were wide with interest.

While the killer had been caught, plenty of loose threads still dangled, and Doro knew tying them all up would take time.

When they reached the car, Ev got in back with Stan while Doro sat up front with Wade. As she looked around, Doro made an observation. "This looks like President's Adams' automobile."

"It is," Wade replied. "We walked to campus. When Mrs. Jones told us about your call and the amount of time that had elapsed before she found us, we asked to borrow it. Even so, we had to stop and get our guns."

"Which was wise," Doro murmured, although Ev's assertion remained in her mind.

After reaching the constable's office, the group shuttled inside, and the prisoner was secured to one of the chairs facing the woodstove. Tee, who had been resting in an old blanket, darted to Doro. After getting petted, the little dog returned to her resting place.

Colleen waited to speak until Doro, Ev, and Wade had shed their coats. "Aggie called. The children are still at your ma's place with their cousins, Constable, so she's coming over shortly."

"Good," Doro murmured.

A chuckle escaped Wade. "The team will all be here."

Stan jerked at his handcuffs. "You don't need to hogtie me like I'm a criminal."

Ev went to stand across the table from the man. "Murder is a crime. So is assault. Assault with a vehicle is, as well."

A flush stained Stan's cheeks. "You're not deputy constable anymore, so why are you involved?"

Wade stood next to Ev and stared at their prisoner. "He's been temporarily deputized, not to mention he's the campus security officer. Two crimes occurred on campus, and another one did just minutes ago. In today's, he's the victim."

Stan's jaw tightened. "You can't prove I harmed Munroe, and I didn't mean to hit Mallow. He stepped in front of my car."

"I saw the whole thing, and you steered your vehicle right at Ev," Doro put in before summarizing what she had heard outside his sister's classroom. "As for the rest, I overheard much of the entire conversation with your sister, and what she said confirmed your guilt. Not only that, Horace MacPherson recognized the smell of sandalwood on the gag you used. So did I."

All color drained from his face as his eyes went wide. For several moments, Stan only stared back at Doro.

"Nothing to say?" Ev asked.

"You won't believe me," Stan muttered.

"Why don't you tell us your story and see," Wade put in.

His sister's appearance interrupted the conversation. Mrs. Spalling, her coat buttoned unevenly and her hair disheveled, rushed toward Stan. Ev put out a hand to stop her. "Please wait right here."

Tears spilled down Mrs. Spalling's face. "He didn't mean to kill Coach Munroe. If you'll only let him talk."

"No one's stopping him," Ev replied.

Stan looked at his sibling. "Bonnie, they're not going to believe anything I say, so why try?" Defeat underscored his voice and clouded his gaze.

"As I said, you have a chance to tell your story," Ev put in. "We're listening."

"Yep," Wade added. "We're fair-minded, so why don't we start from the beginning?" He pulled out a chair and sat down before addressing Bonnie Spalling. "Ma'am, you can sit at my desk, but please don't interrupt."

She nodded and took a seat.

"Doro, will you take notes for us?" Wade asked.

When Ev drew another chair next to hers and sat down, Doro got her writing supplies out. "Certainly."

"I'm not dangerous," Stan muttered.

Since he had killed Munroe, attacked Horace, and run down Ev, his word held little validity for Doro.

Wade drummed his fingers on the battered table. "Start with why you went to Coach Munroe's office yesterday afternoon. Remember, we know you did because Professor Banyon overheard you admit as much to your sister."

For a long moment, Stan hung his head. When he finally responded, his voice was rough and ragged. "Munroe found out Bonnie and Clint are married. That's why he refused to fight against my brother-in-law's firing. Munroe lost his family, and he was jealous of anyone who still had loved ones. I only wanted to talk with him."

A muffled sob left Bonnie Jackson Spalling, and Doro felt a spear of sympathy. Knowing her big brother was in trouble because he had rushed to her defense had to be awful for the young teacher.

"So, you confronted Coach in hope of changing his mind," Wade suggested. "Or you went to threaten him."

Stan's nostrils flared with a sharp intake of breath. "I wanted him to reconsider helping Clint keep his job, and I said he'd be sorry if he didn't. But I didn't plan to kill him." His eyes filled with tears, and he bowed his head. "Munroe threatened to do all he could to keep Clint from getting a coaching job someplace else. He has lots of connections, so he could've done it. He would've done it, so I grabbed his chair. He had the letter opener in his hands and, when he went to hit me, I hit back." Moisture streamed down his face. "Somehow, the opener got between us and..." His voice trailed off. "I don't know. I guess I grabbed for it."

More sobs left his sister, who had put her arms on the desk and laid her head on them. Doro's heart went out to the siblings. Glances at Wade and Ev revealed they were both stone-faced. That did not seem like a good omen, but did Stan Jackson deserve understanding? She was not at all sure. Luckily, the decision on charges would not be left to her.

"Did he die right away?" Ev inquired.

"Yep. The blade must've hit an artery," Stan replied in a husky whisper. "There was a lot of blood."

"There was," Ev agreed. "A jury might believe your story, but how do you explain knocking out Horace MacPherson and hiding him in the attic? The kid was scared and upset."

"I didn't want him to see me," Stan said. "He would've recognized me right off."

A harrumph left Wade. "A blow to the head can be lethal."

"I didn't hit him hard," Stan insisted.

"It was hard enough that he lost consciousness," Ev said.

"And it gave him a goose egg," Doro added.

Stan chewed on his lip. "I didn't want to hurt him, but I was scared and desperate. Everyone thought I was still out of town, so I had an alibi. I needed to get away without being seen. If only Horace hadn't come in and started to look around…"

"How did you know about the attic access? No one else did until Mrs. Jones remembered it," Doro said.

The janitor bowed his head. "I only clean in the fieldhouse when there's extra work. Before the basketball season started, the regular custodian wanted to get everything ship-shape. He knew about the old attic and asked me to go up there to see if there was anything useful. We also checked the pull-down stairs before putting it up again."

"Neither of you mentioned that to anyone else?" Ev asked.

"Nope. No reason to," Stan replied. "I wasn't planning to ever use the place, but it came to mind when I needed to hide Horace. I figured he'd be found."

While Doro continued to take notes, she considered the assertions. Was Stan telling the truth? Or had he committed premeditated murder? When Wade spoke again, she knew her thoughts were not far off-base.

"All of your details are very convenient, which makes me doubt their veracity," the constable said.

"My brother told me the entire story, just like he's telling you. Coach Munroe's death was an accident, and Stan didn't want to harm Horace." Bonnie turned a pleading look on Doro. "You overheard some of our conversation."

With a sigh, Doro faced the other woman. "And I heard what your brother told us now, but that doesn't make it true." Even though, she thought Stan was being forthright, Doro was not prepared to back his story. Besides, would it make any difference? She looked from Wade to Ev, but they remained impassive.

"I'm not lying." Stan's voice rose with every word.

"Maybe not," Wade replied. "At this point, we have enough to charge you in the attack on Horace and with hitting Officer Mallow, which is what we'll do. We need to put together the rest of our evidence and interview you again before deciding what charges to bring against you in Coach Munroe's death. One element is the fingerprints. We'll need to take yours."

Stan's eyes went wide. "I told you I held the letter opener, but killing him was an accident."

"We'll decide that after gathering all the evidence," Wade said.

Ev folded his arms over his chest. "What did you do with the letter opener?"

The suspect bowed his head. "I dumped it in one of the quarries on my way back to Toledo."

"You really went there on Friday?" Doro asked.

After a moment, Stan met her gaze. "I wanted to find another job and a place for all three of us to live."

His sister spoke up. "I have my job."

Stan shook his head. "Clint and I couldn't let you support us."

Bonnie started to cry again. "It would've been better than you being arrested for murder."

Wade got to his feet. "Enough chit-chat. We need to check evidence. Getting fingerprints is a formality, but a needed one."

The constable's statements made sense. Although there was no doubt regarding when and why the coach had died, how remained uncertain. Had the wound been accidental or intentional? That question needed to be answered, and Doc Silven's examination could hold the key.

Chapter Seventeen

Ev and Wade had just returned from locking Stan Jackson in a cell when Clint Spalling rushed in. He took one look at his wife's tear-stained face and red-rimmed eyes and rushed to her side.

The assistant coach knelt beside her chair and took her hands in his. "Don't cry, sweetheart."

His admonition only led to more snuffling from her. When Clint wrapped his arms around Bonnie, she hid her face in his shoulder.

Between sobs, Bonnie choked out what her brother had said and his subsequent arrest. "He wanted to protect me."

"That's my job now," Clint muttered. "I wish Stan had talked to me. I could've told him Munroe wouldn't back off. His rules are all that matter. If you break them, he has no use for you. Not that he had much for a custodian. He made some nasty remarks about Stan, who wasn't too proud to take a lesser job, so we could all be near each other."

Ambivalent emotions tore at Doro, who empathized with the Spallings' situation on one level. On another, she found their behavior suspicious. Marrying in secret seemed odd and dishonest. People who lied about one thing often did not hesitate to prevaricate about others.

"You didn't know what your brother-in-law planned?" Wade asked.

His tone telegraphed strong feelings, which made Doro wonder if Clint had been involved in the confrontation. "You lied to him before you even took the job," she pointed out. "And we all know now that the coach had personal reasons for not wanting an assistant who was married. I may not agree with them, but regret and remorse are powerful factors."

Clint sent a scathing glare in her direction. "Why don't you let the lawmen do the talking?"

"Professor Banyon is an outstanding amateur sleuth," Ev shot back. "She's been involved in a number of investigations, and the constable and I weren't involved in one of them at all. With another, we were too sick to help much."

Ev using her title bothered Doro, and it seemed to widen the gap between them. She could not shake the idea that her promotion, despite his claims, upset him. Something did.

"That's right," Wade added, "so, Doro and Aggie worked on those together."

"Did I hear my name?" his wife asked as she entered the office.

Wade got up with a smile on his face. "You did. Ev and I were saying how you and Doro have worked on two cases with little or no help from us."

After hanging her coat on a hook by the door, Aggie crossed to the big table and sat down. Wade joined her. "Doro is the amateur sleuth. I've been her assistant," she said.

"You've done more than that," Doro said.

Clint put both hands up in the air. "All right. I apologize. It's just frustrating to know my brother-in-law felt a need to protect my wife when that should be my duty."

Bonnie sat back in her chair before running a hand over her face. "When Mother and Father were both down with influenza, Stan promised them that he'd look after me if something happened. After they were gone, it was just the two of us..." As more tears spilled down her cheeks, her voice trailed off.

"How old were you when they died?" Aggie asked, her voice soft with sympathy.

"Sixteen," Bonnie replied. "Stan was twenty. He had two more years of college, but he quit to take a job and support us. When I graduated from high school, I went to normal school for two years and started teaching. That's where I met Clint." Both husband and wife smiled at the memory.

"I was coaching high school basketball then," Clint said. "When the assistant job came up here, I jumped at the chance. Bonnie didn't get a job right off, but both she and Stan did this year. We were all hoping he might be able to finish his degree."

Doro considered the revelations. "You applied for a job here after your husband was hired at the college?" The question was mainly to gain corroboration.

Bonnie nodded. "I was lucky there was an opening for an English teacher this term."

"Didn't your past principal and colleagues know you were married?" Aggie asked.

A delicate flush touched Bonnie's round cheeks. "Back then, we were stepping out, and everyone at school knew that."

Clint patted his wife's shoulder. "Bonnie could've kept teaching at our old school after we wed, but not after children came along."

His wife's blush intensified. "The job here paid Clint a lot more, which is why he didn't tell Coach Munroe we planned to marry right off. How would we have been able to court when we weren't in the same place?"

Clint nodded. "We didn't want to be apart, but that was our only choice until Bonnie got a job here. It was hard being miles away from each other."

Being in love herself, Doro understood their dilemma. Despite his recent odd behavior, not seeing Ev every day would be a sore trial.

"Did either of you know Stan planned to confront Munroe?" Ev asked.

"Of course not," Clint replied. "I would've talked him out of it."

When Bonnie did not respond, Ev addressed her directly. "Mrs. Spalling, did you know?"

"No, I didn't know until Stan came to my classroom this afternoon," she murmured. "I didn't even know he'd come back to town early."

"Neither did I," her husband added. "He went to the city to see friends and look for a job. Or so he said. Maybe he didn't go there at all."

A soft sigh escaped Bonnie. "I believe he left Friday evening or Saturday morning. Exactly when he came back, I don't know. He said this morning, but that wasn't true."

Doro revealed what she and Ev had learned from Mrs. Collier. "Now, I'm guessing it was Stan's vehicle she heard, even though she didn't see it."

"The landlady lets him keep it in the garage since he cleaned the place out," Clint said.

"You were right," Ev murmured to Doro.

Although she kept taking notes, Doro did not repress a grin. At least he was still giving her credit for good detective work. As far as her new job, she would soon ask him outright if it bothered him. Would he admit that? While she considered her concerns, the conversation continued around them.

"Which explains how he could sneak into town early," Wade remarked.

"You said you were only charging Stan with hitting Horace and bumping Officer Mallow," Bonnie began.

Bumping Ev was not quite right, but Doro did not object. As frightened as she had been when Ev hit the ground, the murder case was the major concern. Horace's kidnapping came next. At least the law would see it that way. To her, the image of the car bearing down on Ev was of utmost importance. As was their future together.

Clint swiveled to look at the two lawmen. "You are only charging him with two crimes?"

Wade cleared his throat. "I said we only had enough evidence to charge him with the assaults. Your brother-in-law claims Munroe's death was accidental. He told us that, and Professor

Banyon overheard him tell Mrs. Spalling the same thing. We need to decide on the exact charge."

"I see," Clint said. "But Stan saying that to Bonnie is good evidence."

One of Ev's shoulders lifted and fell in a half-shrug. "Maybe, maybe not. He might just be able to tell the same lie repeatedly."

A gasp escaped Bonnie. "How dare you say such a thing? How dare you say anything at all? You've been let go as the deputy constable. Besides, my brother doesn't lie."

Before Ev could defend himself, Doro jumped in. "First, Constable Lammers deputized Ev again, so he could help on this investigation. Also, two crimes occurred on campus, which is his jurisdiction. Finally, your brother tried to run him down. As for lying. Stan does lie, just like you and Clint have."

Two bright red splotches formed on Bonnie's cheeks. "You don't understand."

"I believe I do," Doro said. "You and Clint were in love and wanted to marry. He got a better job, but he had to hide your relationship to do so. Before you moved here, you married him. Your brother helped you keep the lie going and, when Clint's job was eliminated, you all blamed Munroe." The man deserved to shoulder responsibility for his hard-and-fast, but foolish, mandate about coaches not being married. But he had not deserved to die.

Clint ran a hand over his face. "We didn't blame Coach for my position being cut. What made us all mad was when he wouldn't fight for me. We didn't hide stepping out since Labor Day, but Munroe only fussed a little about that. President Adams had already gone to bat for me, if I decided to court someone. The athletic director's son and daughter are both in Bonnie's class, and they like her. That gave us support. But, after a while, Munroe suspected we must be engaged or married. When he confronted me last week, he said he knew about our marriage. I'm not sure he actually did, but I was so shocked and upset that I blurted it out."

"So, that upset him more?" Aggie asked.

"It did," Clint replied. "I asked if he'd speak up on my behalf, and Munroe laughed in my face. He said a liar like me didn't deserve to be kept on. When Stan, Bonnie, and I went to Sylvania for dinner Wednesday night, I shared what Coach said. I wish I hadn't. It really upset Bonnie."

She clutched at her husband's arm. "I got afraid, but I shouldn't have let it show. Stan was angry on my behalf. If I'd taken it in stride, maybe none of this would have happened. Or if Clint would've stayed at the high school, we would've seen each other although we'd still be saving money to marry." Frustration underscored her words.

Doro swallowed hard over the lump in her throat. "You were in a difficult situation, which would have caused anyone to be upset. Ev and Wade will need to decide on the final charges, and they'll consult the county prosecutor." That was standard procedure.

"We will," Wade agreed. "Now, the two of you are free to go. I'll call if we need to speak with you again."

"When can I see my brother again?" Bonnie asked.

"Call ahead, and we'll make the arrangements," Wade replied

After the Spallings left, Aggie sighed. "What a terrible situation. I feel sorry for them." She laid one hand on her husband's. "We're so fortunate."

"We sure are," Wade said.

"People shouldn't marry in haste. Love may seem like enough, but money is crucial," Ev put in.

Unsure what to say, Doro remained silent. Again, she wondered if delaying their marriage until May would lead to it never happening. Ev loved her, but something stood between them. His uneasiness about the future? The possibility of them both losing their jobs? Her making more money that he did? Doro wished she knew what.

After a moment of uneasy silence, Wade spoke again. "Normally, I'd charge Jackson with murder but his story is plausible." He glanced at Colleen who sat on a stool at the counter leafing through a stack of papers. "Doc Silven should be here shortly, right?"

"Yes," the young woman replied. "When you and Ev left for the high school, I called his house and asked him to postpone his visit until one o'clock."

Before anyone else could respond, the physician bustled into the office. "Good afternoon."

After the others greeted him, Wade gestured to a vacant chair. "I appreciate you coming over, Doc, and changing the time."

Silven pulled off his coat before taking a seat. "The delay let me have lunch with my family, which is a rarity. With school closed for the week, the children are home and full of news to share about goings on." He rolled his eyes. "On my way here, I got more news from folks who are out and about. They said you had Stan Jackson handcuffed when you brought him into the station."

Since word spread fast in a small town, Doro was not surprised by the revelations. "Did folks also see his sister and Coach Spalling coming to the office?"

"A couple mentioned that," Doc replied. "Miss Jackson and Spalling have been stepping out, and her brother was with them quite a few times, so I suppose they were here as support. I hope none of them is involved in Munroe's death."

"We should hear about your examination of the body before sharing details," Ev said.

Doc nodded. "Of course. It's clear Munroe was stabbed, as you already observed. The letter opener was pointed and sharp. I saw it after he cut his hand a while back. Although the wound wasn't deep, the blade hit an artery. An unfortunate happenstance."

The last phrase could support Stan's contention, but how would they know for sure? "You've done autopsies in the past."

"I did a number when I worked in a city hospital," the physician agreed. "And some here."

Ev leaned forward. "Including stabbings."

"A few." Silven's brow furrowed.

"Can you tell if this wound was intentional?" Wade asked.

"We can never know for sure if a wound is deliberate or accidental. Those decisions are up to a jury. This wound was shallow, so it could've been a mishap. Hitting the carotid artery was the lethal blow."

"I see," Ev replied before providing a summary of what Stan had stated and what Doro had overheard. "I was already inclined to believe him, since he didn't know Doro was outside the classroom door."

"I was, too," Wade said. After Doro and Aggie agreed, the constable continued. "Ev and I will consult the county prosecutor before levying charges, but young Jackson is in additional trouble because he assaulted Horace and hit Ev with his vehicle."

The physician turned to Ev. "How bad was it?"

"I'm all right. The bumper grazed me," Ev replied.

"It knocked you down," Doro clarified.

"Nevertheless, no serious harm was done," her fiancé said.

For a long moment, Wade studied Ev. "It looked like you were limping."

"He has been ever since he got hit," Doro said.

Doc scowled. "Are you sure it's not serious?"

Ev drove his fingers through his hair. "I'm a little sore, but more from hitting the ground."

After studying Ev for a moment, Doc shrugged. "If you have symptoms at all, come to the office."

"Sure thing," Ev replied. "Back to Horace. Doro and I interviewed him earlier, and he seemed to be recovering. Will he be all right?"

Doc nodded. "He has a concussion and a bruise, but it could've been much worse. Horace was terribly upset, for good reason. Being bound and gagged in an attic had to be scary. I'm stopping by the MacPherson place on my way home, mostly to ease his parents' minds."

"He seemed calmer when we were there," Doro said. "Tee sat in his lap, which helped." At the sound of her name, the little dog roused from her slumber. Doro petted her. "Go back to sleep, girl. You've already had a big day." As if understanding every word, Tee laid down and closed her eyes.

"Dogs are a tonic," Doc said. "Several of my elderly patients keep going for theirs, I'm sure, and my brood adores the stray we took in. My wife wants to get another puppy from that litter, but we have two dogs and a cat now."

Doro shifted toward Ev. "I didn't know there were more puppies in need of homes. I'll call Mrs. MacPherson since they've agreed to get a dog for Horace."

"That'd be wonderful. The Bakers are caring for the mother and last two pups, but they have a houseful of kids, too. They plan to keep the momma dog." Doc grinned. "As Horace's physician, I'd be pleased to write a prescription for a puppy."

Everyone chuckled, even Wade who had not yet gotten a canine for his children. He patted Aggie's hand. "We've discussed adding a pet. What do you think?"

"The last puppy will have a home," she replied. "With us."

Doc stayed only a few more minutes. After he left, the group returned to the case. Doro glanced over her notes and made a few more. "What charges will you present to the county prosecutor?" she asked Wade.

"Two counts of assault and possibly involuntary homicide," the constable replied.

Ev leaned forward. "That sounds fair to me, but the prosecutor may go for voluntary homicide."

"That won't surprise me," Wade said. "It's his decision."

"It's better than a murder charge," Doro observed, and Aggie agreed. "I hope Clint and Bonnie stay in town."

Aggie nodded. "I hope people treat them well. It's not their fault that Stan confronted Coach Munroe, and it turned out tragically."

"Folks won't blame them for that, but I'm not sure about the reactions to Horace being hurt," Wade said. "Townsfolk are protective of him."

"If the MacPhersons don't blame them, that will help," Ev put in.

"It will," Doro agreed. She snapped the notepad shut. "There's nothing more for us to discuss, so I should get to the library. Even though it's closed until classes resume, I want to get my things in order. A formal announcement about my promotion will come on Wednesday. I'm not moving yet, but I thought I'd start packing." She glanced at Ev with the idea that he would offer to help, but Aggie was the one who volunteered.

"The children are having fun with their cousins at their grandmother's house, so I have a few hours free," she said.

When Ev still remained silent, Doro accepted her best friend's offer. "That'd be wonderful." But not as wonderful as spending time with her fiancé.

Chapter Eighteen

Over the next three days, Doro saw little of Ev. When she did, they discussed plans for spending Thanksgiving with Gramma Rose, as well as a party three days later. Dinner on Sunday would be to celebrate Doro's promotion so Aggie, Wade, the children, and his mother were invited as were Mrs. Jones and Floyd Quartine. Achieving a lifelong dream required celebration, according to Rose McLaren, and Doro agreed. If only Ev would start acting like himself again. That alone would make Doro feel more festive.

On Tuesday afternoon, the group went over the wrap-up of the case. Stan Jackson was charged with two counts of assault and one of involuntary manslaughter, which seemed like the best outcome to Doro. She also learned that Clint was taking the head coaching job, while his wife would continue to teach at the high school. The announcement of their marriage caused a flurry of attention, but most townsfolk were focused on their financial concerns and the coming holiday season. After the

MacPhersons had spoken with the young couple to assure them that no grudge was held, others started to accept the Spallings, as well. All-in-all, Doro felt good about the investigation coming to a successful conclusion. She was less confident about Ev's attitude.

Aggie gave Doro a ride to Sylvania on Wednesday, so she could help with preparations for Thanksgiving dinner. After a brief visit, her best friend returned to Michaw while Doro stayed overnight. Being with Gramma Rose always lifted her spirits, and she looked forward to the holiday dinner and seeing Ev in a casual setting.

On Thanksgiving Day, Ev arrived after the others and left with the group, citing fatigue and a need to get up early on Friday to visit his sister, who lived between Toledo and Cleveland. Although surprised he had not invited her, Doro did not object. Nor did she ask anyone about the decisions from the previous day's Board of Trustees meeting. A call from President Adams had confirmed her promotion, but he had been reticent to reveal other details, citing a preference by the board to delay the announcement of additional cuts until Monday. More jobs would be eliminated. Maybe those involved already knew. But maybe not. Surely, Ev would tell her if his job was gone.

⁂

Late Sunday morning, Doro put the finishing touches on the dining room table. When it was done, she stood back and surveyed her efforts.

"It looks lovely, dear," her grandmother said as she stopped at Doro's side. "Although decorating for your own party isn't usually the way of things."

"I didn't mind. It kept me from ruminating." The admission was out before Doro considered the wisdom of voicing it. For several days, she had maintained an optimistic demeanor. All conversation had been casual.

Gramma Rose patted her arm. "It'll be an hour before our guests arrive. Why don't we sit down and chat?"

"Ev might be here sooner." Doro hoped he would. She wanted to talk with him in private.

"It's a long trip from his sister's place, and you never know about road conditions." Her grandmother led the way into the parlor as she spoke.

After sitting next to Gramma Rose on the sofa, Doro nodded. "I know, and I wonder if his hip is bothering him. It's been less than a week since he got hit by Stan Jackson's vehicle."

Her grandmother's forehead furrowed. "On Thanksgiving, Ev said he hardly noticed it. He wasn't favoring that leg."

"No, but shifting gears and using the clutch on a longer drive could cause problems. If I had gone along, I could've driven part of the way."

Gramma Rose laid a hand on Doro's arm. "You're hurt that he didn't invite you."

A soft sigh escaped Doro. She had not mentioned her feelings to anyone. Doing so might lift some of her gloom. Maybe her grandmother had a better perspective and good advice. "I suppose I am. His sister and I have corresponded, and she's mentioned wanting to meet me. She even said they have two lovely guest rooms, not on the same floor, so it wouldn't have been improper for me to visit."

"I'm sure Ev will invite you to go next time. Besides, this was a short trip for him, and I've enjoyed having you and Tee." The little dog pushed against Rose's leg, so the older woman bent to scratch her ears. "She's always welcome to stay with me, if you go with Ev next time. And when you take your honeymoon trip."

"I don't know when that will be," Doro admitted.

Her grandmother shifted to face Doro. "Over the last couple of weeks, you've mentioned several potential times. I didn't tell you, but your mother sent a letter wondering about the indecision. I haven't replied yet, because I'm not sure myself, and I didn't want to pry."

Doro braced her elbows on her knees and put her head in her hands. "I'm not sure, either," she murmured.

"Oh, my." Her grandmother patted her back. "Are you having second thoughts? You never planned to marry, which you've made clear to us since you were seven or eight and found out wives couldn't work at the college. Policies have changed, but sometimes long-held views don't catch up."

As much as she hated to voice the true problem, Doro thought her grandmother's counsel might be helpful. "It isn't me having second thoughts. It's Ev."

Several moments of silence passed before Rose McLaren spoke. "I'm stunned. He's clearly in love with you."

Doro turned a watery gaze on her grandmother. "I thought so. He's said so. But not lately. Lately, he keeps saying we shouldn't marry until May or later because of economic uncertainty. We both have jobs, and things will get better."

"The economy always has ups-and-downs, to be sure. This down is drastic, even in my long experience." Rose sat back and folded her hands in her lap. "From what I know of Ev's childhood, the family struggled to make ends meet."

"They did after his father died. It's why Ev became a copper so young. Even while he was still in school, he worked to help out."

A faint smile touched her grandmother's lips. "You've never known that sort of hardship, and I'm glad. I haven't, either, but I've seen families suffer and fray because of money troubles. If Ev, who cherishes you, wants to postpone your wedding, it's because he wants to provide for you and any children you have."

Doro took several reassuring breaths. "He's said much the same, but I have a job. A good one."

Her grandmother's forehead furrowed. "When Floyd mentioned your raise in pay on Thanksgiving, Ev fell silent. I noticed he didn't eat much after that."

Thinking back to the holiday meal, Doro recalled the comment. "Ev can't possibly begrudge me earning more money." But maybe he did. She had not had a chance to quiz him on how he felt about her promotion and the extra income.

"Of course he doesn't." Gramma Rose paused for a moment. "In all the excitement about the announcement of your new job, did you ask him about his position?"

"I'm not sure what you mean."

"There were cuts made at the Wednesday board meeting, weren't there?"

Doro nodded. "President Adams won't announce which jobs were eliminated until Monday, although the people involved may know. I'd want to." She chewed on her lower lip. "Ev would've told me if he lost his job."

"Would he?" Gramma Rose asked. "You've admitted the two of you haven't talked a lot lately, and he's acted distant. Maybe he had a hunch, and maybe it was confirmed on Wednesday. If so, he wouldn't have wanted to spoil the holiday for you or the rest of us. Or ruin the celebration of your promotion."

Because Doro knew her grandmother was right, she resolved to speak with Ev privately as soon as he arrived. Getting everything out in the open was best—even if it was hard.

Doro waited impatiently over the next two hours. She hoped Ev would come before the others, but he only arrived ten minutes before dinner. Questions about his sister and her family got terse responses, which led to their conversation becoming stilted. "We need to talk," she said.

His dark lashes fluttered down. When they opened again, his gaze was clouded. "I agree. Later and in private. Right now, everyone is ready to celebrate."

His smile did not reach his eyes, but Doro appreciated the effort and smiled in return. Her grandmother and her friends had gone to a lot of trouble, and she would keep up a good front for them.

Thanksgiving Dinner had involved fewer people than this party, but celebrating her promotion saw every leaf in the dining room table being used. In honor of the event, there was ham, sweet potatoes, and green beans. Aggie brought a cake, and Mrs. Jones supplied rolls and elderberry jam, made from bushes in her garden. Wade's mother contributed pickled peppers and spiced crabapples for the relish tray. Floyd Quartine brought two big bouquets of flowers—one for Gramma Rose and one for Doro. Finding blooms in November was not easy, but the retired library director had beautiful houseplants, which cooperated by providing blossoms over the holiday season.

Although Ev seemed happy about Doro's advancement, he also looked distracted at times, especially when he thought no one was watching him. But Doro watched and worried. And hid her emotions as best she could. Her concern might not have been so pervasive if he had not acted oddly over the couple of weeks. Was he upset over many jobs being eliminated? Had his? Maybe she should have asked after Thanksgiving dinner. Or before. But hindsight did no good.

After eating, the group gathered in the parlor where Doro and Aggie helped serve dessert and coffee. Because Ev had taken the corner rocker, Doro sat beside her grandmother on the loveseat.

"Now, you can get moved into your new office," Floyd said from his seat next to Mrs. Jones. "Let me know if you need help."

"I'll pitch in, too," Aggie said.

"I'm still working out a few details with the murder case, but I can assist afterward," Wade put in. "I didn't want to bring it up at dinner, but the prosecutor filed formal charges in court against Stan Jackson. Involuntary homicide and two counts of assault." He glanced at Ev. "He'd like to talk with you tomorrow, but a telephone call will do."

Between bites of cake, Ev nodded. "Sure thing, but I can go to his office, if he wants."

A frown furrowed Wade's brow. "Not necessary."

Gramma Rose set her cup and saucer aside. "You young people have solved another case in record time. Doro gave me some details over the weekend, no tales out of school, but enough to keep your reputation as a fine sleuthing team intact."

Mrs. Jones smiled. "They are that."

Floyd concurred. "People will be at peace knowing there's no killer on the loose, and it sounds like Stan Jackson is getting off as easy as is sensible."

"I think so," Wade agreed.

"It was another fascinating case," Aggie added. "I'm glad Horace wasn't permanently affected. When Wade, the children, and I got our new puppy, the MacPhersons were leaving with theirs. I don't think I've ever seen a happier family. Except ours." She squeezed her husband's hand as she looked at the faces of their three children, all spruced up for the occasion. The kids grinned in return.

"So true," he said.

Tee, who had been stationed at Doro's feet, woofed. Doro reached down to pet the little dog. "We're a happy family, too." But a glance at Ev made her stomach knot. Although everyone else was all smiles, he was not. She kept recalling her grandmother's words, but Doro wanted to hear from Ev. She wanted to know he still loved her.

~ᵃ⋆

"Are you all right?" Doro asked once they were in his Willys and on the road to Michaw.

"I'm fine." His tone did not support the assertion.

The darkness hid his features, which added to Doro's anxiety. If only she could see his expression. Maybe that would confirm or eliminate her fears. "Are you sure?" Needing some solace, she petted Tee who snoozed in her lap.

A long moment passed before he replied. "I didn't want to put a pall on the weekend's festivities, especially the party to celebrate your promotion."

Her heart rate accelerated. Her grandmother had evidently been right. "What's wrong?" Something was, and Doro wanted an answer. "I'd rather know than speculate, and I realize I should've asked on Wednesday before leaving Michaw." If he wanted to call off their engagement, Ev needed to say so.

A harsh exhalation left him. "I lost my job. The board eliminated the campus security officer position until enrollment is back up. The announcement will be made on Monday, but President Adams wanted me to know."

Doro's jaw dropped as she shifted toward him. "I'm sorry, but you could've told me right off."

"And spoil the holiday and today? How could I do that? We both looked forward to Thursday with Gramma Rose, Floyd, and Mrs. Jones. And with the entire group today. You deserved a special celebration. Becoming the library director has been your dream, and it's a huge accomplishment."

With one hand, she reached out to him. When Ev's callused fingers closed around her softer ones, Doro clung to him. "You don't have to bear troubles alone, not even for a few days. We're a couple, and I want to share everything with you. The good and the bad. I thought you knew that."

His thumb stroked her hand. "I wish you didn't have to share this."

"I'm sorry about your job, but I don't mind sharing the troubles."

"We knew it was possible," he murmured.

"We did." Doro had pushed the possibility to the back of her mind. Ignoring it had been easy while they investigated Coach Munroe's murder. Then, anticipating a festive holiday and her promotion had filled her thoughts. Meanwhile, Ev had coped with the bad news alone. When he went to downshift and released her hand, Doro felt a barrier fall between them again, which was silly. He couldn't safely shift between gears with their fingers entwined. He wasn't slipping away, just being cautious. "Did you tell your sister?"

Several moments of silence preceded his reply. "No. I didn't want to spoil her holiday, either."

At least he had not confided in someone else. "Enrollment will probably be up next fall, and you'll be rehired."

"The board and President Adams expressed that sentiment."

Although his flat tone provided little reassurance, Doro scrambled for something encouraging to say. "You deserve a break, and it comes in time for us to take a longer wedding trip. Maybe we should set a date instead of waiting until spring. There's still time." Long moments of silence again passed.

When Ev failed to respond, Doro pressed on with her previous arguments. "We originally talked about mid-January, and with classes cancelled until then, we could plan a wedding sooner. Maybe around Christmas. If my parents can't come, we'll go to Colorado for our wedding trip." Perhaps the last suggestion would move him to agree.

After another pause, Ev spoke in a rough murmur. "That won't work, Doro."

Something about his ragged tone and implacable profile disturbed her. Despite runaway misgivings, Doro managed a casual comment. "Let's go with January then. There's no reason to wait until May." There were reasons, but she did not wish to consider them.

Ev reached for her hand. "I can't live in campus housing and not work at the college."

"Not even in the garage apartment?"

"It wouldn't be fair to employees, who will be housed in the boys' dormitory next term. Maple Hall is being closed for the rest of the academic year. That was one of Wednesday's decisions. Needless to say, that idea isn't popular, so a couple of the longest-serving bachelor professors will take the garage space."

A sliver of relief helped Doro relax. "Until we marry, you could stay at Mrs. Lammers' boardinghouse. She lost boarders, and most won't be back for the spring term. The mortgage rates are low, and you've saved money for our house. I have, too, but we can delay buying something until you're back at work. Mrs. Lammers has a lovely suite on the top floor that she usually rents to a professor, but it's empty now." Aggie had shared that news.

With his thumb, Ev massaged the back of Doro's hand. "This isn't easy for me to tell you, sweetheart. It's not what I want, and I know it won't be what you want, either."

Despite the warmth of Ev's hand on hers, Doro felt chills ripple through her. "What are you talking about?"

He released her hand and gripped the steering wheel. "I can't be the right kind of husband without a job."

As his assertion echoed in the confines of the car, the chill inside her turned to ice. She recalled Clint Spalling's opinions about having his wife work while he was unemployed. Ev had wholeheartedly agreed with the coach. Most people would. "You're calling off our engagement?" Her voice was so hushed, Doro barely heard herself.

"No. Of course not. We just need to push the wedding back for a while. Maybe beyond May."

"Until your job is reinstated?" Doro asked. Confusion filled her. What if enrollment did not increase within the next year? How long would Ev want to wait? Two years? More? With one hand, she kept petting Tee.

"In all honesty, that may not be for quite a while. There's no sign the economy is getting better. If anything, it's worse than a year ago. You know that."

Denying facts would be futile and foolish, but delaying their marriage indefinitely was unacceptable. She did not care what others thought. "I have a job, and we can find an inexpensive place in Michaw. Several nice cottages are empty, and I'm sure the owners would be happy to rent them out. We don't need to buy a place like we planned."

The ensuing silence became uncomfortable. When Ev spoke, he sounded far away. "I'm not staying at home while you go to work. I'm not letting you support me."

While his assertions did not surprise Doro, they bothered her. When and how would he get another job? "You'll only be without a job for a short time." But would he? Her anxiety ratcheted up.

"I have a couple of offers, so I'm luckier than many people."

Relief had Doro slumping back in her seat. "Good. What are they?" Was the town hiring him back as deputy constable? A part-time salary was not much, but the job would ease his mind.

Again, seconds of silence preceded his response. "One is working for the Toledo Police Department," he replied. "I'd be back to walking a beat like I did at eighteen."

His flat tone telegraphed real reluctance, but what should she say? What could she say? "You stopped in Toledo when you went to see your sister, if you saw her at all."

"I spent Friday night and most of Saturday with her family," he shot back. "But, yeah, I stopped in Toledo on the way home."

"Which is why you didn't ask me to go along." Suddenly, pieces were clicking into place.

"That's right," he muttered. "It sure isn't because I didn't want you along, but I had to see about the copper job."

"That's too long of a drive from Michaw. You'd have to stay in the city." Not that the distance was the big worry. With bank robberies increasing, more and more policemen died battling them, especially beat cops. A sudden memory of gunshots ringing out and Ev crumpling to the ground on a city sidewalk rose in her mind. Prohibition agents fought gangsters, and so did coppers. Far too often, gangsters won.

"Close to an hour in good weather," he said. "In bad weather, I might not get back for days on end. That's no way to begin married life, and I'm not sure I want to take that kind of demotion."

When he did not reveal his other option, Doro felt dizzy with anxiety. "What's the other offer?"

A long moment passed before Ev responded. "Canton Lowery knows about several openings in the Bureau. Unfortunately, none is in Toledo. One is in Detroit, which is only a couple of hours from here. I'd come to visit as often as possible."

The statement hung between them like a lead curtain. Suddenly, Doro felt as if they were in separate universes instead of the same vehicle. "You saw him, too, and you talked about a job when I overheard your telephone conversation."

Ev inhaled and exhaled sharply. "We did."

Emotions battered Doro. "You thought a lot about this long before Wednesday. It's why you and Lowery have kept in touch." Doro did not try to keep the anger out of her voice. "Then, you didn't reveal what happened on Wednesday. You've hidden the truth from me. How long have you thought about going back to the Bureau? Weeks? Months? You promised you'd never go back. You've said that more than once." Doro's voice rose until Tee whined. She petted the dog and lowered her tone. "It's all right, girl." But was it? Would it ever be?

"I don't want to go back. I don't want to join the Toledo force, either, but I don't have other options."

"Yes, you do," she shot back, her voice hushed but forceful. "You could stay here and see what happens. Things could improve any time."

Several seconds of silence passed before Ev spoke again "I wish they would, but it's unlikely, and we both know it. Herbert Hoover isn't doing anything to help people, since he believes the situation will get better without intervention. It hasn't, and it probably won't. I don't pretend to know what will happen. I only know waiting to get another job isn't a wise strategy. If I wait too long, even these positions may dry up, and there may not be other opportunities soon. I know what it's like to struggle to pay bills, because we did that after my dad died. I can't do the same to my own wife and children. I won't do it. Please try to understand."

"Would it hurt your pride so much to stay home while I work for a short time? You've always been open-minded. Why the change now?"

"It isn't a change, Doro. I still see our marriage as a partnership, but I'm looking at the reality around us. I hope the economy improves in the next few months. That's not too likely. If we get married, children could come along right away. Then, you'd have to stay home for a little while, wouldn't you?"

While Michaw College was progressive, having an obviously expectant library director on the job would be out of the question. "I would." Children might well come along after their marriage. She hoped they did, but he was right about little ones creating more needs. How long would she have to take off work if she had a baby? Probably months before and months after. During that time, they would have no income. Her parents would help, but her father might lose his job. A few colleges had already closed, and some were cutting jobs and programs. As a last resort, they could live with Gramma Rose, who would welcome them and babies. But that was not what Doro wanted, either. "I don't like you dealing with all this without consulting me. If the situation was reversed, I wouldn't have hid it from you."

Long moments of silence again filled the vehicle before he responded. "I was wrong not to tell you on Wednesday. You're an adult, and we wouldn't have needed to reveal my job loss to anyone else. The truth is, you probably could've put up a better front than I have." He sighed. "I'm sorry. Sweet heaven. I don't want to go away. I want to stay here. With you."

The raw anguish in his voice evoked a memory within Doro. Only a short time ago they had talked about Clint hating to leave town, Ev had voiced his own emotions. *I'll feel the same if I have to leave here.* "Did you think you'd be let go when we were in the coach's office?" For her, the possibility had been amorphous, not solid. Had she been fooling herself? Evidently.

He bowed his head for a second. "I was afraid that would happen, which is why I understood Clint's pain. I looked forward to marrying you in a few weeks. Now, who knows how long we'll have to wait." A harsh sigh escaped him. "I should've admitted I've been talking to Lowery about a job with the Bureau. I am sorry."

"It's such a dangerous job." As she considered how dangerous, Doro remember what he had said to Stan Jackson during the man's arrest. "You've been shot twice, and you've had to shoot criminals, too, haven't you?"

His harsh exhalation was audible. "I wasn't planning to shoot Stan as he laid on the ground, and I've never fired at someone who wasn't holding a gun on me." His voice was rough and raspy. "I haven't killed another person, either, and I hope I never do. I thought you knew that."

"I do," she whispered, "but your words stunned me, and they painted a clear picture of what you faced as an agent. What you'll face when you return to the Bureau."

"When I return? You're resigned to that happening?"

As anger battled with sadness, Doro reached out to touch his shoulder. He had admitted to being wrong, which made a small concession possible. "Detroit isn't impossibly far, and maybe you'll be able to move to Toledo."

As Ev slumped back in his seat, he brought her hand to his lips and pressed a kiss there. "If I take a job with the Bureau, I'll make it clear I need to be transferred to Toledo as soon as possible. And I definitely won't go farther than Detroit, so we'll still see each other. I'll come home whenever I can. I'm sure Mrs. Lammers will keep a room open for me. Like you said, a lot of her boarders aren't coming back for next term."

"That's good." Doro tried, but failed, to inject enthusiasm into her words. "When are you making a final decision on which job to take?" From what he said, she figured he already had.

"I'm driving into Toledo in the morning. First, I'll talk with Lowery again. He'll call his friend in Detroit, and I'll arrange to go up there. The Bureau is my first choice."

That news provided some relief. "When would you start?"

"Maybe before Christmas."

The three-word response sent her spirit plummeting. "So soon."

"President Adams said I can stay in the garage quarters until the first of the year, but there's not much sense in delaying," Ev said. "My employment with the college ends on the thirtieth of this month. That's today."

"Today," she echoed. "Have you already packed?"

"No, like I said I don't have to get out immediately." Ev pulled to the side of the road and turned toward Doro. "I want to spend as much time as I can with you. I don't want to leave you, but this isn't about want. It's about need. They won't hold the job for me, and there are plenty of other guys as qualified as I am who will jump at the opportunity." He slid one hand behind her neck. "It's possible the top agent in Detroit won't want me."

"He will," Doro said with certainty.

His fingers slid through her sleek bob. "If he offers the job to me, do I have your blessing in taking it? I need to hear you say so."

She wanted to say a resounding *no*, but Ev supported her in all her endeavors, and she could do no less for him. "Of course, you do." When he bent forward, Doro put both hands on his shoulders and leaned toward him. Long moments passed before they drew apart.

When they did, Ev petted Tee's head. "I'm glad she'll be with you. I hate to leave my two girls, but at least you'll be together."

Tears pricked her eyes, but Doro blinked them back. "We'll be fine."

"I know."

His husky voice made Doro put one hand to his cheek, his damp cheek. "Oh, Ev."

"So much for being fearless, huh?" he asked in a hoarse whisper.

"It takes a special kind of courage to feel things so deeply and to let those feelings show," Doro murmured as she lifted his hand to her face and let her own tears fall.

After several silent moments, Ev put the car into gear and drove on. As the Willys sped on into the darkness, neither spoke but Doro no longer felt like a wall stood between them. In a short time, they might be miles apart, but their heartstrings were tied together forever.

"The Festive Fantasy"

At the end of <u>The Hounded Hoopster</u>, Doro and Ev part due to circumstances beyond their control. Sad about the separation and worried about Ev, Doro and Tee spend Christmas in Sylvania with Gramma Rose. On Christmas Eve, Doro falls asleep only to have a vivid dream.

Is it only a dream? Or does it foreshadow the future? Read the story and decided for yourself.

You can access this story at https://read.bookfunnel.com/read/oyl2pg25ec

Sneak Peek of "The Surly Secretary"

Chapter One

Dorothea Banyon collapsed into her desk chair and thanked heaven it was Friday afternoon. Although she loved being the new library director at Michaw College, the job came with challenges. Both professional and personal challenges tested her. Almost of their own volition, her fingers reached for the token of love and connection that she wore daily, the North Star she touched when bolstering was needed. But when she put her hand to her neckline, Doro started in surprise. She ran her hand inside the neckline, but her locket—the beautiful gold locket that was a link to her mother—was gone. As panic set in, Doro she rushed to search the nooks and crannies of her office, but the locket was nowhere to be seen. She mentally reviewed her work, which had taken her to all parts of the library. Before she got halfway done, a tap sounded at her door. Doro groaned. She did not want company right now.

"Come in," Doro called out.

A blonde young woman, her expression solemn, stepped inside. "May I have a few minutes of your time, Professor Banyon?"

Despite wanting to search for her locket, Doro nodded. "Of course, Naomi." She gestured to the empty chair across the desk from her. "Tee has taken over one of the seats."

"I see," Naomi murmured. When the little black dog wagged her fluffy tail, the young woman scratched her ears. "I always love when you spend part of the day with us, Miss Tee."

"She loves it, too. Staying in my place for an extended time is hard on her, since she's used to walking the campus with Ev." Just saying her fiancé's name brought a lump to Doro's throat.

"It must be hard to have him far away," Naomi said, her voice soft with sympathy.

Not seeing Ev for weeks was worse than hard. "It is, but how can I help you?" This was not the first time the student clerk had come to her looking grim, so Doro could guess the source of the problem.

When Naomi perched on a chair, Tee curled up again and dozed off. "You know Miss Bensen has found fault with my work."

Indeed, Doro did know since she had observed the secretary's behavior for three weeks—observed it and tried to curtail it with little success. "I've spoken with her about criticizing you. It isn't easy being the only student clerk. Usually, we have several, but our budget is tight. I didn't think the library would be so busy this term, since enrollment is down, but it seems to be a popular place for students and professors." Being shorthanded meant she, Marjorie Bensen, and Naomi all had more to do. Naomi pitched in without complaint. Unfortunately, Miss Bensen complained endlessly about doing anything beyond what she perceived as secretarial duties, which was next to nothing.

"The library is warm and inviting," Naomi said. "Students enjoy being here because you're good to us. You help us find resources, and there's no constant shushing."

A grin lifted Doro's lips. "Director Quartine wasn't a shusher, either." Her boss, who had retired at the end of December, had been both mentor and friend to Doro. Some days, she wished he was here to handle Miss Bensen, who gave Doro trouble at work and at home, since they both lived in Wheaton Hall, the residence for female employees. Naomi's voice broke into her troubled thoughts.

"I follow the rules, but Miss Bensen makes her own," the girl said.

Since the statement was true, Doro did not disagree. "What happened now, Naomi?"

The young blonde wiped at her eyes with the back of one hand. "Miss Bensen scolded me for talking to a boy from my English class. She said I should flirt on my own time, but I wasn't flirting, Professor Banyon. He was working on a term paper and asked where the books on the Spanish-American War were."

"Did you tell Miss Bensen what went on?"

"Yes, and she said he should use the card catalogue, and not bother me."

Doro fought to keep her expression impassive. "What you did was fine. We often help students locate material."

A watery smile took some of the anxiety from Naomi's face. "Then, Clark won't be banned from the library?"

"Banned? Of course not. Why would you think that?" Doro asked.

"Miss Bensen accused him of distracting me, and she won't allow it. If he does it again, she'll see he can't use the library, and he needs to come here for research. All students do."

Doro clenched her hands in her lap until her fingernails scored her palms. "Miss Bensen can't ban students from this building. I'll speak with her before she leaves today."

"Thank you. I love this job, and I need it." Naomi's blue eyes glittered with moisture. "My dad still has his position, but my folks are pinching pennies in case he loses it like so many others have. Every bit extra helps."

"I understand," Doro murmured, and she did. Since the stock market crash in October 1929, some sixteen months earlier, many Americans had lost their employment. Her fiancé, the former campus security officer, was among them.

"Professor Banyon, I'd rather not be here when you speak with Miss Bensen. Can I leave a little early? It's after four o'clock."

"That's fine. I'll speak with Miss Bensen after you're gone." Not that it would do much good. The secretary held a years-long grudge against Doro. Would bringing it out in the open help? Doro did not think so.

"Thank you. Clark slipped a note to me. He wants to take me for supper at the diner." All traces of distress were gone from Naomi's pretty face.

"How lovely," Doro said.

"He might ask me to go to the Sweetheart Dance." Hope shone in Naomi's gaze. "I hear it's magical."

Memories brought tears to Doro's eyes, and she blinked to keep them away. Her attention moved to the framed photograph on the corner of her desk. Taken at last year's dance, the image of her with Ev was precious but bittersweet. "It is."

Naomi followed Doro's gaze. "Is Officer Mallow coming for the dance?"

When Doro looked back at the girl, she forced a smile. "He'll try, but his job keeps him busy."

"Because Prohibition agents have so many bootleggers to investigate," Naomi murmured.

"They do," Doro agreed in a solemn tone. Before she could say more, Miss Bensen appeared in the office door. "Do you need something?" she asked the secretary.

When Naomi turned to face the newcomer, she jumped up. "Excuse me. I have to go."

The girl pushed past Bensen and disappeared before Doro could ask if Naomi had seen the locket.

A harrumph left the secretary. Somewhere in her mid-thirties, the secretary wore a perpetual frown along with her typical attire—severe suits with skirts ending below her knees. Serviceable Oxfords completed her work attire. Doro never saw her in anything less formal. Not even on the weekends. Her mouse-brown hair, pulled back into a tight bun, completed her stern appearance. Miss Bensen was most definitely a shusher.

The secretary put her hands on her hips. "Why did you let that foolish girl leave early when there's work to be done?"

Doro throttled her anger. "Sit down. Please."

"I'm fine where I am." The woman glared at Tee. "I came to report Naomi lollygagging with a boy earlier."

After a long, low breath, Doro gestured to a chair across from her desk. "Sit down. We need to talk." The secretary's scowl intensified, and she hesitated long enough for her action to register as reluctance bordering on insubordination.

When the woman finally took the chair, she gestured at Tee. "Why is that little mutt here again? She shouldn't be, but she shouldn't be in Wheaton Hall, either."

Doro gritted her teeth. "Tee lived in the faculty residence before you did."

The woman's nostrils flared with a sharp intake of breath. "And got fleas all over."

Again, Doro fought for control. "She doesn't have fleas."

"All mongrels have them." Miss Bensen scooted her chair away from where Tee slept before glowering at Doro. "That girl flirting with boys in the library and that little mutt all over this place." She gave a slight shudder.

Although Doro prided herself on being pleasant, her hackles rose when a loved one was attacked, and Tee was a loved one. "Let's move on. We've discussed your treatment of Naomi in the past. We've also discussed the fact that you do not set the rules in this library. Students will not be excluded on your say so. In addition, your responsibilities are what I say they are, not what you choose to do. Is that understood?"

Fire flamed in Miss Bensen's brown eyes. "You are quite full of yourself, aren't you?"

Doro gritted her teeth. "No, but I've been faced with various issues due to your attitude. We've discussed you refusing to allow professors and their classes to the library. Several have complained to me."

"More women who are filled with self-importance because they have men's jobs."

Doro clenched her jaw until she thought her molars might crack because the secretary's statement hinted at the source of her anger. Several years earlier, Doro had been hired as a librarian instead of the woman's nephew, a man who needed the job according to Bensen albeit behind Doro's back. "Michaw College has always been progressive, and hiring women as faculty members is in line with that." Her nostrils flared as she inhaled deeply. After releasing the breath, Doro continued. "I've tried to work with you, but you refuse to cooperate. If your attitude doesn't improve, I'll be forced to go to President Adams. As you know, jobs are scarce, and several secretaries lost theirs last year. They would surely be thrilled to return.

The color drained from Miss Bensen's angular face. "How dare you?"

With her tolerance drained, Doro lifted her chin. "I dare because I'm your boss, and you'd be wise to remember that."

Those words dangled in the air for several moments before the secretary jumped to her feet. "I won't listen to threats."

Tee's head went up, and a low growl ensued. The atypical behavior surprised Doro. "It's all right, girl." When the dog did not quiet down, Doro hurried to scoop her up before returning to her chair and keeping Tee in her lap. "It's not a threat..." Before she finished her statement, a knock interrupted, and Doro noticed another middle-aged woman, her expression disapproving, standing there. Doro's heart sunk. Not only was Gladys Fairchild a notorious gossip, she was a dear friend of Miss Bensen.

"You shouldn't be threatened, Marjorie," she said. "I'm going to speak with the provost about this harassment." Her narrowed gaze focused on Tee. "And about that mongrel being here all the time."

Doro's stomach knotted. Why, oh, why had Miss Fairchild come along? She could twist the smallest disagreement into a major catastrophe. Since Doro detested drama, she attempted to calm roiling waters. "Miss Fairchild, your friend needs to follow library rules, not make up her own or refuse to perform necessary duties. I'm sure the provost would agree with me. As for Tee, she has permission from President Adams to be in the library and in Wheaton Hall."

The woman's scrawny neck swiveled until she was facing Miss Bensen. "It's almost four-thirty. I got off a bit early which is why I stopped, Marjorie. Surely, your boss," she said, putting an emphasis on the last word, "could let you have a bit of extra time for once."

Miss Bensen nodded. "I'm not feeling well, so I need to go home. Our little student helper already did."

After several deep breaths, Doro agreed, mostly because she wanted peace. "All right, but before you go, have you seen my locket? I lost it sometime today. Maybe when I was searching the stacks."

Miss Bensen stared daggers at Doro. "We had a crowd of students in-and-out all day. One probably found it and stole it. That wouldn't happen if you didn't allow them to swarm all over the place."

"Students need to conduct research for papers," Doro pointed out. As she spoke, a memory came to her. "Your nephew was here around lunch time. While he waited for you, he was all over the library."

The older woman's face went red. "How dare you accuse Russ of taking your necklace?"

"I didn't accuse him." Despite her protest, Doro wondered if the man might have snagged the item. Although she did not know him well, Russ Bensen frequented speakeasies. Did he gamble and lose at them?

A harrumph left Miss Fairchild. "If you don't get your locket back, you have only yourself to blame. Come on, Marjorie. Let's go."

After the two women were gone, Doro burrowed her nose into Tee's soft fur and fought back tears. As she did, the diamond in her engagement ring caught the light and winked up at her. Like the locket, it was a token of love and connection. But tokens were no substitute for the presence of loved ones.

꙳

An hour later, after retracing her steps in a vain attempt to find her locket, Doro locked up the library and headed toward Wheaton Hall. Watching Tee prance along, tail wagging, was a small solace. Clearly, the icy wind and snowy landscape did not bother the dog, but Doro felt chilled to the bone. Or maybe to the soul. Escaping to her snug apartment, where she and Tee could relax in peace was her strategy for this Friday evening, but the fates were against her. Her foot was on the first step when Polly Lenard appeared.

"Doro, do you have a few minutes to talk?" the slender brunette asked.

Although reluctant, Doro nodded. "I have a little time, if you don't mind Tee coming along."

Polly bent down to pet the dog's head. "Certainly not. Beulah is already waiting at my place, and she loves dogs, too, so Tee is more than welcome."

Doro followed Polly up two flights of stairs and into her apartment. Fatigue, more emotional than physical, weighed her down. While the suite was smaller than Doro's place, it was homey.

"I made tea," Beulah, a redhead in her early thirties, said. "And I put out cookies." She gestured to the low table in front of the fireplace.

"How kind," Doro murmured as she shrugged out of her coat, which Polly immediately hung on a hook by the door.

After the three women settled with refreshments, Tee curled up in front of the grate, and Doro addressed the other two women. "What did you want to discuss?"

The pair exchanged a long look before Beulah sat forward in her chair. "It's Miss Bensen again. On Monday, I called the library to arrange for my classes to visit next week, and she said it was impossible. No reason given." The woman clasped and unclasped her hands." I have freshmen, and not all of them are proficient at doing research. This early in the term, I like to help them."

"I have the same situation," Polly put in, "and Miss Bensen told me the same thing when I telephoned."

Taking calls was part of the secretary's job. Refusing to co-operate with professors was not. "I didn't know about either of your requests, and I'm sorry for any inconvenience. I'll speak with her but, in the future, talk to me about visits." Relief shone in both of their gazes.

"Thank you," Polly said. "She makes everything so difficult. Even here in Wheaton Hall, she's a tyrant and so is Miss Fairchild."

"They're ruining life in this residence," Beulah added. "Most of us don't eat downstairs anymore because they hold court with the other secretaries. Even though there are six of us professors, not counting you, and only four of them, they make constant snide remarks about women knowing their place. Which they think is subservient to men. I don't understand how women can be so nasty to other women." She glanced at Tee who was sound asleep. "Or dogs."

"I don't understand it, either," Doro murmured.

Sympathy soften Beulah's gaze. "I don't envy you having to see Miss Bensen in the library and at home."

"Neither do I," Polly agreed.

"Thank you. She tries my patience." Doro wanted to unburden herself but stopped. Such complaints should only be shared with those in her close-knit circle. Unfortunately, that circle was broken. With her best friend married, her parents in Colorado, and her fiancé in Detroit, Doro had never felt more alone. Surely, things would get better.

Chapter Two

Following the discussion with Polly and Beulah, Doro and Tee holed up in her apartment. After feeding the little dog, Doro fixed a sandwich and tea for herself and settled next to the fireplace. The soft sofa, piled with pillows, provided a comfortable place to relax. Tee leaned against Doro with her gaze fixed on each bite.

"You are a beggar," Doro with a chuckle. Tee's tail wagged merrily. "And you don't care." After tearing off several bites of turkey and bread, Doro fed them one-by-one to the dog, who greedily consumed every morsel. "Can I have a little more?" Tee's response was to lie down and stretch out. Doro laughed again.

Following the light repast, she propped her feet up and tried to focus on a book, but her mind wandered. Doro gave up and simply stared into the flickering flames until she dozed off.

When she and Tee woke later, they took a long walk around campus before returning home. The frigid air gave the dog energy, but Doro was eager to get in her pajamas and under a pile of blankets. She breathed a sigh of relief when they stepped inside Wheaton Hall, where warmth enveloped her. Before starting up the stairway, she bent to pet Tee. "I'm glad I have you, girl." Tee woofed and twirled around like she understood every word.

Just as Doro reached the steps, Gladys Fairchild came down the narrow side hall from the kitchen. A scowl darkened the woman's face. "That dirty mutt shouldn't be in college housing."

Tee's happy woof turned into a loud yelp. When the little dog pulled forward, Doro gripped the leash handle tighter. "Tee, stop that."

"She's mean, too," Miss Bensen added as she followed her friend. "And a yapper. I'm sick of hearing her bark all night."

"She doesn't bark at night. In fact, she hardly barks at all." While that was true, Tee failed to support Doro's assertion. Instead, she barked louder. "That's enough, girl."

"It's more than enough," Miss Bensen went on. As she spoke, she shoved a foot at Tee, which only increased the dog's distress.

"Don't you dare kick her," Doro shouted.

"Your dog is a vicious menace who ought to be put down," the library secretary said.

"You're right, Marjorie. She's tried to bite me, too," the other woman added. "I'll talk to the provost about getting rid of that thing permanently."

"Good." Miss Bensen glared at Doro. "You think you're so special because your father taught here for years, but he's gone. So is your beau. He hasn't been back, has he? He's probably found a more compliant female, and one who doesn't make more money than he does."

The low blows threatened to fell Doro, but she fought back. "Ev works long hours." When Tee barked, Doro picked her up. Despite being held, the little dog continued to yap.

"Awful little noisemaker," Miss Bensen muttered. "She should go."

"She was here before you were. Maybe you should go." Doro gripped Tee tighter and tried to calm her down. A gasp followed, and she suddenly realized they had an audience. One young secretary, an acolyte of Bensen and Fairchild, stood on the landing.

Bonita Rowling, a small brunette, stared at Doro. "What a thing to say."

Without another word, Doro brushed past Bonita and rushed upstairs. As soon as she reached her apartment, Doro sank on to the sofa, held Tee close. "They won't take you away from me, girl. I'd quit my job first." Her dream job. The one that now made her hate going to work.

⚬⚬⚬

When she woke near dawn, Doro rolled over and tried to doze off but to no avail. After thirty minutes, she got up and dressed. Perhaps a brisk walk would lift her spirits. A peak out the window revealed bright sunshine. Although the temperature might still be below freezing, the sun would help.

After Doro grabbed her coat, cloche, and Tee's lead, the little dog dashed to the door. "Fresh air and exercise will do us both good."

Within moments, the pair was outside. Before they took more than a few steps, Doro donned her gloves. "It's cold." Tee wagged her tail. "Luckily, you have a built-in coat." With every breath, a cloud puff left Doro's mouth. "At least it isn't snowing. Let's head toward the park. You like that."

Tee pranced along ahead of Doro, occasionally stopping to sniff. After entering the park, Doro heard raised voices coming from a copse of trees about twenty feet from the front gate. A man and a woman seemed to be arguing. She stopped in her tracks. When they began to wrestle, Doro called out for fear the woman would be overpowered. "Stop." A pop sounded before the man rushed toward the parking area. Since the woman was on the ground, Doro darted to her. By the time Doro looked up again, the man was speeding off in a cherry red Auburn Speedster. She narrowed her gaze. Was there another figure in the vehicle? Her study was interrupted by low moans coming from the woman. As Doro dropped to her knees next to the crumpled form, recognition hit her. "Miss Bensen, what happened?"

The older woman reached up and grabbed at Doro. "Help. Shot." Her voice, rough and raspy, was barely audible.

Doro bent closer. "Who? Who shot you?" The man, in a coat and hat, had not looked familiar to her, and neither had the car.

"Catch them..." The words came out in a slow, hoarse murmur. When her right hand flailed around, a pistol became visible.

Doro gasped. "Let me have the gun. We can't have it going off again." Was the shooting an accident? She could not be sure, but Doro did not want any more bullets flying. When Miss Bensen's grip on the pistol slackened, Doro snatched it way and laid it aside.

"What?" She settled back on her haunches. A closer revealed the shoulder of Miss Bensen's coat was soaked. "Let me try to staunch the bleeding. I have a scarf and hanky." Neither seemed enough to do much good, but she tried. Almost immediately, the material grew damp. "I've got to get help for you."

Miss Bensen clutched Doro's hand with surprising strength. "No...don't leave."

Frantic with worry, Doro glanced around, but no one was insight. Even in the dead of winter, a Saturday morning brought out a few walkers. Silently, she prayed someone would come soon. "Hold on."

"I thought...I thought...he cared about me," the older woman mumbled. "He didn't..." Her voice trailed off as her eyelids shut.

"Who do you mean?" When Miss Bensen said no more, Doro started to rise, but the woman clutched at her again. "Miss Bensen, you need help."

"Don't leave...don't want to...die alone."

Since the secretary's voice was increasingly weak, Doro was torn.

"In my pocket..." Miss Bensen's hand shook as she opened her fingers.

Doro stared in surprise. "My locket." When she reached for it, the other woman gripped it tight.

"He found it...planned to blame me...need to silence me. Why...Doro...why?"

The words made no sense to Doro. Out of the corner of her eye, she saw Bonita approaching. "You need to go for help. Get Doc Silven right away." She did not spare a glance. Instead, Doro kept putting pressure on the wound.

"Doro...no...why..." Miss Bensen's ragged voice intruded.

"What happened?" Bonita asked as she came closer.

"Miss Bensen has been shot," Doro replied. "We've got to get help."

The other secretary's gaze ran over Doro. "You're covered in blood and your locket is in her hand." she gestured with one hand. "There's a gun."

"She was shot, and I was trying to help." Beneath her hands, Doro felt Miss Bensen go slack. She stared down to see the woman's head fall to one side as her mouth fell open. "Oh, no."

Bonita spoke in a rasping whisper. "You wanted to get rid of her, and now you have. She's dead."

Join Doro and Ev in their most challenging and dangerous case yet!

Her dream job becomes a nightmare when Doro clashes with a churlish underling over job duties, library rules, and Doro's little dog Tee. Following a confrontation between them, the woman is shot. When Doro sees her nemesis with a stranger, she calls out. The killer escapes but not before shooting Doro's nemesis. As she reaches the body, Doro grabs the gun before it goes off accidentally—a grave error. Although she tries to help the victim, a witness sees only Doro covered in blood with a weapon at her side and Doro's lost locket in the woman's hand.

After becoming the top suspect, Doro is suspended from her job. She vows to clear her name and contacts her fiancé Ev, who is now back with the Prohibition Bureau. Much to her surprise, she learns he is investigating a bootlegging operation with ties to college employees—including the murder victim. Ev is already undercover as a gangster, so Doro joins him as his moll. As the pair navigate the two cases, they find themselves in more peril than ever. Ev puts it all on the line to protect Doro, and she rides to his rescue when their real identities are exposed. Join them as they go into the world of flappers, bootleggers, Prohibition agents, and speakeasies.

You can preorder the book from various digital retailers. Links are at https://dslangbooks.com/books/the-surly-secretary/

Thank You!

Thank you for reading <u>The Hounded Hoopster.</u> I hope you enjoyed it. Please take a few minutes to rate or review it. Ratings and reviews are important to authors. Thanks in advance!

For more about Doro's sleuthing adventures, please visit my website, where you can sign up for my newsletter, if you have not already done so. News about future releases, promotions, other authors', historical tidbits, and more are in the monthly missives. https://dslangbooks.com

Each is a standalone whodunit, and the first, <u>The Catalogued Corpse</u> is free. You can find links to various digital retailers at https://dslangbooks.com/series/All of the ebooks are also available through my online store, the Bijou'd Boutique. You get 20% off your first order with coupon code FIRSTORDER.

The next complete book in the series, <u>The Surly Secretary</u> will release on February 1, 2026. A sneak peek follows the end of this book.

About the Author

A retired teacher and tutor, D.S. Lang started making up stories to entertain herself as an only child, and she is still making them up. Now, she puts them in writing. She is an avid storyteller and reader. A lover of language, D.S. has published over 10 books with more on tap. Her aim is to write novels that blend history and mystery with dashes of drama, splashes of humor, and touches of romance to create charming stories with authentic details.

Set during the post-Great War period in small-town Ohio, the books welcome readers into an exciting period of American history, when women were navigating new roles, and the country was dealing with Prohibition and the aftermath of war. Her two historical mystery series give readers whodunits to solve along with intrepid amateur women sleuths and their colorful teams of associates. A lawman is always in the mix, but the lady detective takes center stage.

If you're looking for something a little different, like history and mystery with a light love story (ending with a series HEA), try one of D.S. Lang's books. For more, sign up for her newsletter at https://dslangbooks.com

Doro Banyon Cozy Historical Mystery series

The Doro Banyon series has a cozier tone than the Arabella Stewart books. History and mystery still mesh as amateur sleuth Doro solves whodunits with a team of colorful characters in smalltown America during the 1920s. Travel back in time to a college campus and crack cases with them!

Prequel-<u>The Lost Exam</u> (free when you sign up for my newsletter)

Book 1-<u>The Catalogued Corpse</u>

Book 2-<u>The Murdered Matron</u>

Book 3-<u>The Jammed Judges</u>

Book 4-<u>The Problem Professor</u>

Book 5-<u>The Bottled Bootlegger</u>

Book 6-<u>The Doomed Doctor</u>

Book 7-<u>The Hounded Hoopster</u>

Book 8-<u>The Surly Secretary</u> (releasing on February 1, 2026)

Book 9-<u>The Angry Angler</u> (coming in May 2026)

A Valentine's Day short story, "The Vintage Valentine," is available to my newsletter subscribers. In it, college librarian and amateur sleuth Doro takes a break from detective work as she prepares for a romantic evening at the annual Sweetheart Ball with her would-be beau, Everett Mallow. Will this be the night when they go from stepping out to courting? Or will a snowstorm interfere? A vintage Valentine plays a role in this standalone story, which is not a mystery but has a thread of suspense.

You can sign up for my newsletter at https://dslangbooks.com

Arabella Stewart Historical Mystery series

The Arabella Stewart Historical Mystery series is set in small-town Ohio after the Great War. Bella returns home from serving as a U.S. Army Signal Corps operator to find her family resort and hometown in dire straits, and the murder of a neighbor adds to the trouble. Much to the dismay of Constable Jax Hastings, an Army veteran, Bella turns amateur sleuth to solve the case. As the series continues, Bella and Jax vanquish the shadows of the war, while solving a series of whodunits with a team of colorful characters. Love and laughter occur along the way. If you love history and mystery mixed with touches of humor, romance, and drama, this series is for you!

Book One-A Precarious Homecoming

Book Two-A Lingering Shadow

Book Three-A Lethal Arrogance

Book Four-A Baffling Absence

Book Five-A Fatal Reunion

Book Six-A Surreptitious Undertaking

Book Seven-A Treacherous Accusation

Book Eight-An Uncertain Ceremony

Two prequels for this series are available to my newsletter subscribers. Sign up on my website: https://dslangbooks.com You can unsubscribe at any time!

Doro's Cranberry Salad

Cranberry Salad

This is an old favorite in my family, and I love it. You may use a similar one. It's the recipe that I imagine Doro would have used. As Mrs. Jones says in the book, it is tasty.

One bag (about 16 ounces) of fresh cranberries
Two oranges (peeled)
Two sweet apples (cored, not peeled)
8-16 ounces of walnuts (shelled)
One package of black cherry gelatin mix (regular or sugar free)

Run the fruit and walnuts through a food processor or old-fashioned meat grinder. Combine with gelatin mix and about half the water called for on the package. For a festive look, use a mold. Let set overnight. It is great for Thanksgiving, but I enjoy any time of the year.

Author's Series Notes

At one time, there actually was a Mitchaw, Ohio (sometimes called Mitchaw Corners). It was the birthplace of many of my relatives, including my dad. At its height, Mitchaw was an unincorporated village surrounded by farms. Like many other small, rural communities, it has disappeared as a separate entity. Now, it is part of Sylvania Township, and subdivisions have replaced most farms.

The town never had a college, nor was it as large and bustling as the Michaw in the Doro books. That is a big reason I dropped the "t" to change the spelling. However, Sylvania is a very real city. It is my hometown and where I still live. Since the 1920s, when this book is set, it has gone from a small village of around 2000 to a small city of 19,000. The township's population is approximately 50,000.

Author's Notes

C ollege sports were dramatically different before the
NCAA (National College Athletic Association) began
to set uniform rules for scholarships in the 1950s. Early on,
schools provided assistance to athletes through various means
including part-time jobs and pay-to-play. A 1929 Carnegie
Foundation report highlighted the prevalence of subsidies.
Some of the players in this book receive such help. At the time,
it was not illegal. During the Great Depression, donors often
helped athletic programs stay afloat as budgets were cut.

www.ingramcontent.com/pod-product-compliance
Lightning Source LLC
Chambersburg PA
CBHW030350020726
47493CB00003B/759